GREYSTONE'S DILEMMA

GREYSTONE'S DILEMMA

A NOVEL

JODY C. HEYMANN

Bullion Books

Houston, Texas

FIRST U.S. EDITION

Library of Congress Cataloging-in-Publication Data

Heymann, Jody C.
  Greystone's dilemma : a novel / Jody C. Heymann.
    p.   cm.

  1. College teachers — Texas, South — Fiction
PS1924.H634   G3 2000

ISBN: 0-9651376-4-3

Library of Congress Control Number: 00-90417

Published in the United States of America by Bullion Books, Houston, Texas

Printed in the United States of America

For Shirley Peddy, Stan Ellis, Terry Ellis, Leslie Matney, Debbie Hammond, and Hans Heymann.

This book is also lovingly dedicated to the memory of David Ellis.

ACKNOWLEDGMENTS

My thanks go to the following persons for their kind assistance and encouragement, as well as for their many valuable suggestions and criticisms.

My sister, Shirley Peddy, has been an inspiration to me and a mentor. By words and example, she encouraged me to write and has never been too busy to discuss the manuscript, critique it, and finally edit it, even though she was immersed in her own projects.

A word of acknowledgment goes to one of my early readers who offered me so much support and constructive criticism: Lucy Gonzales; and to Charmayne Wilson, Deenie Roper, and Ann Lopez for their perceptive reading and support.

Special thanks also go to my sons, Stan and Terry, and daughters, Leslie and Debbie, for being such astute readers and for putting so much effort and spirit into their insightful counsel.

No writer can do her best work without a reader who is willing to take the time to do a careful reading and editing of a manuscript, chapter by chapter, and line by line. I want to thank Susan Hayes for her editorial assistance and encouragement, as well as for her work in overseeing the production of the book.

My profound appreciation goes to John Heymann for educating me on legal matters.

My thanks also to others who have read the book and offered suggestions, criticisms, and support: Red Peddy, Larry Matney, Mark Hammond, Lynn Ellis, Jewell Ellis, Fred Sternberg, and George Trevino.

Finally, I want to give my special thanks to my husband, Hans Heymann, who makes all things possible for me. He is my role model and has taught me — by his good example — that when you truly look, you will see, and when you really listen, you will hear, both good lessons for the writer.

GREYSTONE'S DILEMMA

PROLOGUE

He had brought her a single, perfect yellow rose and laid it on the table before her as a peace offering. She thanked him grudgingly and left it where he laid it. On looking back, he had expected something entirely different from the evening. He had invited her to dinner on the island at an elegant new restaurant that she had wanted to try. She fancied herself an expert on the local dining establishments. He had received her offer to drive their own cars with some relief because he felt that now if she got angry or difficult, he would have the means for a hasty departure. Recognizing the edge in her voice when he had talked to her about his plans for the evening, he knew that she was quite perturbed with him. When he questioned her about it, she promised that she would not create a scene or embarrass him. So he had carefully picked out the yellow rose, her favorite flower.

After the waiter took their drink order, he looked around admiring the room. It had been a perfect choice with its rich paneling, parquet floors, and original paintings by talented local artists. These surroundings clearly called for dignified dress and behavior. He noticed with disappointment — as he had a cautious nature — that there were at least two tables with people whom he recognized. He nodded and smiled at them, and they waved at him. Then he saw one of his married friends sitting near the window at a table that had a direct view of his own. At least he was not within hearing distance.

Their eyes met and he perceived the discomfort on his friend's face. The fellow was out to dinner with an attractive young woman whose long blond hair was pulled back from her face. It was definitely not his wife Marcia.

When their drinks arrived, wine for her and a beer for him, he started to propose a toast, but she would have none. Instead she asked him to call for the waiter as she had made her selection. She ordered the most expensive item on the menu, a lobster, and looked at him as though she were punishing him. He ordered the lobster too in order to get rid of the waiter before she created a scene. By this time his patience was gone, and he told her to say what she had come to tell him, so they could at least enjoy their dinner afterward.

She gave him one of her looks. He had seen them all. And then she started to speak in a low, irate voice. Instead of leaning forward so he could hear her better since the noise in the room was distracting, he eased back in his upholstered chair and tried to listen. At the same time he wanted to appear nonchalant to any observer. She talked on endlessly, and he noticed that she had not touched the expensive merlot she ordered. He wanted another beer and signaled the waiter. While he waited for his drink, he tried to answer the charges she threw at him, but with each remark he made, she raised her voice to a higher level. Looking quickly around the room at the other tables, he decided not to speak again. He wanted nobody to overhear her diatribe. Although he was used to her scenes in private, he couldn't risk this behavior in public.

She finally noticed he wasn't responding to her questions. She became more enraged and accused him of mocking her. He thought to himself, she's out of control again, and he turned off her words — he was always able to do this — and just sat observing her. An uncommonly pretty young woman, he mused, with her long, dark shining hair and flawless skin. Her large brown eyes were edged with long lashes. Most of her admirers thought them fake, but he knew better. Tall and slender, she looked stunning in her short, black slip dress. If she didn't live in the Texas Coastal Bend, she might have been a model and not had to wait tables at a crummy restaurant to pay for her college education. He used to think she was beautiful before she lost her temper all the time. When she grew angry, her expression changed, and she became quite ugly. He watched her mouth moving, but he wasn't listening to the words. He knew he had heard them before many times. Then he leaned forward to listen again. She was accusing him of lying to her about something. He wasn't sure about what. He lied to her frequently about everything. He could feel himself growing even more impatient. It was time to put an end to this. He told her to stop or he was leaving the restaurant. She looked at him with contempt and reminded him that they had lobsters coming. He started to rise to show her he meant what he said.

When she saw him push back his chair, she jumped out of her seat, picked up her wine glass, and threw the merlot at him. It had been an extra large wine glass, and the deep red wine splattered over him and the table. She then set the glass down at the edge of the table, reached to retrieve her purse on the floor, and accidentally knocked the empty wine glass on the hardwood floor, breaking it. For a few seconds she stood there, staring at the mess she had created, and then she turned and walked quickly from the room. He could feel every eye turned toward them; the restaurant employees and the other diners were swivelling their heads back and forth like spectators at a tennis match. He sat down and reached for her napkin — his was covered with wine — and quickly mopped his face and clothes. The waiter appeared suddenly with a busboy to pick up the broken glass, gather up the table cloth, and reset the table. He saw the look of pity on everyone's face, even his friend's, and looked away.

He had finally had enough of her. Enough of her rage, her threats, and her shameful behavior that always led to her feelings of guilt, remorse, and contrition. He decided that this was the last time she would threaten or humiliate him. Now she was taking their battle public, and he would not have it. He had a family and a reputation to protect. He should have stopped her tantrums long ago. He had been too good to her, too easy on her, and now she was out to destroy him. She had already begun spreading lies about him. And there was nothing he could do to stop her from talking. She was no longer just a nuisance; she'd become instead someone dangerous to him and to others. He would not let her wreak havoc on his life, even if it meant getting rid of her permanently. He smiled at the thought of it. The thought of her dead. Perhaps she could be the victim of an accident. Or she could meet with some other violent end, maybe even be murdered by one of her nemeses, as she liked to call them. He enjoyed each scenario as it popped into his mind and smiled at his own ingenuity. Possibly, like her father, she might even take her own life. She certainly had threatened suicide before. He thought about how easy this was going to be. He gazed at her empty chair and picked up the yellow rose and crumpled it in his hand. The petals dropped helplessly on the white cloth, and he brushed them aside. So much for her, he thought, looking at the torn petals; so much for that. Then he raised his empty glass, and the waiter, recognizing the signal, brought him another beer. When the lobsters arrived, he decided to stay and enjoy them. He had more thinking to do and some plans to make.

❧ I ❧

"A young woman was here looking for you. I told her you would be back shortly."

"Maybe she was looking for you."

"No, I offered to help her, but she said she'd come back later. She wanted to see Professor Jeremy Greystone."

That was me.

"If she were one of your students, I'd probably have recognized her."

"I can't imagine who she can be. Did she say what she wanted?"

The first speaker is the young teacher I share my office with, Royall Phillips. He has been recently placed in my quarters, much against my will, because of a shortage of space. Since I have one of the larger offices in the corner of the hall, there is enough room for another desk, filing cabinet, and bookcase. Our two desks are placed so that we are looking directly at each other. Royall is extremely neat in appearance. His desk and every other part of his work space, however, are not. He neither opens his mail nor unpacks the books sent to him from the publishing companies. His side of the room is always a mess, and he only partially cleans it whenever I lose my temper and insist. He is afraid of me as he hates confrontations. Just then the bell rang and Royall sauntered off to one of his classes.

5

I sat down and began to sort through the envelopes I just brought from the mail room. The window shades in the office were open, revealing an overcast late October afternoon. The dark, windy day suited my mood.

The community college where I teach in Corpus Christi has served this South Texas metropolitan area of nearly 300,000 people for about sixty-five years. It has the reputation of offering its student body a quality education, although it's relatively far from the large urban centers of Texas — Dallas, Houston, and San Antonio. Let me set the stage: Corpus Christi is on the Gulf of Mexico and is known for its outdoor recreation of swimming, fishing, windsurfing, and sailing. Its cultural advantages are limited, however, by its distance from other large cities and because it leads nowhere except to the Gulf. It does have a port and some beaches, as well as an excellent symphony orchestra, some art museums, and other tourist attractions. Although there are several nice parks, it is too hot and windy to enjoy them most of the year. Most of the residents of this city seem to have come here from somewhere else. Why am I here? The answer will become clear as the story unfolds.

I live in a large old apartment building on the west side of Ocean Drive. My small view of the water is worth the noise from the constant traffic below my windows. There are four little rooms — two bedrooms, one of which is my study, a living-dining room, and a kitchen. Since I do not entertain very often, I have paid little attention to the decor. I find that what most people call decorating is rather imitative or derivative of what they see in movies, television, and magazines. I prefer simplicity. I am not a collector of sentimental remembrances, so there are no personal objects lying about.

Since he is part of this story, I will describe Royall. He has recently received his Ph.D. in American literature from a rather respectable institution, but in the pursuance of his degree, he has neglected the procurement of some much needed common sense. What he has instead is luck, which miraculously gets him out of one muddle after another, whether it be

6

with the college administrators, his colleagues, or students. No matter what difficulties he creates for himself, he somehow comes out all right; in fact, usually better than all right. Part of this is due to his Nordic good looks. Royall could be the poster boy for skiing advertisements, and he has received more than one mash note from adoring coeds who refer to his "fine blond hair and sea-green eyes." There is, I am told, an innocence about him that encourages women to want to take care of him. He has many friends — mostly unmarried young men like himself who teach in every building in the college in a variety of disciplines. What annoys me most about them is that they are always hanging around the office waiting for him to go with them on their endless pursuits of pleasure. The two that come to the office most often are Steve White from the math department and Bill Walker from history. Steve sprawls in the one easy chair I like to think of as my reading chair, his long legs making it impossible for anyone to move across the room. Bill likes to sit at my desk, but, of course, jumps up quickly when I enter. So far there was nobody else around this afternoon, so I thought I could get some work done. I teach a variety of freshman and sophomore English courses, and there is always grading to do.

I was about to start reading some exam papers from my American lit class when one of my colleagues from across the hall appeared in the doorway.

"Are you too busy to talk for a few minutes?" Jim Butler asked.

"Come on in."

Jim is another member of the English department. We have a casual friendship, mostly only greeting each other as we pass in the hall. He rarely comes by my office, and when he does, he usually just stands in the door for a brief exchange of pleasantries. Jim is one of those teachers who seem more relaxed with students than with his colleagues. He is always giving his better students extra attention and helping them apply for awards and scholarships. He has a nice, quiet wife, shy like him, and two bright sons in high school. Jim sat down in my reading chair and for a few moments hesitated before he began to speak. Then he mentioned the name of one of the women enrolled in my American lit class.

"I believe you have one of my ex-students in your lit class — Sharon Ames?"

"That's right."

"I 'd like to talk to you about her if you have a minute."

"Has she been complaining to you about the class?"

"No, nothing like that." He paused and then spoke uneasily. "This is really hard to talk about. I might be betraying a confidence."

"Then maybe you shouldn't tell me. You know me, I don't like getting involved in students' lives."

Jim looked distressed.

"I'm not criticizing anybody who does."

"I know, Jeremy, or I wouldn't be here, but she does need help, and I don't seem to be able to do it."

"If you can't help her, what makes you think I can?"

"She speaks about you and the class sometimes. I think she really respects you."

"If it's about grants or scholarships, I'm the wrong person to ask. I know next to nothing about financial aid."

"That's not what I mean at all. I think I'd better go. Don't mention this to her." Then he quickly rose and started toward the door.

"Wait a minute. Sit down and tell me what this is all about." Jim turned back, but just then Steve White stuck his head in the door.

"Is Royall back from class yet? Can I come in and wait?"

Jim brushed past Steve as he was leaving, "I'll talk to you later, Jeremy."

Before waiting for me to say no, Steve entered my sanctuary, plopped down in the easy chair, and threw one leg over the arm. Glaring at him made no impression. He was in the mood to talk or at least be entertained while he waited for Royall. Grading exams was now out of the question.

"What's going on in the English department?"

"Perhaps a better question is what's happening in Math?"

"You mean the petition being circulated by some remedial students?"

"Read all about it in the *Spectator.*"

"Well, don't believe everything you read in the school paper."

"So there's no truth in any of it?"

"I'd say more like half-truths. The students are asking for a new math lab like yours in the English Department. The trouble is that it takes more money than the budget allows. And then, of course, the state congressional body can't agree on how to deal with the whole remedial issue. So now it's not simply a Math Department problem; it's politics." Steve is always involved in such issues because he is a member of the Faculty Council. He keeps us all informed on what is happening all over the campus, whether it involves the president, the faculty, or the students.

Before I could comment about the evils of school politics, Royall walked in, followed by two admiring young women students. There were too many in the room by now for my taste, so I picked up my papers, waved at them all, and left. On my way to the faculty parking lot, I passed Sharon Ames in what looked like a heated discussion with some other students. I wondered if their arguing had anything to do with the problem Jim had come by the office to talk about and if he planned to return and finish what he'd started to tell me.

The drive back to my apartment along Ocean Drive revealed a spectacular view of the city. The sky was overcast, but the water was a dark blue-gray. To the north I could see the downtown skyline of office buildings and further north, the Harbor Bridge, one of the main routes in and out of the city. Ocean Drive is the most beautiful and popular boulevard in the city, not only to tourists but also to the disparate communities that call Corpus home. In many ways this gulfside metropolis is two cities trying to become one in spite of its residents. Half of the population is Hispanic, and the other half is a combination of other racial and ethnic groups, mostly Anglos. It's this multicultural quality of the area that fascinates me most.

After pulling my old Honda into my assigned spot in the apartment parking lot, I went by my mailbox. There were the usual bills and a letter from my sister. As I entered the apartment, I could hear the end of a message in a woman's voice on the telephone answering machine. I will get to that later. I dropped the bills on my desk in the study and decided first to read the letter from Joan.

Dear Jeremy,

You are probably wondering why I am writing you this letter when it would be simpler to just pick up the phone. I have a favor to ask of you, and I don't want to hear your first response. I'd rather you read this letter and think about it before you answer.

You know that Sybil and I have remained close friends in spite of your divorce from Grace. Sybil and I were friends before you ever married her younger sister. But we had this conversation already ten years ago, and that is not why I am writing you now. Do you remember Sarah Wilson, Sybil's daughter, your niece? I know that she was only a niece by marriage, but you always said that she was a nice kid even if she were a tomboy. Sarah has accepted a job with one of your local television stations and is moving to Corpus Christi. Could you take her under your wing for just a short time until she gets settled in a place of her own? She will have so many questions about moving to a new city, and especially to a place as insular as Corpus. People do not accept newcomers there easily, perhaps because they think they are only temporary residents and will soon move on.

I have given her your office address and phone number, and I am sure that after you are reintroduced to each other, you will want to help her.

I'm enjoying my new school in Dallas. This may be the place I'll put down some permanent roots. Let's get together during our winter breaks either here in Dallas or in Corpus. I remain always your devoted sister.

Joan

No! My answer is no, absolutely no. I will take no responsibility for some young woman who decides without any encouragement from me to move here. I don't want her here. I moved to Corpus to get away from Grace and everyone connected to her. This Sarah is no relation of mine. She's no longer even a connection through marriage. I can just see all her relatives swarming like bees down here to pay her visits. Then probably one of the obnoxious group will decide to move here just to be near her. I'll have no part of it. For all I know one of them who show up will be Grace herself, heaven forbid. When we divorced I promised myself that I would never under any circumstances see her or any of her relatives again. So the answer is positively no. How dare my sister give this person my address and phone number, even if it is only to my office. If she shows up, I'll get rid of her fast.

My sister is the only family I have left since our parents died. She is five years older than I am, but does not look forty-five because she is small and slender with short brownish hair and large, inquiring eyes. Like me she is an English teacher, but she has followed a different path from mine. Instead of choosing one school and remaining in one place, she has chosen to be a world traveler. She goes to other countries that she wants to see, finds a job there teaching English, and stays as long as she finds her life there satisfactory. She develops no ties to any of these places except for the people she meets along the way. She picks up strangers wherever she goes. These she calls her friends, and they are a motley crew. She is not very discriminating. I have met some of them, and others have called on the phone when they are back in the States to let me know that Joan is well and thriving. I have never encouraged these phone calls since I do not enjoy carrying on small talk with strangers. In spite of her constant moving, we have kept in pretty close touch as Joan is a letter writer. Sometimes she finds herself in places where she does not have access to a public phone, but there is always a way for her to post a letter or have someone carry it out to be mailed later. Recently she has returned to Dallas and is teaching in a high school. She says she is ready to put down some roots, but I've heard her say that before.

She has obviously taken up with Sybil again, and now she expects me to help her friend's daughter. She can forget that. I do not take in stray people, just stray animals, whom I find more appreciative. Right now I share my apartment with two orange cats, which I consider better company than most people I know. They arrived one day on my doorstep and adopted me despite my reticence. Anthony and Cleopatra brushed against my leg, letting me know that it was time for their dinner, so I went into the kitchen and prepared their evening meal. Then I looked in the refrigerator to see what I could eat. There was a bowl of spaghetti left over from last night that looked promising, so I decided to pop it into the microwave and cut up some vegetables for a salad. Just when I was putting the food on the table, the phone rang. I was pretty sure I knew who it was.

"Jeremy, didn't you get my message on your machine?"

"I just got here."

"I was hoping you could come over for dinner tonight, or if you'd rather we could go out for some Chinese."

"Sorry, Margaret, I'm staying in tonight and having leftovers."

"Save them for another time. I really want to see you."

"I'm not very good company tonight. Besides I have some grading to do before classes tomorrow. I'll give you a call some time this weekend."

"That's not good enough, Jeremy. It sounds to me like you're putting me off. Don't you want to see me too?"

"And if I said I didn't, would you believe me?"

"No, I wouldn't."

I could imagine her smile as she added, "You couldn't be that cruel. You know how I feel about you."

"I just got home and I don't feel like going out again."

"I could come over to your place. I could cook dinner and then we could grade papers together."

"That never works. You finish yours in half an hour and then want to talk. The answer is still no."

"I won't beg you. I know how you hate that. Goodnight, Jeremy."

Margaret is a good friend, but she wants more from me than I'm willing to give. She says she wants a relationship. I call it a ring through my nose. I neither want nor need to be tied down to anyone. My marriage and divorce taught me that much about myself, and I refuse to get entangled like that again. I realize that Meggie, as she is called by most, is very different from Grace. Grace is a narcissist and thinks only about herself. We met in high school but did not get seriously involved with each other until our last two years at the University of Texas. She was a slender blond who dressed like all the other fashionable Dallas girls. She looked fragile and gentle. She was neither. Her only reason for marrying me was to get away from her mother, whom she resembled in both looks and temperament. I can't remember why I married her. When she did not have her parents to fight with any longer, she turned her rage on me. I could do nothing to please her. Since I do not take abuse gracefully, it was a doomed match from the start. I can remember nothing pleasant about the marriage. We stayed together for five unhappy years until it came to us both one day that we did not have to continue living like this, and we parted, but not as friends. We had stayed together too long for that. The only good that came out of the marriage was our not having children.

Meggie, on the other hand, is different. Less striking in appearance than Grace, she is loving and loyal and puts up with all my moods. She is almost as tall as I am with reddish hair, green eyes, and a pleasant, lightly freckled nose, which she sometimes tries to cover with face powder. She teaches accounting in the Business Administration Department. Meggie, who is forty years old like me, was also married once a long time ago to a naval aviator named Joe, who died in a landing accident aboard an aircraft carrier. Unlike me, she remembers only the good times in her marriage and says that she wants to marry again. She also hints that she would like to marry me, although I give her no encouragement.

I looked at the spaghetti that had become cold while Meggie and I were talking and decided to put it back in the microwave. After I finished eating, Tony and Cleo joined me on the sofa expecting some attention. I imagine at times that they read my thoughts, but in reality they were now telling me that it was time to brush them. Afterwards I began working on the papers I needed to grade before my classes tomorrow. I turned on some Chopin études and spent the rest of the evening without further interruptions.

❧ 2 ❧

The next morning as I entered the English Building, I heard muffled voices coming from Jim Butler's office. Usually when the office doors are closed, it is impossible to hear voices, so whoever was in there was speaking loudly. I entered my own office in the middle of a conversation between the inevitable three, who promptly stopped talking when I arrived. Bill jumped up and gave me my chair, and both he and Steve left to go to their classes.

"Don't you have a class this morning, Royall?"

"My students are in the library working on papers."

"Anything new happening around here?"

"Why ask me? I'm always the last one to know anything."

"Your friend Steve is on the Faculty Council. He always has the news before anyone else."

"As a matter of fact, he says something is going on. It seems that there is a sexual harassment case on the campus right now. Don't ask me who because I don't know. I don't think even Steve knows right now."

"I guess we'll hear about it soon enough. It's hard to keep any secrets around here. I'm off to class."

The class went well. We were discussing Jonathan Edwards' work as it compared to Benjamin Franklin's, and Sharon Ames was among those who took part in the discussion.

When I returned to the office, Royall was just leaving.

"That young woman I told you about yesterday came by the office again. I told her when you'd be back, but she said she had an appointment and couldn't wait."

"Did you ask her name this time?"

"No, and she didn't offer it; she said she'd be back later."

The phone rang and it was Meggie.

"Are you going to take me out to lunch today to make up for the horrid way you treated me last night?"

"No, I said that I would call you this weekend if you're not otherwise occupied."

"What is wrong with today? I need to talk to you about something important."

"All right, if it's important, let's meet at La Mesa at 12:30."

After my last class Sharon Ames stopped me in the hall and asked if she could speak to me. We entered the office, and she sat down in my easy chair, dropping her satchel of books beside her. She seemed anxious and ill at ease.

"Do you mind if we talk with the door closed, Mr. Greystone?"

"I usually keep the door open, Miss Ames. Is there a reason why you'd like to close the door?"

"What I'm about to tell you is quite personal, and I don't want anyone else to hear me."

Since this was the first time that she had asked to confer with me, I had never seen her up close before. She was looking directly into my eyes with a measuring expression to see how her words were affecting me. She was a young woman who seemed comfortable with men. She had sultry good looks with dark brown silky hair and large brown eyes. She was wearing the usual jeans, but she wore them with a natural style. I was always cautious with women students. I wanted no misunderstanding that my intentions were anything but professional. Occasionally a student would ask to shut the door, and I would comply, but always with some trepidation.

"This isn't easy for me to talk about."

I guessed by the way she was hesitating that what she had come to say had nothing to do with my course.

"Are you sure that I'm the right person to hear this? Maybe you would be more comfortable talking to the Dean of Student Affairs."

She shook her head and looked down for a minute as if she were deciding what to do. Then she looked up directly into my eyes and in her soft, clear voice began to speak.

"There is a professor in this school, for now he will remain unnamed, who is following me wherever I go. He turns up in the hall outside of my classes. He gives me gifts. At first they were just books he thought I could use as an English major. Then he started giving me other books on history and philosophy. Finally I told him that I could not accept any more books. So then he began to buy me presents — a watch, for example, to make sure I got to class on time."

"What kind of relationship have you had with this man?"

"He was my professor at one time, but I'm not in his class this semester."

"Is he trying to date you?" I realized immediately that I had used an antiquated expression.

She smiled slightly and then continued. "No. Not directly, I mean he hasn't mentioned our going out. Besides, he's married and has children. And he knows I have a boyfriend."

"Are you saying that without any encouragement from you this man is following you around and giving you gifts?"

"That is exactly what I'm saying, and my boyfriend is angry. I'm afraid he is about to do something terrible if this professor doesn't leave me alone."

"Have you talked to anyone else about this?"

"I've told another teacher and some students, thinking that there is some safety in other people knowing what's going on."

"And what do they say?"

"So far nobody has done anything to help me. They listen just as you are doing right now."

"If you won't reveal the name of this man, how can anyone help you?"

17

"I don't know. I don't want to ruin his career or reputation. I don't want to ruin my name around here either. People will think that I brought this on myself, that somehow it's my fault."

"Has he written any letters or notes to you expressing his feelings for you?"

"Yes, in the beginning he did."

"Where are they?"

"I destroyed them. I was afraid my parents or my boyfriend would find them."

"So if he denies what you're saying, it will be your word against his."

"Sometimes I feel that unintentionally I said or did something to give him the wrong impression. I talked to him about a problem I was having at home that was getting in the way of my studying. He was very sympathetic. I shouldn't have told him. I've never talked about that before with anyone, not even my boyfriend."

She stopped then and looked at me, and I could see tears in her eyes. I handed her the box of tissues I kept on my desk, and she took one. All of a sudden I remembered the time. I looked at my watch, and it was 12:45 P.M. I was supposed to meet Meggie at La Mesa fifteen minutes ago.

She had seen me glance at my watch and asked, "Am I keeping you away from something?"

"I'm supposed to meet someone, and I'm already late. Can we meet in the morning at the same time and talk some more? Maybe if I think about it overnight . . ."

We both stood up at the same time, a tacit signal that our meeting was over. She reached down to pick up her book satchel, and for a moment I could see a look of agony in her eyes that she could not conceal. Then she thanked me and rushed out of the room.

The drive to La Mesa took about fifteen minutes in midday traffic, but it seemed faster. I couldn't get Sharon's conversation out of my mind. What could this man be thinking to prey on this young woman? I'm not so naive that I don't know that such things happen. I wondered who the man was and if I should talk to him. I don't like complications, especially in other people's lives. The first thing she will have to do tomorrow is give me his name. I was pulling into the parking lot as Meggie was coming out the door of the restaurant. We spotted each other about the same time. By now it was one o'clock, and she probably thought I wasn't coming. She came toward me as I got out of the car.

"Sorry I'm late. I just left a student conference."

"I thought it must be something like that. You ought to carry a cellphone, so you can call me when you're tied up."

"I'll be the last one you know to carry a cellular phone."

"So you always say. One of these days someone's going to drag you kicking and screaming into the twenty-first century."

"Yeah right. Let's go back in and I'll buy lunch."

After the waiter had taken our order of beef caldo, my favorite vegetable-beef soup, Spanish rice, and beans, I looked at Meggie. She was especially attractive today with her long wavy red hair framing her face. She wore little makeup, but she needed no enhancements with her natural coloring.

"Well," I said, "What is so important it couldn't wait till Saturday?"

"There is something we need to talk about right now. I have been thinking about it a lot lately. It's about us. Things have to change. I know how much you hate this subject and how you avoid life's little complications, but it's time that we make some alterations in our living arrangements."

"I'm perfectly satisfied with my living arrangements. If you are suggesting marriage again, we've been through this a dozen times, and you already know my answer. It doesn't work for me. I don't wish to try it again."

"You've been divorced from Grace ten years now. I'm very different from her. I know I can make you happy. We're good for each other. You can't tell me that all you feel for me is friendship and lust. I don't believe that, and neither do you."

"Some very good relationships are based on just those two items."

"Then if you won't marry me, why don't we try living together for a while?"

"We've been through that also. My place is too small for two, and I don't want to give it up. I like my apartment. I like looking out my windows and seeing the bay."

"Then keep your apartment; visit it whenever you like. But move into my house. There's plenty of room for you and the cats."

"Cats are territorial. They hate moving. Besides they would not be pleased when they saw your dog."

"Harold loves everyone. I'm sure he'd be glad to have the company."

"Harold doesn't love everyone. He hates me. So you think we would be one big happy family. Oh, Meggins, what a dreamer you are."

Just then the waiter brought our food, and I hoped the conversation was over, at least while we ate, but Meggie was not ready to give it up yet.

"If this is your final answer, then I'm seriously going to consider moving to Austin again."

"And give up your teaching job here?"

"I got another call from Frank Garza that the accounting job I applied for last year is opening up again. I might as well take it. He said they would wait for me to finish this semester."

I put the spoon down and looked at her. She had threatened to leave Corpus before, but this time she looked like she really meant it. I didn't like the idea of Meggie moving away, but I also wasn't ready to marry or move in with her right now. Yet she was right. We were good for each other. This was something else that I would have to think about. I don't like making such decisions impulsively, and I told her so. I asked her if she would wait a little longer before giving Frank Garza her answer. She said she would.

After lunch we returned to the campus to attend the various committee meetings that typically take up most of the afternoon. Occasionally my mind would wander to my meeting with Sharon Ames or to my conversation with Meggie. Everything seemed uncertain and up in the air. I hated these feelings. I like being in control of my life, but at this moment that control was slipping away. I tried to type a note to Joan on my computer, but decided to go home and call her instead. She has to stop this Sarah Wilson from trying to contact me.

As I was leaving the building, I saw Jim Butler walking ahead of me. When I called to him, he turned and waited for me to catch up.

"There was a young woman waiting outside your office around 1:30, Jeremy. She asked when you would be back from lunch, but I didn't know. She said she would try to see you again tomorrow morning. It's probably about early registration for next semester. Aren't you the one who advises all the English majors?"

"I'm the one." I started to bring up the conversation I had with Sharon, but decided not to mention it if he didn't say anything. He didn't.

When I arrived home, I called Joan but got only her answering machine. I left a message for her to call off her friend's daughter. I was not the Chamber of Commerce or the Welcome Wagon. Then Tony, Cleo, and I went into the kitchen to see what we could drum up for supper. After we ate I turned on the Jupiter Symphony for a little accompaniment while grading the American literature exams, but I had too much on my mind to concentrate, so I put them away again.

Questions kept invading my thoughts: Why did I let Sharon Ames go without trying to help her? Who is the man she is protecting, and why is she shielding him? What does her boyfriend know? And who is he? What trouble is she having at home? What was Jim going to tell me about her when he came to my office? Then my mind would jump to my unresolved questions about Meggie. Should I move into her house for a trial period? Would my cats survive such an arrangement? Should I let her move to Austin? It would be a good professional move for her. Would it be right to stand in her way if I cannot make a commitment? Am I capable of making a commitment?

That night I dreamed I was running through a long, dark tunnel that opened into a large labyrinth. As I tried to find a way out, I kept getting deeper into the maze no matter which way I went. There were murmuring voices, but I didn't know who or where they were coming from. Then I became aware that I was being followed, slowly at first, then chased, but I couldn't tell who was chasing me. I ran as fast as I could, though I didn't know where I was going. Some of the rooms I found myself in were dimly lit. I could hardly see where I was. I bumped into furniture and walls. At last I saw Meggie walking far ahead of me. I tried to catch up to her, but the faster I ran, the farther away she moved. The noise level increased to raucous laughter and screams. Then suddenly I was alone and cold, standing on the wet sand at the edge of the bay, watching the endless waves breaking on the shore. I awoke to the loud sound of thunder overhead. Rain was splashing hard against the windows from the force of the wind. I was glad it was Friday. The campus would close early this afternoon for the weekend.

3

It was a cool Friday morning and still raining when I reached the office. Royall would not be in for an hour as his classes were scheduled later than mine. I had to decide where to meet with Sharon, so we would not be interrupted. I looked behind my chair and saw that my umbrella was still there. Across the street was the Student Center. There was a lounge in a corner of the building that would probably be vacant until the lunch hour, but around noon it always filled up with faculty members. Or we could go to one of the small glassed-in study rooms on the second floor of the library. Nobody would interrupt us there. The library sounded like a better idea. I still didn't know how I was going to help her. Much depended on what she told me today about the man who was harassing her. I needed to know more of her story. If she wanted my help, she'd have to trust me.

Just as I was getting my books together to go to class, there was a knock on the door. Perhaps Sharon had decided to come early. I told the person outside to come in, and looking up from my desk, watched as a young woman entered.

Standing before me was an almost familiar face, someone I hadn't seen in over ten years but remembered at once. She had changed from the scrawny, boyish-looking twelve-year-old whom I used to watch play ice hockey when I was married to her aunt. Her hair was much fuller, longer, and darker now,

23

the waves falling well below her shoulders. Her eyes were such a deep blue they seemed almost black at first glance. She had grown tall, and she was as slender as ever. When she smiled at me her full lips revealed perfect white teeth and dimples. Sarah had grown into a beautiful young woman.

"Uncle Jeremy?"

"Sarah, what a surprise." Seeing her standing there, looking so familiar, reminded me of how much I had always liked her as a child. I stood up and shook the hand she offered.

"I hope you don't mind my showing up here without an appointment, but I did want to surprise you."

"Not at all, Sarah. Joan told me you were moving to Corpus, but I'm still surprised, and I'm delighted too. Look at you, all grown up. Please, sit here."

I gestured toward my easy chair. I thought I was beyond responding so frivolously to a pretty young woman, but here I was saying again how glad I was to see her.

"Yes, I'm happy to be here too. I've always liked Corpus Christi, and now I'll be here for the next year or two. I've just begun to intern at KCOR, and I can't wait for my first real assignment. This is such a great opportunity. Do you know how hard it is to break into television news, especially for someone right out of college?"

"I've heard that. So how did you get the job?"

"One of my best friends at SMU was Betsy O'Ryan."

"I see. Her father owns the station."

"She introduced me to him in Dallas. He was looking for interns, and he offered me this chance. I'm going to work hard to prove to him that hiring me wasn't a mistake. I know I can do it."

"Sounds like a real opportunity to me. I'm sure it's a tough, competitive business."

"The biggest problem is the salary. They don't pay interns much. But I'm not complaining. I'll get by. But first I need a place to live that's not too expensive. And since I'll be working day and night, a place that's safe."

"This isn't Dallas, but you're right. A young woman living alone needs to be careful."

Aside from her good looks, there was an innocence about her, a girl next door quality, and suddenly it seemed very natural that she should come to me for help.

"A foolish consistency is the hobgoblin of little minds."

"What?" she looked at me, wondering where that fit into the conversation.

"Oh, it's just something that Emerson once wrote," was my only comment. I was doing exactly what I had said I would not do. But then Joan had asked me to look after Sarah until she was settled in her own place and knew the city a little better. All of a sudden that seemed like a reasonable request.

"All I remember is 'Simplify, simplify, simplify,' but that was someone else, wasn't it?"

"Thoreau, as a matter of fact, but you were close."

"Yeah, weren't they pretty good friends?"

I nodded, enjoying the moment.

Just then the bell rang, and I automatically stood up to go to class.

She rose also, ready to leave.

I asked her, "Would you like me to help you look for a place to live this afternoon?"

"Are you sure you can spare the time to do that?"

"I'll make the time. Is two P.M. all right? Why don't we meet here?"

"That's nice of you. I'll be back at two. Thank you, Uncle Jeremy." With that she left me to gather my things and make my way to my classroom.

After three hours of freshman composition classes, I returned to the office to find Royall there. He was putting his papers together, getting ready to leave. I asked him if he were going to spend the weekend grading.

"I'm going out of town this weekend. Marian and I are going to spend the next couple of days in San Antonio. We're going to take in the River Walk, art museums, bookstores, and who knows what else."

Marian happens to be Royall's latest girlfriend. I can't remember if she's the redhead or the blond. Royall goes through so many young women that I try not to develop any relationships with them. Then I don't feel sorry for them when he stops calling, as he always does when he's ready to go on to his next conquest. He picks women who fall hard for his superficial charms, but they never hold his interest long. Something is always wrong with them. They're too serious; they aren't thoughtful enough; they talk too much; they never say anything interesting. He believes in serial monogamy, one woman at a time, and there is never a shortage of new ones.

I'm glad that Royall is leaving early. Now I can see Sharon in the office. Fridays are getaway days at Corpus Christi Community College. After a heavy workweek, everyone who can leaves the campus by midday. Of course, the Faculty Council chooses this day for its monthly meetings to give the rest of the faculty the opportunity to attend, but today a meeting is not scheduled. I looked at my watch and saw that it was 11:30. Sharon should arrive any minute now. I decided to use the time grading. At 12:30 I began to think that she wasn't coming. Maybe she had second thoughts about talking to me. Perhaps she was able to work things out herself. I should be relieved, but I wish she had come by to let me know.

At one o'clock I went across the street to the Student Center to pick up a sandwich and a newspaper. I left the office door open since there was no one in the building except the janitor. Richard liked to stop by when he was at this end of the hall and talk a little. As I ate, I browsed through the classifieds to see what furnished apartments were available. The pickings were pretty slim. The Naval Air Station was expanding, so there was a shortage of living quarters in the area. Apartment construction had not caught up with the demand yet. Another problem, of course, was the modest rent Sarah could afford. Most of the apartments in the safer areas of the city were probably too expensive for an intern's salary. I scanned the unfurnished listings and found they too were limited. They weren't that much cheaper, and there would still be the extra cost of leasing furniture.

I made a short list of the most promising ones. When I noticed the time again, it was ten past two. Maybe I was going to be stood up by both young women in one day. I still felt uneasy about Sharon's not coming by the office to let me know that things were under control. From what I had observed in class, she seemed responsible enough. Just then I heard footsteps moving quickly down the hall, and Sarah, wearing designer jeans with her hair pulled back in a pony tail, rushed through the door.

"Sorry I'm late, Uncle Jeremy, but I got held up at the TV station. The station manager wanted to give me my first assignment. Nothing exciting. I also met some of the others on the staff. People are so friendly here. Everyone's offering help."

"I'll bet they are." Then as she perched on the arm of my reading chair, I added, "I didn't know you TV types could work in jeans."

"We can't, but I'm off for the rest of the afternoon. They know that I need to find an apartment. I can't wait to move out of that hotel. It's too expensive."

I grabbed the list and we were on our way. We drove from one apartment complex to the next without much luck. Nothing was suitable. The apartments that Sarah could afford were dreary or located in areas that would not be safe for her. By now I was feeling responsible for seeing that she found the right place.

Finally around six o'clock we went by my apartment to feed the cats. Sarah made friends with them immediately; they were even more interested in her than their supper. She sat down in a large chair by the window, and Cleo, the shy one, jumped into her lap. Tony leaped up on the back of the chair to get his share of attention.

"I love your apartment, Uncle Jeremy. The view of the city and the water is marvelous."

"That's Corpus Christi Bay. You should see it on a clear day."

"I wish I could find something like this. Do they have any vacancies in this building?"

"Not that I know of. This place is really only big enough for one person, but if you want you can sleep on the sofa in the study until you find something." That was said impulsively before I had even thought about it. Now I hoped she would say no. I didn't mind someone spending a couple of nights, but what if once she moved in she didn't find a place of her own? What if it took weeks, months to find the right apartment? What would Meggie say when she found out that a young woman was living here? It would be hard to explain that Sarah is my niece when I'm divorced from her aunt and haven't been in contact with any member of her family in over ten years.

"If you really don't mind, I'd love to stay. It will only be for a few days until I find my own apartment. Joan told me how nice you were, but I never expected this. Thank you, Uncle — do you mind if I call you Jeremy? Our relationship is a lot different now from what it was when I was twelve years old."

"I'd like that better too. Now let me drive you back to the college, so you can pick up your car and go to the hotel and check out." After I dropped her off, I had grave doubts about Sarah's moving in, but now it was too late to back out. I drove back to the apartment and tried Joan's number again. This time she answered.

"Why do you do these things to me?" I asked after I had told her what had happened.

"Actually, Jeremy, I never expected you to invite Sarah to move in. That was your idea. I know how you value your privacy."

"It all happened so fast. Right now she's getting her things from the hotel, but she ought to be back here any time."

"I'm sure it won't be for long — just until she finds an apartment. I've stayed with you before. It wasn't so bad, was it?"

"That's different. Remember, I know you. I don't have to remind you that she's practically a stranger."

"I'm sure after a couple of days in that small apartment of yours with only one bathroom, she'll no longer be a stranger, and trust me, she'll be very anxious to move."

"And what if you're wrong? You understand that people in the building are going to get the wrong impression. And how am I going to explain this to Meggie?"

By now Joan could hardly control her amusement. "That won't be easy."

"I'm glad you're finding this so entertaining."

"It'll work out."

"I don't think so."

"There goes my bell. Sorry, Jeremy, I'm having some people over for dinner tonight. I'll get back with you later."

And with that Joan was gone, and I had to decide what to do about Meggie fast before Sarah returned.

I dialed Meggie's number, hoping she was in. She answered immediately, and I could tell that she was glad I called.

"Can you come right over? There is something I need to tell you." I knew this was rushing her unfairly, but I wanted her to hear about Sarah from me before Sarah moved in.

"What about? Can't you tell me over the phone?"

"No, I can't, and I have to see you now, if you can make it."

"You sound so strange. You're scaring me." There was a pause and then she said, "All right, I'll be right over."

The drive from her house would not take long as she lived only a few blocks away. I was sure that she thought I was calling her about our discussion at the restaurant. Five minutes later she arrived, and after a quick greeting, I led her to the comfortable chair by the window. She sat stiffly waiting for me to begin.

As quickly as I could I told her about Joan's giving Sarah my office number and how I had tried to head Sarah off from contacting me. By the time I reached Joan, I explained, Sarah had already arrived and come by the office looking for me. Meggie sat and listened without asking questions, without any outward response at all. I tried to read her eyes to decipher what she was thinking, but she simply looked at me and said nothing.

"I spent the afternoon with Sarah looking for an apartment, but without results."

"I'm not surprised."

I stopped and looked deeply into her eyes. "You haven't really said very much."

"What else haven't you told me?"

"Because she is on such a short budget, I told her she could move in here till she found a place to live."

"I thought this apartment's too small for two people."

"Is that all you have to say?"

"You're free to do whatever you want. There are no strings to our relationship, if it can be called that. I do have a suggestion though, if you want to hear it."

"You know I do."

Just then there was a knock on the door, and I opened it to find Sarah standing there, her arms loaded with clothes. After making the introductions, I went down with her to her car to help her bring up her remaining suitcases and other possessions. I realized that she had brought all her portable property with her in this move, and I wondered how it would all fit into the apartment even for a few days. Among her belongings she had a desktop computer and printer, stereo equipment, and a TV. In just a few minutes she had totally invaded my space.

The three of us sat down together in the living room to decide what to do next. Meggie asked Sarah questions about her new job, about school, about Dallas, and Sarah seemed forthcoming in answering all her questions. Then Sarah asked Meggie about Corpus Christi — all the questions that a young newcomer might want to know about shopping and doctors and modes of entertainment, and Meggie was ready with the answers. I was pleased that they got along with each other so well. Meggie addressed most of her conversation to Sarah, ignoring me, but I accepted that as part of my penitence.

It was time for supper, and I suggested calling out for a pizza, and they both agreed. While we waited for our dinner to arrive, Sarah rose to begin finding places for her belongings. At this point it looked hopeless. Meggie finally decided to offer some relief. She gave me and Sarah a choice:

"Sarah, you can come home with me for a few days until you find an apartment. I have much more room. You can move into my guest room with its own big closet and bath. There will be room for your things even if it is a bit crowded. Or Jeremy, you can move into that room until Sarah moves out. It's up to you both to make the decision. I'm just offering you the room, nothing more." With this she looked directly at me.

"That is a most generous offer. Don't you think so Sarah?" I was thinking, a way out, yes!

"Most generous," Sarah answered. "Which way would you prefer to do it, Jeremy? Meggie?"

It was obvious that Sarah saw the hopelessness of the space situation as clearly as I did. And she hadn't even investigated the bathroom yet.

"Maybe Sarah had better come home with me. Do you like dogs as much as cats?"

"Anything with four legs. Thank you, Meggie. I'd love to accept your offer. I promise I'll find something right away."

Meggie looked at me to see if I had any comment to make. I was too relieved and too grateful to do anything but mouth a thank you.

"Look what time it is. Do you mind if I tune in the news on KCOR?" Sarah, of course, wanted to watch her new station perform. They were the typical group of locals that I usually choose to avoid, but I didn't mind anything tonight knowing that this would not be a regular occurrence. As we were watching the banal TV chatter, the pizza arrived, and I went to the door to retrieve it. When I got back, the others were talking about a small news item that had just been presented. Some young college woman had disappeared. The police said that they couldn't consider her a missing person for forty-eight hours.

"This is just like Dallas, only on a smaller scale," said Sarah.

"She probably has run off with her boyfriend and will be back Monday," I answered.

"I don't know. I always get a funny feeling when a young woman disappears," Meggie commented.

"Now that is the kind of story that I want to cover. Something high profile."

"Patience, young one," I said to Sarah but looked at Meggie to see if she was all right with the new arrangements. I still couldn't read her expression.

After the pizza, we all helped reload Sarah's car, and after the two women drove away, Tony, Cleo, and I luxuriated in the privacy that had almost been lost.

❧ 4 ❧

Saturdays are always catch up days for me. I take my laundry and cleaning in, go to the grocery for food and supplies, run by the bank, and do all the leftover errands that I never get done during the school week. While I was out this morning, I debated about whether to go by Meggie's and see if the two women were getting along all right. I still felt guilty about Meggie's having felt obligated to invite Sarah to stay with her. I was also concerned that Sarah might innocently repeat some gossip she might have heard about me from her mother or Grace. I decided I'd better go check things out.

Meggie answered the door and invited me in for a cup of coffee. As I entered the living room, Harold began barking and then tried to run behind me to take a bite out of my ankle, his usual greeting when I arrived. Meggie returned to her seat at the table in the breakfast room, and I slid into an empty space beside Sarah in the booth. They had just finished breakfast and offered me one of the remaining bagels.

"How are you getting on with Harold?" I asked Sarah.

"Very well, but I can see that he doesn't like you very much."

"Harold can tell that Jeremy is a cat person," Meggie said in defense of her dog.

"Meggie has invited me to take my time moving," Sarah

33

said, looking very much at home in her short, colorful cotton robe.

"I'm rather enjoying the company, and there's plenty of room here. I even have an old table I can set up in your room, if you want to use your computer." I noticed that Meggie was addressing all her conversation to Sarah and looked at me only occasionally.

The conversation continued to go like that, so after I finished my coffee, I rose to leave. Sarah walked me to the door, and I asked her,

"Do you need some help today looking for an apartment?"

"No thanks, Jeremy. Meggie said she would drive me around today, and my friend Betsy is keeping her eyes open too."

"Then it sounds like you have everything under control, but if you think of something I can do, let me know."

"I appreciate what you have done already — especially introducing me to Meggie."

With that I left, wondering when I would get the chance to see Meggie alone. The remainder of the weekend went by peacefully. I didn't pick up a newspaper or turn on the TV. I neither called nor heard from anyone, and so I finally completed my grading and caught up with my reading.

When I returned to the office on Monday morning, Royall was already there working at his desk.

"I came in early to prepare for my classes. I never thought about school all weekend," he said barely looking up from his book.

"How was the trip to San Antonio?"

"Wonderful. The room at the hotel was beautiful. It overlooked the Riverwalk. The restaurants were excellent, especially the Mexican food. We even did some shopping. I think I'm in love."

"And how were the museums and the bookstores?" I said ignoring the last remark.

"We didn't spend much time in them. We were too busy enjoying our time together — no schedules, no demands from anything or anyone. It was fun just sitting together out on the balcony, drinking wine, and talking. Marian and I have so much in common."

I decided not to ask what that would be. This was not the first time that Royall thought that he was in love with a woman. As I have mentioned before, the feeling passes.

When I entered the room for my first class, I heard the students talking about the young woman who had disappeared during the past weekend. One of them said that he heard that she was in one of my classes. I asked what her name was, and he said, "Sharon Ames." I had been at the door to get the pizza Friday night and had missed hearing her name on the broadcast. Neither Meggie nor Sarah had mentioned it when they talked about the young woman who had disappeared. Sharon Ames missing. I could hardly believe it. I went through the motions of teaching my classes, but always in the back of my mind was my meeting with Sharon. I wished again that I had not let her go without offering her more help. Where is she now? Why did she run away? How come she didn't tell her family where she was going? Why doesn't she let anybody know she's all right?

That evening I wanted to talk to Meggie about a number of things. When I called, she was at the grocery store, but Sarah invited me to come over. She wanted me to meet someone visiting her at the house. When I arrived Sarah introduced me to Betsy O'Ryan. Betsy with her short brown hair and blue eyes was as plain as Sarah was beautiful. But she had all the self-assurance of a young person who had been given the advantages of an upper-middle class upbringing. It was obvious that she and Sarah were close friends, and Betsy enjoyed listening to Sarah's impressions of her father's television station and the people who worked there. Sarah said that she was especially surprised that one of the weathermen had a job. He seemed to know nothing at all about weather.

"Even I know that Corpus is going through a serious water shortage, but all he talks about is that the sun is shining and that it's a good day for the beach."

Betsy said, "Oh, you mean Ramón. I know. He starts out on Mondays and begins the countdown on how many more working days till the weekend. He must have something on the station manager to keep his job." She laughed and said that although she had studied journalism at SMU, she was not going to work for her father. She had been around the station all her life and needed a change. "Anyway," she continued, "I've been accepted by The University of Texas Law School, and I'm moving to Austin in January."

I waited a while longer, and when Meggie did not show up, I decided to leave. As I was about to rise, Sarah asked Betsy if she knew Sharon Ames.

"I've known Sharon since we were in the first grade at Fisher Elementary. We went all through school together."

"What do you think happened to her?" I asked. "Has she ever run away before without letting anyone know where she is?"

"No, that's not at all like Sharon. When the rest of us went through our wild stage during high school, she stopped hanging out with us. She always had to go home."

"What kind of home does she come from?" I was glad to finally find someone who could answer some questions.

"That's the strange part. She used to come over to our houses, especially when we were pretty young, but by the time we entered middle school, she stopped coming and didn't invite us over to her house either."

"Does she have any brothers or sisters?"

"She has a younger brother, Ted. I think he's still going to the University of Houston."

"When have you talked to her last?" There were dozens of questions I wanted to ask.

"Not in years. I should have kept up with her better, but after we graduated from high school, I went on to SMU, and she didn't go to college. When I was home on holidays, I never saw her. Diana Parker lived next door to Sharon. She knows a lot more about her than I do."

"I don't even know Sharon," Sarah added, " but I can't help being concerned about her. I'm sorry the police aren't doing more to find her."

"She is of age, and there aren't any signs of foul play. I'm sure the police think she left of her own free will and she'll return when she's ready," I said.

"I'd like to believe that too, but going away like this without letting anyone know is not like the Sharon I remember." Betsy said.

"What bothers me is how she looked the last time I saw her."

"What do you mean — how she looked?" Sarah wanted to know.

"She looked pretty upset. She made an appointment with me for the following day to continue our conversation, but she never kept it."

"She left town instead," Betsy said. "Maybe something important came up."

"But wouldn't her family know?" I asked.

Just then Meggie walked into the room, her arms full of groceries, and we all got up to help her.

"Are you staying for dinner, Jeremy?" she asked.

"I came over to invite you to have dinner out with me. There are some things we need to talk about."

"Not tonight, Jeremy. I told the girls I would cook my famous chicken and rice, an old family favorite. But you can join us if you wish. There'll be enough for one more." She looked at me indifferently.

"I'll take a rain check," I said. "Maybe I'll see you later?"

"Not tonight," she said and went into the kitchen, Harold following at her heels.

On my way home several thoughts kept running through my mind. I decided that I would pursue my personal investigation of Sharon's disappearance. I needed to know whether she planned to return to my class or if I should drop her to keep her from failing the course and ruining her excellent GPA. But I had other more personal problems. Meggie was still acting rather cool towards me. I wasn't used to that from her. Not that it really bothered me, but we have known each other a long time, and I count on her friendship. She is the one person I like to bounce ideas off of. She has great insight, and tonight I had wanted to talk to her about Sharon Ames.

❦ 5 ❦

On Tuesday I invited Sarah to have lunch with me. I wanted to find out what her plans were for finding an apartment. I also wanted to discover what she had been telling Meggie about me that might have created this new distance between us.

When I walked into my American lit class, I hoped to see Sharon sitting in her regular seat. I had heard no more about her on the television news nor had I read anything in the newspaper. Surely she had come back by now, and all the worry about her had been for nothing. But she wasn't there. Most of the students do not keep up with the news, so nobody seemed concerned that she was absent. The class was a good one, and the discussion about Benjamin Franklin and his *Autobiography* was quite animated. Then I answered questions about their paper due on Thursday. I kept thinking that Sharon would have to borrow somebody's notes when she got back. I also hoped she would not miss the essay deadline. After the bell rang a cluster of students came up to my desk to continue asking questions. Some were about Franklin, while others asked about the paper due Thursday. They followed me out of class and continued the discussion for at least ten more minutes. Then I returned to the office to find Sarah and Royall laughing and talking as if they were old friends.

"You two know each other?"

"We introduced ourselves," Royall answered not taking his eyes off Sarah.

She was wearing a light wool suit the color of her eyes. I could see by the way Royall looked at her that he was impressed.

"I had no idea that you had a niece."

"There's a lot you don't know about me."

"I'll have to get Sarah to fill me in."

We talked about Sarah's moving to Corpus and her new job for a few minutes more, and then she and I left the office to go to lunch. When we were seated near the window in a restaurant overlooking Corpus Christi Bay, Sarah said,

"I never get tired of watching the water." She didn't speak for a minute while she stared out the window. Then she said, "It reminds me of a poem, 'Neither out Far Nor in Deep.' *The people along the sand / All turn and look one way / They turn their back on the land / They look at the sea all day.*"

"I didn't know you liked poetry."

"Not all poetry. I do like Robert Frost. I wrote a research paper about him once."

"He's one of my favorites too."

"Tell me about Royall."

"Right now I can tell you that he's in love."

"That's too bad. He seems nice. An English teacher just like you."

"That's probably all we have in common."

"He's too young for me anyway."

"Now that he isn't. I'm sure he's at least five years older than you are."

"That's not what I mean. I like older men. They're more interesting."

"Do you have a boyfriend in Dallas?"

"I just ended a relationship with someone there."

"Would you care to talk about it? I'd like you to fill in some of those lost years for me."

"I'm not ready to talk about it yet. He was too young and

immature. He's involved with someone else anyway. At least he doesn't have to lie about it anymore."

"Speaking as your long lost uncle, I'd say he wasn't near good enough for you."

"You're not at all like Aunt Grace described you, Jeremy."

"And how is that?"

"Oh, I don't want to say. But I'd like to know you better too."

"What do you want to know?"

"For one thing, how serious are you and Meggie about each other?"

"I'm not sure. We're still trying to figure that out. As of now, we're just friends."

"There's a lot to Meggie. I wouldn't take her for granted if I were you."

"Did she tell you that I'm taking her for granted?"

"Of course not. We don't talk about you at all, if that's what you're wondering."

"What I've been wondering is how long you're going to stay at her house."

"She's not anxious for me to move. But I won't overstay my welcome."

"Harold doesn't bother you with all his poodle demands?"

"Harold's a joy. Meggie says he's a good judge of character, and I think she's right."

We spent the rest of the lunch talking about her job. At this point she was doing small chores for everyone around the station, but she was anxious to work on her own assignments. What she was hoping for was to get out in the field as a reporter. I told her that she would get her wish before too long. She had all the qualities necessary to be a TV journalist, as well as the education. In the meantime she should take every assignment seriously. She had her dues to pay.

"Since I have the time, I'm going to inquire on my own about Sharon Ames' disappearance," Sarah said.

"I'm not sure I would do that if I were you. There may be issues that Sharon would not want made public."

"What issues?"

"Personal information about herself."

Her elbow leaning on the table and her chin resting on her hand, Sarah looked at me with inquisitive blue eyes and said, "This story sure has my reporter's curiosity aroused."

"And something else. Even though this isn't as important as Sharon's disappearance, there could be something that might involve the college unnecessarily in a scandal."

"Jeremy, I may be inexperienced, but I check my sources carefully. I'm not going to do anything that will hurt Sharon or your precious college."

"Then if you find out anything, keep me informed, and don't do anything reckless. Since I'm the only family you have here, I feel responsible for you. I don't want the whole Dallas clan and my sister heading down here because something terrible has happened to you."

"You're not responsible for me. What all of you should remember is that I'm an adult now and fully capable of taking care of myself."

Properly chastised, I turned to less personal subjects. After lunch I returned to the office and decided to look for Jim Butler. A student was leaving his office just as I was about to knock on his door.

"Come on in, Jeremy," Jim said. "I was wondering when you were going to come by."

"I don't believe we talked since Sharon Ames came by my office. Did she tell you about our conversation?"

"No," Jim answered, "I'm sure I never saw her after you spoke to her."

"What do you think would make her leave town right in the middle of a semester? What do you know about her, Jim?"

"I know that she was not happy at home when she was living with her mother and stepfather. She told me her mother was an alcoholic. She belonged to all kinds of clubs and organizations, and she didn't work. She said for some reason, which she never explained, her stepfather didn't want to continue paying for her education. It's not that he couldn't afford it; he's a rather prominent businessman in the community."

"I don't even know who her stepfather is."

"Harvey Stone. You know, Stone's Realty."

"Doesn't he also own a dozen apartment complexes throughout the area?"

"That's him. Plenty of money. He lives in that large Mediterranean-style house on Ocean Drive."

"Where does Sharon live now?"

"Last time I heard she had moved into one of Stone's apartments. I don't know if she pays rent or not. She was looking for a job to help pay for her tuition and books."

"Did Sharon ever tell you about a professor who was harassing her?"

"I know nothing about that. What professor? How was he harassing her?"

I told Jim the little I knew and how Sharon was going to return last Friday to my office to tell me the rest of the story. Jim just sat quietly and listened. He was rather surprised that Sharon would confide in me and not him about something like that when he had known her so much longer and thought of himself as one of her mentors. I didn't understand that either. Finally I asked him if he knew Sharon's boyfriend.

"No, I did see them together once in the Student Center. I don't remember much about him. They were on the other side of the room."

"What did she tell you about him?"

"She said he was hot-tempered, jealous, and controlling. She was afraid to say hello to friends when he was around. She told me she was going to break off the relationship."

"When did she tell you all this?"

"I think it was one of the last times I saw her. He was giving her a lot of trouble about someone."

"Jim, what had you started to tell me in my office the other day when you came by?"

Jim began to speak, then paused, and looked uncomfortable.

"I think under the circumstances of Sharon's leaving, I'd rather not say. Remember, I don't want to betray any confidences."

"I don't expect you to, but you did come by to talk to me about something you thought was important."

"I've decided to wait until Sharon returns and check with her. If she says it's all right to speak to you about it, then I will. Otherwise, I don't know anything else I can tell you."

"Do you think anything has happened to Sharon that the police should know?"

"I have no idea, Jeremy. You saw her after I did. What do you think?"

"I don't know what to think. But if you hear anything at all, please let me know."

When I returned to my office, Steve White was sitting at my desk. He and Royall had been talking about Sharon's disappearance. Steve got out of my chair and stood leaning on the door frame. He was saying that Sharon was in his advanced calculus class, and he couldn't understand what happened to her. She had taken two other mathematics courses from him last year and never missed a class. Last Friday she wasn't there for a major exam, and she didn't show up yesterday either.

"She's in your class too, isn't she, Jeremy?" he asked.

"She sure is, but I can't help you. She's not attending my classes either. Maybe Royall knows something about her. He seems to have a line on all the good-looking women that come into this building."

Royall glared at me. "I do know who Sharon Ames is," he said. "She hangs around the English Lab sometimes with some of the other English majors. I also saw her one morning last week picking up an application in the English office for some job in the department. And, of course, I know she's Jeremy's student, so that makes her off limits."

I asked them if either one knew anything about her

boyfriend. They both said they knew nothing about him. After I finished my work in the office, I left the two of them bantering about how they were going to spend the evening.

Soon after I arrived home, Meggie called and said that she was on her way over. I tried to tell her that I just got in and had some things around the apartment to take care of, but she said that she would be there in half an hour. Her voice sounded more strained than usual, and I presumed she was still angry about something.

Thirty minutes later the bell rang, and when I opened the door, Meggie marched in looking like she had finally decided to let me know what was on her mind. She got right to the point.

"What I resent about the whole matter, Jeremy, is not Sarah. I like her. It's just your usual callous way of handling everything."

"And what way is that?" I decided not to go on the defensive yet.

"You knew that Sarah was here and looking for you, but you never mentioned anything about it until after you had invited her to move into your apartment."

"I had no idea that I was going to do that."

"The Devil made you do it?"

"She had no place to stay, and it was only going to be for a few days."

"Then you call me and expect me to give you some kind of approval. You've told me a hundred times that I can't stay over here."

"You'd hate it here. It's too crowded for two."

"That makes a lot of sense. Then what really got me mad was that you were behaving like some love struck teenager trying to pull something over on his mother. Sorry, Jeremy, I won't assume that role, even for you."

"You misunderstood the whole thing. I was just doing my sister a favor."

"Then you're more blind than I thought you were."

"If you don't understand how innocent all this is, I'm

45

sorry. But you're the one who said there were no strings attached to our relationship."

"So that's how you want it?"

"Doesn't that mean we're both free to get involved in other relationships without asking permission?"

"Right. I'd better go." Meggie got up to leave, but I didn't want things to end like this. I went over to her and took her hands in mine. She looked up at me, and I took her in my arms and kissed her lips. At first she did not respond, but then I felt her arms around me. I kissed her again on her lips, her eyes, and her neck. In a few minutes we were in the bedroom. I helped her slowly undress while she unbuttoned my shirt. She kissed my chest. She stood naked in the dim light of late afternoon. She always seemed most beautiful like this. She had no inhibitions, no shyness, and I pulled the rest of my clothes off and dropped them on the floor beside the bed. As always our arguing was forgotten in our lovemaking. From much experience every curve of our bodies fit together, and later we lay in each other's arms, our legs entwined. We spent the rest of the evening talking, making love, resting, and making love again.

Finally we were both hungry and went into the kitchen to see what was in the refrigerator. I was glad that I had gone shopping over the weekend. There were bacon and eggs plus all the makings for sandwiches. We decided the sandwiches would be faster. Meggie looked lovely in my white terry cloth robe, her hair falling in waves around her face. I couldn't take my eyes off her. Looking up at me, her sandwich in her hand, she asked,

"Why can't it always be like this?"

"It can," I told her.

"No, it can't," she said. "You always do something to spoil it."

6

At home the next evening the telephone rang about 10:15. It was Sarah, who called to tell me to turn on the KCOR news. I told Sarah that I would get back to her later and quickly turned on the TV. The body of a young woman, identified by her family as Sharon Ames, had been found earlier in the evening, buried in a shallow grave in the sand dunes on Padre Island. The police had turned the body over to the coroner's office to determine the cause and the time of death. A reporter was interviewing a family who had been visiting the area on their vacation and had accidentally discovered the body while they were beachcombing for driftwood and shells. In the background was a shot of a bodybag being removed from the scene. Sharon dead. For the next few minutes, I found it hard to breathe. What had I done. I had turned her away when she came to me for help. She might be alive today if I had responded differently. By now the news anchor was moving on to another story, so I clicked off the set with the remote control. I sat, I'm not sure for how long, unable to move.

I had remained home this evening to work on a paper I was submitting to an English conference. Mozart's Piano Concerto No. 11 was still playing merrily in the CD player. I had been writing about the use of telecommunications in the teaching of English courses. That seemed unimportant now. Someone had died because I was too absorbed with my own

47

plans. I had told Sharon to come back tomorrow because I was late for a lunch date.

The phone rang, and when I picked it up, a very distraught Jim Butler asked,

"Jeremy, have you been watching the news?"

"Yes, I just heard about Sharon."

"Who could have done such a thing?"

"I can't answer that. Do you have any idea?"

"No, of course not."

"There's nothing we can do tonight. I'm going to bed, Jim; I'll talk to you in the morning."

I looked at my watch. It was 11:30, too late to call Sarah back tonight. I would talk to her tomorrow. I had a hard time falling asleep and must have tossed until it was almost morning. Then suddenly I found myself walking on the beach, watching a small sail boat drifting out to sea. I recognized the solitary sailor. It was Sharon. I ran into the water and then dived and began swimming as fast as I could toward her, but the boat kept drifting out of reach. I began to tread water, and when I looked back on the shore, I saw a young woman walking along the edge of the water. She was waving at me to come back. I looked back again at the boat, but now it was empty. The woman on the shore signaled to me again. Was it Sharon? I swam closer to see who it was. Now a man was standing beside her, but it wasn't Sharon. Sarah and Jim were standing together waiting for me to return to shore. But where was Sharon? I couldn't return until I found her. Then sirens in the background began their insistent blaring, and soon police cars converged upon the area. I awoke to the ringing of my alarm clock. I dragged myself out of bed and, more slowly than usual, began to get ready for school.

While I drank my usual morning cup of strong coffee, I searched the paper for details that the TV news story had omitted. There was little more. The article did reveal approximately where on the beach the body had been found. It was ten miles farther south than the more popular public beaches. Since there was no blood at the scene, the police assumed that she had died somewhere else and that her body had been dropped there. Sharon had been shot, and near her body, covered with a small layer of sand, a .38 Special was found. Whose gun it was the police did not say. They announced that they were revealing no more information until they completed their preliminary investigation. Sharon's five-year-old white Mercury Sable was also missing. Beside the story was a recent picture of Sharon, looking young and attractive with her large, searching eyes and expressive mouth, revealing the hint of the smile I had sometimes seen when she was absorbed in a class discussion. She seemed to be looking at me now, appealing to me again to help her.

Royall was not in the office when I arrived, and Jim had not shown up yet in his office either. I was glad I didn't have to talk to anyone before the bell rang for the first class. When I entered the classroom at eight o'clock, I could hear bits of the students'conversation. One group was talking about the possible condition of a body found on the beach. Padre Island has a large population of coyotes always foraging for food, and it's a constant problem for people who bring their dogs to the beach. The coyotes would hardly ignore a human body if it were exposed on the sand. Someone then reminded the others that Sharon's body was concealed in a shallow grave. Another group of students were speculating about what Sharon was doing so far from the main beach in late October and with whom she had gone there. I could hear the words "drugs and alcohol." Always there are those who imagine that they know more than they really do. A police science student, who seemed to be better informed than the rest of us, said that the police had not labeled this a murder case yet. There were other possibilities, such as an accident or a suicide. The police department was asking anyone who might have any relevant information to come forward. For a few minutes I wondered if I should call them. Then I decided I would just be getting in the way of their investigation. I didn't have any real information that could help them.

Later when I returned from my classes, Royall was working at his desk. He looked up and said, "That's really too bad about Sharon Ames."

"Yes, it is. Has there been any more news about it?"

"Just that the gun was a .38 Special Smith and Wesson and belonged to her stepfather."

"I'm sure the police will have the whole story in a day or so."

"From what I hear from other students, she was pretty straight — no drinking or drugs."

"I was just grading one of her papers. She was a good writer. I wonder if her family would like me to send it to them."

"I'd wait and let some time pass."

"You're right. I'll just hold onto it for a while."

Just then the phone rang, and I picked it up to hear Meggie's voice.

"Jeremy, I'm sorry to hear about your student. I know you were concerned about her."

"I can't help but feel that I might have prevented this."

"You're giving yourself too much power. None of this has anything to do with you."

"The day we met for lunch she was in my office. She was the student I was talking to. I told her to come back tomorrow."

"I thought she was the one."

"I need to talk to you. How about lunch today?"

"I'll see you at 12:30. Is the Country Inn all right? It's quiet and we can have some privacy."

I tried to call Sarah at Meggie's house, but she had already left for the television station. I wasn't sure that she could talk to me there, so I decided to wait until this evening to get back to her. Then I checked to see if Jim was in his office. Two young men were on their way out the door, so he waved me to enter. "Well, Jeremy?"

"Jim, you may have some information that could help the police solve this case. Don't you think you should tell them what Sharon told you?"

"I don't think I can, Jeremy. I have no proof that any of it is true, and it would hurt a lot of people."

"Do you still say that it has nothing to do with any of our colleagues?"

"As I told you already, she never complained to me about any of her teachers. What she did say concerns someone else. I'm still not going to talk to you about it. I might tell the police if I think it will help them, but right now I'm going to wait and see what happens. Nothing I do will bring Sharon back, so I'd rather not get involved."

Jim and I talked for a few minutes more, and then I noticed the clock on his wall revealed it was 12:15. It was time to meet Meggie at the Country Inn. I was glad there were no committee meetings this afternoon. I had thought for a while that I would go home after lunch and work on my conference paper, but I was no longer in a very creative mood.

I arrived before Meggie and was seated in a comfortable booth by a window, overlooking a sumptuous garden. October is always a beautiful month in Corpus. The weather finally cools off, and some long awaited October showers bring out every shade of green that living plants can display. This is a tropical part of the country, and bird-watchers come from all over to see birds of every variety. Other than California, Texas has more species of birds than any other state in the nation. If I sound like a bird-watcher, that's because I am one. I like nothing better than to take my high powered telescope and binoculars to the many areas around the city to watch my feathered friends in their natural surroundings.

While I stared through the window and waited for Meggie, something kept repeating itself in my mind: "I'd rather not get involved. I'd rather not get involved." I could understand Jim's desire to stay out of the whole mess. Hadn't that always been my credo too? I turned my thoughts back to the garden and observed a couple of mourning doves sitting on the edge of a birdbath. At last Meggie appeared. Dressed in forest green, a color that brought out the natural beauty of her red hair, green eyes, and clear skin, she looked especially

51

lovely today. She slid into the booth across from me, and I moved over so that I could look directly at her while we talked.

For the next few minutes we were engrossed in the menu. After we ordered some house white wine and chicken Caesar salads, I looked up at her. I wasn't sure how much I wanted to tell her. She decided to let me take my time and not push me to speak. One of Meggie's virtues is that she doesn't have to fill every moment with conversation. She isn't afraid of silence, and without ever meaning to, she has taught me not to fear it either. As I observed her calm presence across the table, I realized that she was the one person I always went to when I needed to talk to someone. I knew that I could count on her clear mind and good judgment to tell me what she thought, whether I liked it or not. Slowly I began to tell her the story that Sharon had told me. Meggie listened as she always does without interrupting me or asking questions. When I finished, I asked her if she knew of any teacher at the college who had been accused recently by a student of sexually harassing her. She said that she didn't know of anyone, but that the Faculty Council was working on a new sexual harassment policy and that there had been quite a lot written about it lately in the city newspaper. The faculty and the administration were at odds, and the Board of Regents had ordered them to work together and come to a consensus by the next board meeting.

"I'm surprised you haven't heard about it."

"I have. I've just had other things on my mind lately."

She smiled and said softly, "I know."

The waiter brought the wine and some of the restaurant's famous garlic bread. Meggie took a slice and put it on her plate, but I was more interested in the wine. It was an excellent chardonnay.

"Do you think the students are aware of the harassment controversy?" I asked her.

"They are if they read the papers. It's been on television too."

I then told her about my conversations with Jim. She was

surprised that Sharon had not told Jim what she had confided to me.

"Very strange that she chose you alone to tell this story to," she commented.

"I don't think I am the only one, but I don't have any idea who the others are." I then spoke out loud something gnawing at the back of my mind.

"Do you think that Sharon didn't say anything because she was referring to Jim? She was in his class last year, and he does have a wife and a couple of kids."

"Do you think he's the type to get involved like that with a student?" she asked.

"No, I've never seen any sign of it."

"From what I know about Jim Butler, I don't think so either. But then how can any of us know for sure what goes on behind closed office doors?" She was silent for a minute and then added quietly, "No, I don't think it's Jim."

The waiter arrived then with our lunch, and so for the time being, we dropped the subject.

Our conversation then turned to Sarah. I asked Meggie how long she was going to let Sarah stay with her. Meggie said that she didn't mind Sarah staying for as long as she wanted, but that it was Sarah who seemed anxious to move.

"I think she has a boyfriend whom she doesn't want us to meet," she said.

"That's unlikely. She just broke up with someone in Dallas."

"I may be misreading the signs, but I don't think so."

"You must be. As far as I know, she didn't even know anyone in Corpus, except Betsy, when she moved here."

"Maybe Betsy introduced her to someone. Anyway, I'm just guessing, but the way she sprays on perfume when she leaves the house at night sure makes me wonder."

"If she's meeting someone, why is she being so secretive?"

"I have a feeling that she wants to maintain her privacy."

"From us?"

"From you — especially."

"Now you're really letting your imagination run amuck. If I seem the least bit interested in Sarah, it's only because Joan expects me to look after her."

"Right, it's for Joan."

"Well, she is my niece."

"You may pull the wool over everyone else's eyes, even your own, my friend, but spare me, please."

"You're jealous of my relationship with Sarah."

"I suppose this is another one of your male fantasies. How charming."

Meggie had a way of half smiling at me during these verbal exchanges so that I could never tell exactly how flippant or serious she was being. I decided to let the comment pass. I was in no mood to fight with her today, especially in so public a setting, so I changed the subject. We finished our lunch in peace, and I walked her to her car.

"I may have time to come by later, if you're not busy." I said.

"I need to groom Harold tonight, but that shouldn't take too long. Do come over, but don't expect Sarah to be there. Most likely she'll be going out."

"All the better."

I opened the car door for her, closed it, and watched her drive off in her shiny black Mustang convertible, thinking that one day soon I would have to find the time to take my Honda in for its regular wash and wax job. I've been so preoccupied lately that I've let that and many other chores pile up. I hate messes of all kinds, and that includes dirty cars.

❀ 7 ❀

"It's small, but I have a place for my computer, a window that looks out on an old park, and a wonderful neighbor, Miss Annie Clark."

I was sitting across the table from Sarah a little over a week later as she described the apartment she had recently moved into. She had called me earlier in the morning to see if I was available for lunch, saying that she had some new information I might be interested in. We had agreed to meet at the Silver Spoon, a popular eating place located in a strip mall in the southeastern part of the city. We had just settled into a comfortable booth when a crusty waitress took our drink order. It wasn't the decor nor the friendliness of the waiters that brought customers back to this restaurant regularly; it was more likely the fast service and large helpings of well-prepared food. A few regular customers believed that they had their own tables and that nobody else should be allowed to sit at them during the lunch hour. It was rare not to see a friend or relative dining nearby. Many local celebrities also made the café a customary hangout.

"I wish you had let me know you were moving. I might have been some help," I said, putting the menu aside. After being a customer for many years I could recite it by heart.

Sarah looked up from the menu. "I had plenty of help.

You don't have to look after me anymore, Jeremy. I'm beginning to know my way around this city."

She looked elegant today in a brown check suit, her hair pulled away from her flawless face in a French braid. Her eyes swept over the room as I suppose a reporter is wont to do.

"There's John. He's on our six o'clock news."

"He eats here all the time. He's usually at that round table over there with some other local luminaries. I suppose one of these days you'll be sitting there too."

"I'd much rather be sitting right here with you," she said smiling.

Sarah has the ability to focus her attention on whomever she's with and make a person feel that she's exactly where she wants to be.

"What does Meggie think of your apartment?"

"She hasn't seen it yet. When I'm all settled in, I'll have you both over for dinner."

"And what is the important news you wanted to tell me?" I asked.

"You said to keep you informed about the investigation of Sharon Ames' death. Well, I do know something that might interest you."

No news about the case had been announced by the media for several days, but Sarah had access to the latest information through the station. She went on to say that Sharon's body had been released to her parents, and they had chosen to have a private family graveside service.

"And what about the investigation?"

"The coroner's office found gunpowder residue on Sharon's hands."

"This only means she shot a gun before her death."

"Because of the gunpowder and the way the bullet entered her body, the coroner believes that she probably shot herself."

"Then the case is closed?"

"Once the coroner declares it a suicide, it's hard to keep the investigation open."

"What about the police? Are they satisfied that this was a suicide?"

"I'm not sure, but it seems that the active part of the investigation is over."

"But I thought the police announced that Sharon didn't die on the beach."

"They did. The coroner says that because of the lack of blood at the scene and the blood trails on the body, she was moved there after she died."

"And the gun?"

"The gun was wiped clean of fingerprints. Whoever handled that gun also knew how to clean it."

"But if it were a suicide, why would anyone bother with the gun at all? Why take it to the beach?"

"I don't know. Perhaps whoever moved her body wanted the police to know that Sharon committed suicide with her own gun."

"So the case is really closed?"

"Of course not. The police will keep the investigation open until there are explanations to all the unanswered questions."

"And I bet there are plenty of those."

"You're right. They found out that Sharon's mother and stepfather have large insurance policies on Sharon and her brother."

"How large?"

"I think Sharon's policy is worth $600,000 if she didn't die by her own hand."

"So, of course, her parents say somebody else killed her."

"That's right or it could have been an accident."

"The good old Texas gun accident."

"Really, Jeremy, accidents with guns happen all the time."

"But usually the body doesn't go to the beach."

"You sound just like her brother Ted."

"You've met the brother?"

"He was at the funeral."

"I thought it was a small family graveside service?"

"Betsy was invited and asked me to go with her. I've met the whole family."

"What was Sharon doing with a gun anyway?"

"Her stepfather let her keep one of his .38 Specials in her apartment for protection. There had been some problems in the apartment complex with break-ins."

"Did Sharon know how to use a gun?"

"She did, but Harvey said he'd give her some extra lessons at the indoor range. Sharon, however, told him her boyfriend was a hunter and familiar with guns. He would teach her himself."

"You're already on a first name basis with Harvey Stone?"

"Oh, didn't I tell you? The apartment I rented is in the same building where Sharon Ames lived. Harvey owns it."

That evening back in my apartment, I tried to work on my paper, but I couldn't concentrate. I scrambled three eggs for supper and put a couple of slices of bread in the toaster. Then I heated water in the microwave for instant coffee. This was one of my favorite suppers, but tonight I wasn't hungry. The cats had already finished their dinner and were sprawled out comfortably on the living room sofa, waiting for me to come in and pay attention to them. I couldn't stop thinking about Sarah. I had made no response when she told me that she had moved into the same building where Sharon had lived. Since she had made it a point not to discuss her move with me before she took the apartment, I knew that she wouldn't take any advice from me now. She had told me often enough that she could take care of herself. I reminded myself that this move of hers was none of my business. It was clear to me that she was getting as close as she could to the Stone family in order to do her own investigation of Sharon's death. I wasn't sure yet what I wanted to do about these latest circumstances, but I was sure that Sarah had watched too many TV movies in which young reporters solved murder cases.

Restless and unable to settle in one room, I finally turned

on the TV to watch the ten o'clock news. A reporter, standing in front of a large apartment complex not too far from the beach on Padre Island, was pointing to a white Mercury Sable parked along the street. A resident had called the police to report that the car had been there over two weeks. No one was sure when the car first appeared. It wasn't unusual for those who lived in the apartments to ignore a parked vehicle because visitors were always coming and going. The police had identified the car as belonging to the deceased Sharon Ames. They were questioning everyone around to find out if anyone knew who drove the car to the apartment complex. The car was locked and there was no key inside. As the news segment ended, the vehicle was being towed off to the pound by a police wrecker.

The next morning I found myself at Meggie's door. It was Saturday, and I had left my apartment to run the usual weekend errands. For a minute sitting in the parked car in front of her house, I was sorry that I didn't have a cell phone as I dislike dropping in on anyone unannounced. I rang the doorbell and waited, and soon I heard Harold's sharp, irritating bark coming closer. When the door opened, out he ran as fast as he could across the street toward one of the neighbor's houses. Harold wanted to be a street dog like most of the other dogs in the neighborhood. His dog door to the back yard only whet his appetite for freedom, so whenever he could, Harold escaped. Meggie, still in her light blue terry cloth robe, chased after him as he took off running down the block as fast as he could. This was not the first time I had helped her retrieve the ungrateful mutt. The more we tried to catch up with him, the faster he ran. Whenever Meggie called his name, he turned to look at her without slowing down, his long black ears flying behind him. It took ten minutes and several blocks before we finally caught up with him and carried him home.

"Have you ever thought of replacing him with a cat?"

"If I had a cat, I'd probably have to run after him too."

"You do spoil your animals."

"And my friends."

We were now sitting in the breakfast room having a cup of coffee. There was nobody else around for the first time since Sarah had moved in. Meggie, leaning forward, her head resting on her hands, elbows on the table, looked for a moment deep in thought.

"What would you like to do for Thanksgiving this year?" she asked.

"Is it already time to think about that?"

"I thought you liked Thanksgiving and just hated Christmas."

"Hate may be too strong, but it's the entire holiday season I dislike. It's all part of the conspiracy to perpetuate the happy family myth."

"So now you believe in conspiracies?" She laughed and pulled the blue robe that was falling open closer around her.

"Right. Take Thanksgiving, for example. All over the country people gather together with relatives they don't really like, bore each other to death with small talk or argue about old grievances, all the while stuffing themselves with food that's too rich for them. Then the men gather in front of the TV to watch football and drink beer while the women clean up the mess in the kitchen. I won't even begin to describe Christmas."

"Does that mean we're not spending Thanksgiving together?" she said, laughing.

"Pay no attention to me. I have a truant disposition."

"So what's really bothering you this morning?"

"It's Sarah and her moving into the building Sharon Ames lived in."

"I've been concerned about that too." She stood up to go into the kitchen to get some Danish she had been warming. The short robe showed off her long, beautiful legs.

"It's also time that I find out the whole truth about Sharon. There was a moment when I might have helped her, but I let it pass. Now I just want to know what happened to her and why. It's the least I can do for her now."

"But what can you do that the police can't?"

"I'm not sure. But now I've heard that the coroner has ruled her death a suicide, and I don't know if he's right or not. Somehow I don't believe it's as simple as that. I don't believe Sarah thinks so either."

"Sarah's just a hungry young reporter looking for her first big story."

"Whatever her motives, Sarah shouldn't be going after this story alone."

"You're right. She shouldn't. So if there's any way I can help, let me know."

"Then come over here right now, and I'll show you what you can do first."

With that we both rose from the table, and Meggie moved toward me. I pulled her closer and kissed her. Then, with my arm around her shoulders, we walked to the sofa, and I gently pulled her down beside me. We lay together quietly for a while, and I buried my face in her shoulder. She was wearing the lightest of floral perfumes. I whispered, "You are delicious."

She answered, "I love you so much."

"I know. I love you too." Holding her in my arms and kissing her, I realized that there were times when I never wanted us to be apart. Although the sofa was narrow and full of pillows, we didn't move into the bedroom. The sofa was not only too narrow but too short, and we had some difficulties getting positioned so we could lie together comfortably. Part of my joy in Meggie has always been her spontaneity. She is never a passive lover, and our love making is never dull. For now no matter what problems I was experiencing, actual or imagined, being with her made me feel whole again. Then why, I asked myself for the hundredth time, couldn't I make that final commitment?

✿ 8 ✿

It was nearly evening on the following day when the phone rang, and I heard Joan's cheerful voice.

"How do you feel about company over the Thanksgiving holidays?"

"I'm always glad to see you," I said. "What are your plans?"

"I'll fly in Wednesday night, rent a car, and drive over to the Regis. I'm going to ask for a room facing the water."

"Why not stay here?"

"This time I'd rather stay at the hotel. I'm bringing someone along."

For a minute I couldn't speak. My first thought was that she was bringing Grace along so she could spend the holiday with her niece. Then I imagined that if it wasn't Grace, it was probably one of her other peculiar friends. Whoever it was, I was not pleased.

"Who is it?"

"You don't like surprises very much do you, Jeremy?"

"You know I hate surprises. Whom are you bringing?"

"Someone you'll be very glad to see — Angela."

I was immediately relieved. Of all Joan's friends and acquaintances, Angela was my favorite. A history professor at a community college in Dallas, she was reserved, yet congenial, charming, and compassionate. I had first met her the year we both started teaching at the community college in Dallas and

62

had introduced her to Joan. They became instant friends; in fact, they were more than just friends. I hadn't seen Angela in the years that Joan had been away traveling.

"So Angel's coming. I look forward to seeing you both."

After Joan hung up, I called Meggie to tell her that Joan and Angela would be in for the holidays, and Meggie sounded quite pleased.

"Why don't they stay with me?"

"You're not a hotel for all my relatives and friends."

"I'm very fond of Joan. I'd love to have her here, and I can't wait to meet Angela."

"They've already made up their minds that they want to stay at the Regis in a room overlooking the bay."

"Now we can have a real Thanksgiving. We'll invite Sarah. She can bring her new boyfriend. We can ask Royall too since he's alone, unless he's going home for the holidays."

"I have no idea how Royall will be spending Thanksgiving. He's probably planning a skiing trip with his latest love interest."

"Then you don't mind if I ask him anyway, do you?"

"No, sweet Meggins, ask whom you will."

The next day when I returned to the office after my first class, Sarah called.

"Jeremy, I just heard from Meggie. I'm so glad that Joan and Angela are flying down Wednesday."

"They'll be glad to see you too. Did Meggie tell you to bring your new boyfriend to dinner?"

"I can't bring him cause I'm working every day through the holiday weekend."

"Aren't we going to see you at all?"

"I'll be over at Meggie's for Thanksgiving dinner, but afterwards I have to get right back to the station. Remember I'm just a lowly intern."

"As if I could forget. How is life at the apartment?"

"That's really why I called. I need to talk to you about something."

"Can you meet me today for lunch?"

"I was hoping you'd ask. Where and when shall we meet?"

"How about the White Kitchen. If we get there about 11:45, maybe we'll beat the crowd."

The rest of the morning went by quickly. Students were in and out of the office between classes turning in research papers, so I didn't have a chance to ask Royall if he would be at Meggie's for Thanksgiving. He was busy with his own students too. At this time of the semester, they come by more often to confer about their work and grades or to be advised on which courses to take next semester. When I finally looked up, it was 11:40. Royall was on the phone, so I waved good-bye, grabbed my books and papers, and rushed out of the office toward the parking lot. I had five minutes to get to the restaurant.

As soon as I entered, I saw Sarah sitting at a table in the front.

"Sorry I'm late."

"I just arrived a minute ago myself."

The waitresses in the White Kitchen are known for their good service, and one approached us now with water, menus, and a basket of garlic toast. The White Kitchen, like the Silver Spoon, is a popular lunch spot in Corpus with its own group of regulars, but they usually don't begin coming in until after twelve. The decor is simple, all blue and white, including the dishes they serve their excellent lunch specials on. Today they had a stuffed flounder platter with wild rice that appealed to both of us. After the waitress brought our coffee, I looked up to see Sarah watching me.

"What?"

"Sometimes you amaze me."

"What have I done now?"

"The way you have given me my space. For a while I didn't think you could do it, but now I feel we can really be friends. I'll be able to talk to you without your asking me personal questions or going off into parental-type lectures."

64

"I feel like I'm being set up."

"You're too smart and too good looking for me to take advantage of you."

"Stop that. I won't have you practicing your feminine wiles on me."

"I'm not. I'm just happy today."

"Is it too personal a question to ask why you're so happy?"

"I've just been assigned my first spot as a reporter. It's not much, but I'll be on the local news tonight for about thirty seconds interviewing a teenager who rescued a cat off the roof of an office building."

"I'll be sure to watch. Is that what you wanted to tell me?"

"You asked me about what was happening at the apartment, and I thought you might want to know what I've found out about Sharon since I moved there."

"I'm very interested. In fact, I've decided that I'm going to do a little investigating myself."

"What do you plan to do with the information when you get it?"

"I'm not sure yet, but Sharon came to me for help, and I won't be satisfied until I learn the truth about what happened to her. The police don't seem to be pursuing the case any longer."

"That's true. The coroner's report put an end to that."

"So what have you discovered?"

"I'm coming to that, but first let me start at the beginning." She sat up closer to the table and lowered her voice as if she wanted to be sure that nobody at a nearby table could overhear her. "I had trouble with the air conditioner when I first moved in, so after work one evening, I called the manager. Instead of sending the handy man, Jeff, who usually fixes everything, Harvey Stone himself came by the next day before I left for the station. He gave me his card with his private phone and pager numbers. He then told me that he would get the air conditioner repaired immediately, and by the time I returned home that night, it was fixed."

"It's all in whom you know. But it's been so cool and pleasant the last few weeks. Why do you need air conditioning?"

"I can't sleep at night unless it's cold in my bedroom. I always have the air conditioner on at night. I can't open the windows in that apartment. It's not safe."

"I wish you had chosen some other place to live. Why do you think Stone gave you his private numbers? I'm sure he doesn't do that for all his tenants."

"I can guess, but that's only the beginning of the story."

Before she could continue, the waitress arrived with our dinners. For the next twenty minutes we paid attention to the food. The stuffed flounder was broiled to perfection with a crabmeat stuffing. The wild rice was a savory addition to the fish. Corpus Christi fish can compete with any in the country. The fish in South Texas have an especially delicate flavor. Broiled or baked, trout, redfish, and flounder require only the lightest seasoning and a little lemon. No sauces are necessary. Later the waitress returned to ask us whether we wanted dessert. We decided to have another cup of coffee instead.

Throughout the dinner we had lapsed into small talk about Sarah's work and my classes. Her job at the station was going reasonably well. She was getting more assignments that were leading to her immediate goal — to be a regular reporter on one of the local news broadcasts. She said she needed to work on a significant story to prove her ability. I understood her impatience but assured her that her time would come soon enough. Then it was my turn to talk. Sarah listened while I told her about some students who were doing very poor work, neither reading nor turning in their written assignments. She responded to my comments with the students' point of view. She suggested that teachers ought to remember that sometimes less is more. They need to focus on the most important things they think students should know. She compared teaching to reporting.

"You can tell people everything you know, but at some point they stop listening."

"I've been trying to learn how to do this for years, but it's one of the toughest things a teacher can master. Some never do. How did you get so wise?"

"Now you're laughing at me."

"On the contrary, what I'm really thinking is how much I respect your opinion."

Then the waitress came back to the table to refill our coffee cups and clear away our empty plates. Finally with only our cups of coffee in front of us, Sarah looked across the table at me and said,

"Now I've got a story to tell you."

And so I listened.

"It must have been eight o'clock when the phone rang the same evening that the air conditioner was repaired. I recognized Harvey Stone's voice immediately. He asked if the air conditioner was working all right, and I assured him that it was. I thanked him for taking care of it so promptly, and he said, *I like my renters to be comfortable. So any time you need something, you have my numbers; call me directly.*

"I said that I would and was about to hang up when he asked me if I had time to go somewhere and talk. I know he's married, but he didn't make the offer sound like a date, just a drink and a little small talk. At first I turned him down. I told him that I was too tired, but then I thought that this might be a good way to ask him some questions. He could tell me about Sharon from the family's perspective. So I agreed to meet him at a small restaurant and bar called The Pub. You know the place. I changed into something casual since I was still in my work clothes. When I arrived at the bar, he was already sitting at a table waiting for me. He got up when he saw me and we shook hands. Then we sat down by an artificial fireplace, and I watched the flames throwing strange shadows across his face. I wondered if meeting him like this had been a mistake. I know this is how reporters research a story, but it was my first time. I could see he was watching me. I looked at him and thought, he's attractive for a man his age, and he knows it.

He's tall and slender with thick wavy white hair and steel blue eyes that seemed to look right through me. He wore a plaid shirt and Diesel jeans. His loafers looked expensive too. Guccis I think. The waiter came almost immediately to take our order. I asked for a glass of the white house wine. He ordered a scotch and water.

"I could tell that he was pleased that I had changed my mind about meeting him. He said, *What is a pretty young lady like you doing renting an apartment in such a rough part of town?*

"It's a matter of economics. My job doesn't pay enough for me to live anywhere else."

What do your mother and daddy think of that?

"My family's in Dallas. They haven't been down here to visit me yet. But they'd understand."

So you're alone here in Corpus?

"Not really. I have my work and my friends."

I suppose that includes a boyfriend?

"It's a little too soon to call him that, but yes — there is someone."

Lucky fellow. I hope you and I will be friends too. I noticed you at my stepdaughter's funeral. Did you know Sharon?

"No. I've heard a lot about her. I came with Betsy O'Ryan."

Yeah, they were old friends. Her daddy still owns the TV station you work at, doesn't he?

"That's right. I just want to tell you, Mr. Stone, that I'm really sorry about Sharon. Betsy told me how much she liked her."

Thanks. I raised that girl. She was only five years old when I married her mother. She was like my own daughter. Haven't I told you to call me Harvey?

"Do you have any idea how it happened, Harvey?"

It was either a suicide or an accident. I'm betting it was an accident. There wasn't a note. She wasn't the type to do something like that on purpose. I told the police that.

"What was she doing with the gun?"

How would I know, pretty lady; I wasn't there.

"Did the gun belong to you?"

I gave it to Sharon several months ago. As long as she insisted on living on her own, she needed some protection.

"Did she know how to use it?"

How come you ask so many questions? Are you writing a news story about Sharon for your station?

"I'm only an intern, Harvey. I'm just curious about how she died because she was so young. Was she familiar with hand guns?"

I told her I would take her to the shooting range — there's an indoor one you know — but she wouldn't hear of it. Said her boyfriend knew all about guns. He was a hunter. I said okay as long as someone gave her lessons.

"He held his glass up, and a waiter quickly responded by bringing him another scotch and water. The waiter asked if I was ready for another glass of wine. I nodded and he disappeared behind the bar. When he returned with my drink, he brought a bowl of mixed nuts and placed it between us on the small table."

"How did you like her boyfriend?"

Ben Haynes. I can't say that I did. She never told us too much about him except that he was a pipe setter in the oil fields, and he's going to school to be a welder. Neither her mother nor I thought he was right for her. He was always hanging around. I told her that I felt like I was supporting him too.

"How did she take that?"

She didn't like it one bit. She never could take any criticism, even when she was a little girl. I said she'd better get rid of him, or I would stop giving her money for school.

"So did she?"

He lived in a small rent house near the college, and she took some of her things over there and moved in with him. She said she was going to get a job and pay for her own education. I asked her to take her things out of the apartment, so I could rent it, but she wanted to keep them there a little longer.

"What did you tell her?"

I had a feeling that things weren't really so good as she pretended between her and Ben, although she covered it up pretty good. I'm rather adept at reading people. "He looked at me for just an instant as if he were letting me know that that went for me too. Then he continued." *I decided I'd give her a little time. I thought if I stopped putting pressure on her, she'd get rid of him and move back to the apartment.*

"Was Sharon having trouble with anybody else that you know of?"

You mean at the apartment or at school? Not that I know of. She was a good student. I always said she was the smartest one in the family. Always brought home A's in everything.

"Are you sending Ted to school too?"

Yeah, nobody else is going to do it. Ted's a good kid. He's never given me trouble like his sister has.

"So Sharon was a lot of trouble?"

Not always. Sharon and I were really close while she was growing up. Things changed after she got involved with Ben and moved out of the house.

"Harvey signaled the waiter again for another drink, and he came by the table to ask if I wanted one too. I was still nursing my second. I've never been much of a drinker. For a minute there was a lull in the conversation, so I thought it was a good time to ask him why he had invited me to have a drink with him. He had a ready answer like a man who was used to hearing that question from women."

Maybe because I like to know who's living in my apartments or maybe because you're so good-looking. I have a weakness for pretty young women.

"Does your wife mind your buying drinks for other women?"

I've never asked her.

"For a minute there was silence."

"Do you mind my asking about her?"

Not really. Sharon looked a lot like her mother. Linda was quite a beauty in her day too. Comes from an old Corpus fam-

ily. Not rich, but married into lots of money. Then she got too much of everything too fast and couldn't handle it. Now she's spoiled her looks with too much boozing.

"Does she still drink?"

If I went home right now, she'd be crashed in her room. "He looked at his gold Rolex watch with its flashy diamond bezel." *Teresa has probably cleaned her up by now and put her to bed.*

"Teresa's your maid?"

My maid and her best friend, or should I say the only real friend she has left.

"That must be pretty hard on you and the children."

It's the main reason Sharon moved out of the house. She told me she just couldn't take it anymore.

"Has Linda tried getting help?"

We've tried everything — Betty Ford, AA, you name it. I would've thrown her out years ago except for the kids.

"He signaled the waiter again, this time for the check. Then we walked out together, and he took me to my car."

Can I call you again?

"I don't know. I'm usually not up this late at night when I'm working. The camera is very unforgiving."

Maybe I can buy you lunch next time.

"I don't date married men, Harvey."

You might have some more questions about Sharon you want to ask me.

"And you don't mind answering them?"

"As he opened the car door for me, he smiled and said, *I'll be looking forward to it.*"

She stopped speaking, and I knew the story had ended. My first response was to tell her that I thought she shouldn't be having drinks late at night in a bar with a complete stranger. But guessing what her response would be, I decided I'd better take a different approach.

"Here's the way it looks to me. Harvey sees an attractive young woman on her own and is testing the waters to see if there is anything in it for him."

"Maybe so, but remember, I have my own agenda."

"So, will you see him again?"

"If I think he has more to tell me, I probably will."

"Then next time ask him more about his relationship with Sharon. When she was having trouble with someone harassing her at school, she didn't go to him. If he was such a good father, I wonder why not. She told one of my colleagues in confidence that she moved out of the house because she was unhappy with both her mother and her stepfather. He also said that her parents had stopped giving her money to pay for her education."

"He did want me to think that he was a good father to both his wife's kids."

"He's not going to admit any blame for what happened to Sharon," I said. "Then, of course, there's the boyfriend, Ben Haynes. I wonder how he fits into this puzzle."

"Maybe she moved out of the house to have more time for him. Obviously the family didn't approve of their relationship."

"I'm going to see what I can find out about him."

"Do you think he might be involved in her death?"

"I'm sure the police have already interrogated him. But there are some questions I'd like to ask Mr. Haynes myself about their relationship and if he knew who the teacher was who was harassing her."

"Were they still living together when she died or had she moved back to her apartment?"

"I don't think the police report ever made that clear."

"I'll ask Harvey next time I talk to him."

"That reminds me, what about this boyfriend of yours Stone was asking you about?"

"I knew you couldn't last. That subject is off limits to you too," she said in a firm but friendly voice.

"What's wrong with him? Why are you being so secretive?"

Looking somewhat amused, she was about to answer and then thought better of it. Instead she glanced at her watch and reached for her purse. It was time, she said, to get back to the station. They were quite strict about lunch hours, and hers was over.

I returned to my office but could not get the conversation with Sarah out of my mind. I was intrigued by all the unanswered questions. I wished that the police had not put their investigation on the back burner, but since they had, I was determined to proceed with mine. I wasn't quite sure where to begin. Perhaps it was time to see Jim Butler again.

❀ 9 ❀

Jim's office door was open, and the young man sitting with him looked vaguely familiar. Jim introduced me to Ted Ames, Sharon's younger brother. The familiarity came from his resemblance to Sharon, especially the shiny dark hair and large brown eyes. He had just arrived for the Thanksgiving holidays and decided to drop in on some of his old teachers. The summer before he left for the University of Houston, he had taken a few classes at the college. Jim was telling him that he was too good an English student to major in engineering.

"Thanks, but I was never as good in English as Sharon."

"Did I ever say that?" Jim asked.

"Not in so many words, but I knew that's what you were thinking."

Jim nodded toward the other chair, and I sat down. He asked me if I wanted a cup of coffee. He kept a large thermos and all the fixings on his worktable beside his desk. They both were holding cups.

I shook my head and added that I'd just had lunch. I told Ted how sorry I was about Sharon. He thanked me and said how much he wanted to find out what happened to her.

"Then you don't believe it was a suicide or an accident?"

"No. Sharon would never take her own life. Our father committed suicide. We were very young when it happened. He shot himself. When we grew older we used to talk about it all the time. She called it the worst kind of cowardice. Sharon stayed angry at him for a long time after he died. I'm positive she'd never shoot herself."

"It's happened before," Jim said, and I guessed he was referring to the Hemingways.

Looking at Ted, I could tell that his sister's death was an open wound, yet he wanted to talk about it.

"Could it have been an accident?" I asked.

"No. I don't believe that either." Ted leaned forward in his chair and looked directly at me. "We grew up around guns. Our stepfather is a hunter and gun collector. He taught us how to handle guns safely to avoid accidents. Sharon wasn't as interested in them as I was, but she knew how to handle a loaded gun. Our stepfather insisted that she keep the .38 Special in her apartment for protection."

"Why would she need protection?" I asked.

"Because of the neighborhood. Neighbors had told her that there had been some recent robberies and break-ins, so when Harvey offered her the gun, she took it."

"Did she keep it loaded?"

"Of course, she did. It had to be ready to use if she needed it. But it was Ben, her boyfriend, who liked the gun. He acted as if it were his."

"Did Sharon practice shooting it?" I asked.

"When we were young, she was a pretty good shot. We have a ranch in Live Oak County and spent a lot of time there while we were growing up, especially during the hunting season. We shot all kinds of weapons out there."

"Did Sharon hunt?"

"She never enjoyed it like some women do. Our stepfather had several hunting parties every year. Sharon went out to the blinds sometimes when he insisted, but she said she'd never shoot at anything with a face."

"Did she shoot at targets?" I asked.

"All ranch kids love to shoot at targets," Jim said.

"I guess you shot handguns too," I said.

"Sometimes. My stepfather always had one around for

protection. He hates poachers, and there are plenty of them when you have a ranch that you don't live on all the time. One of the ranch hands told me he saw Harvey kill a man once and bury him somewhere in the brush. I don't know if that's true or not. I do know he once warned a man he caught poaching on the ranch that if he found him on his property again, he'd shoot him."

"Did he ever come back?"

"As a matter of fact he did."

"And did your stepfather shoot him?"

"No, the story goes that he took his gun away from him and beat him within an inch of his life with the butt of his own rifle."

"I thought that only happened in the movies. Did the guy press charges?"

"He never did. Harvey gave him money to keep him quiet."

"What about the .38 Special he gave to Sharon, had she kept up with her shooting?"

"Not too much, but she still knew how to handle it. I saw the gun at her apartment once when Ben was cleaning it. It was a beautiful piece, and both of us were admiring it. Except for that one time, I never saw it again. I think she kept it in a nightstand near her bed."

"Maybe she was cleaning it when it went off."

"She wouldn't be cleaning it unless she shot it. Besides, that gun wouldn't go off unless someone pulled the trigger. Like I said, it was obvious that it was Ben who liked the gun. He's the one who took care of it. He liked to shoot it too. He used to go to the indoor range and practice."

"Did she go with him and shoot?"

"Sometimes. I'm sure she did. I once heard him try to talk her into getting a license to carry it."

"I hope you don't mind my asking these questions. Sharon was my student. I share your concern that we haven't heard the correct story yet."

Ted looked over at Jim, who said, "Jeremy was one of

Sharon's teachers. She came by to talk to him in his office right before she disappeared."

"I didn't know that." Ted looked at his watch and said, "I'd better get going. We're leaving for the ranch in a couple of hours to spend Thanksgiving there."

"Do you have time for one or two more questions?"

"If they're brief, but remember, I've been away at school."

"Did Sharon ever mention that she was being harassed by one of her professors?"

"Never. She did say that she had become friends with some teacher. She said he was easy to talk to. He was encouraging her to leave Corpus Community College and go to a university away from home. He kept giving her books and college catalogs, but she hadn't made up her mind yet."

"Did she tell you his name?" Jim asked.

"She may have, but I can't remember it right now. I might recognize the name if I heard it."

"As far as you know, how was she getting along with Ben?"

"It's hard to say. Like most couples, they had their ups and downs. She told me things about him she didn't want our parents to know." He paused and added, "If he didn't have a good alibi . . ." Ted stopped in mid-sentence and stood up.

"I know you have to go," I said. "But can we get together again before you return to Houston?"

"Give me your phone number, and I'll call you." he said.

Jim handed me pen and paper, and I wrote down my name, address, and phone number and handed it to Ted. Then he was out the door.

"All right, I'll take that cup of coffee now."

"So you're planning to stick around for a while?"

"I'm not leaving until I get some answers from you."

"What do you want to know, Mr. Holmes?"

"You know darn well what I want to know."

"You want to know what Sharon told me in confidence."

"If you don't tell me, don't you think you should tell someone?"

"You mean the police? No, I can't do that." For a minute he sat there thinking about what he should do. "You're right," he said at last. "I should tell somebody." Then he looked out the window, remembering, and slowly began to speak,

"She came by the office one day last spring pretty depressed. I asked her what was bothering her, and at first she didn't say anything. When I asked her if it had to do with her family, she said that it did and that she was moving out of her parents' house as soon as she could find a place of her own."

"Because of her mother's drinking?"

"The drinking was part of the problem. Her stepfather was trying to control her and threatened to stop paying for her and her brother's education unless she did what he said. She said she wasn't worried about herself, but she wanted to make sure that Ted finished school."

"What did her stepfather want from her?"

"For one thing, to get rid of her boyfriend. Neither he nor her mother approved of that relationship."

"Was that all of it?"

"She said that she and Harvey had been close at one time, but she had just found out that he was having an affair with some secretary in his office."

"I guess it's always a shock to discover your father's a womanizer."

"This secretary was about Sharon's age. She said that he was buying her expensive gifts, taking her on business trips, and dining with her at his private clubs."

"How did Sharon find out all this?"

"In many ways this is a small town. Harvey was seen by lots of people, including some of his office staff. Somebody told her."

"Did she talk to him about it?" I said.

"She said she did. At first he denied everything. When she refused to believe him, they had a terrible fight. She said that when he lost his temper like that, she was afraid of him."

"Was he violent with her?"

78

"Sharon said that her stepfather was capable of hurting people and getting away with it. He knew policemen, judges, and lawyers. She said that nobody in this part of the country would ever convict him of anything. He had the money to buy his way out of trouble."

"So she was moving out because she was afraid of her stepfather?" I said.

"Partly." Jim picked up a pen and twirled it between his forefinger and thumb. "It was more complicated than that. He wanted her to get rid of her boyfriend; and, at the same time, she acted like she resented his relationship with this secretary, and not just for her mother's sake."

"So what are you suggesting?"

"Maybe that she was jealous or possessive. I'm not sure. It sounded to me as if she and Harvey Stone had a rather muddled father-daughter attachment."

"He'd been the only father she had most of her life. Why would their attachment seem so strange to you?"

"I'm not sure. I asked her what was going on, and she said that if anyone ever found out, there would be a scandal this town would never forget. When I tried to get her to tell me what she meant, she refused to say any more."

"Was she trying to tell you that there was something physical in their relationship?"

"I don't know. But you can see why I couldn't tell the police or anyone else about it. She was never explicit, so I wasn't sure exactly what she was implying. An unproved story like that, not even an allegation, could really hurt a lot of people."

We talked a few minutes longer before I returned to my office. I needed time to think about what Jim had just told me. In my mind I could hear Sharon's voice, saying over and over again, "Help me; please help me." And I answered aloud, "I'm so sorry I let you down." I was glad no one was around to hear me talking to myself.

It was quiet in the English Building. The campus was getting ready for the Thanksgiving holidays. Some students who had long trips to make to their homes in other cities were already on the road. Others who would remain in town were getting ready for out-of-town guests and shopping for turkey and all the trimmings. I thought about Meggie at home getting ready for a houseload of people, mostly my friends and relatives. I called to see if she needed any help with the preparations. She sounded glad to hear from me but said that she and Sarah had everything under control. I was glad that she and Sarah had become friends and that Sarah wanted to help even though she wouldn't be around much this weekend.

I decided to go home and finish grading research papers before the company from Dallas arrived tomorrow. After dinner Cleo and Tony would not let me work. They kept stepping all over my papers, which made grading impossible. They behave this way during periods when I'm too busy to give them attention. I tried to work on my conference paper, but then they jumped up on the computer table. I could have locked them out of the room, but they always manage to punish me when they feel neglected, and by now I was out of the mood to work. Finally I sat down with them in my big living room chair and started clicking my remote through the channels to find something to watch on TV. Nothing looked promising, so I closed my eyes to rest for a few minutes.

Before long I found myself on an unfamiliar ranch in the country. I was walking, holding a Smith and Wesson .38 Special in my right hand. Since I don't own a gun, this seemed strange to me, and I kept wondering whose gun it was. It was just about evening. I saw the sun disappearing below the trees in the brush. I didn't know whose ranch it was or why I was walking. I kept looking around, trying to find my car, but it was nowhere in sight. Had I had an accident? Had the car broken down? Lost, I walked along a sendero, one of the paths someone had cleared with a tractor, looking for a ranch house to ask directions. I passed a deer blind on the left side of the path and noticed a deer feeder made from an old oil drum, standing on the right side of the sendero a hundred feet away. Just as I was passing beside it, I heard a loud explosion and realized that a gunshot had hit the drum, spilling corn on the ground. The noise terrified me. Someone was shooting a gun behind me.

I jumped into the brush to get out of the line of fire. It was hunting season, but I felt that this hunter was not aiming at a deer and that I was probably the target. Another shot was fired, this time into the brush not far from where I was standing. I started to run through the brush along the sendero. It was difficult and slow-going because of the thick growth. The ground was uneven and full of cacti, bristles, and thorns. They were tearing at my clothes and scratching my face and hands. A twig slapped me across my left eye, and the scratch began to bleed. I concentrated on my running and tried to ignore the pain and the blood running into my eye. When the brush became too thick to go any farther, I had no choice but to step back on the sendero. My car was still nowhere in sight.

Suddenly standing in front of me, I saw a tall white-haired man, holding a rifle. He looked at me angrily and said, "Drop the gun and move away from it. You're poaching on my property. Do you know what happens to poachers?"

"I'm not poaching. I'm lost. I'm just looking for my car. I think it broke down around here somewhere."

"It's down that sendero," he said, pointing in the direction I was walking. "Waste no time getting off my property or you might get hurt."

I looked down the sendero, but I couldn't see the Honda. By now blood from the scratches was running down my face. I tried to wipe it out of my left eye with my torn shirtsleeve. The rancher walked over and picked up my gun. When he did this, I started running in the direction he pointed. After I was a mile down the path, I looked back. There was nobody behind me. Then I saw my Honda, sitting on the side of the road. As I rushed toward it, I heard another shot in the distance, followed by a man's strident laughter. The key was in the ignition, and, to my surprise, the car started easily. I drove for what seemed like hours in the dark, looking for the main gate, but the senderos kept leading me in circles. There were no stars to light the way. I looked down at the fuel gauge and saw that the car was almost out of gas. I tried to stay calm, but it was becoming clear to me that I would never escape from this labyrinth until I fulfilled some mysterious quest, which I had been sent to do. Then suddenly a loud rumbling noise started in the engine. I wanted to pull over to the side of the sendero and open the hood to examine the engine, but I couldn't risk stopping. I had to get off the ranch before I ran out of gas. The engine noise grew louder, and the car sounded as if it could go no farther. When I finally pulled over on the side of the road, I sat behind the wheel, frantically wondering where to go and what to do next. My eyes were burning. I closed them for a minute. The engine was still running, and the noise coming from it was loud and insistent. I forced myself to open my eyes. Suddenly I was back in my living room. Tony was sleeping on the back of the chair, next to my head, and Cleo was curled beside me. I don't know how long the TV had been blaring. The station had gone off the air for the night. I turned off the set, but I could still hear Sharon's voice saying, "Help me."

The only way I could help her now was to search for the truth.

❦ 10 ❦

At nine o'clock Thursday, I awoke suddenly, glanced at the clock radio on the night stand, and jumped out of bed. I was late to class. Then I remembered it was Thanksgiving. What had happened to Joan and Angela? I had expected them to arrive yesterday and was sure they would have gotten in touch with me as soon as they arrived. I walked into the kitchen and had just turned on the coffeemaker when the phone rang. Joan said that she and Angela were about to have breakfast at the hotel and asked me to join them. I took a shower, got into some jeans, and drove up Ocean Drive to the Regis. By the time I arrived thirty minutes later, they were in the dining room having fresh orange juice and coffee. Joan rose and came over to me her arms outstretched. She never changes. Slender, a few inches over five feet tall, she has brown hair, cut very short, and sparkling blue eyes. She was wearing a tweed skirt and sweater and looked twenty years younger than she was.

"All your traveling agrees with you," I said.

"Thanks, but I think I'm going to stick around for a while," she answered.

"I bet we have Angel to thank for that." That was Joan's and my special name for Angela.

I hadn't seen Angela for several years; I couldn't remember exactly how many. She was much thinner than I remembered.

83

Her short hair was now streaked a lovely shade of gray. She was wearing slacks and a black suit jacket. When I reminded them that I had expected them yesterday, they laughed and said that they had arrived too late to call last night. Joan said they had been waiting for me before they ordered breakfast. The waiter came by and convinced us to try the buffet. The Regis has an elegant buffet with choices to satisfy any appetite. I decided on bagels, lox, and cream cheese with fresh fruit on the side. Joan chose the Belgian waffles with cherries on top, and Angel asked the omelette chef to prepare a mushroom and onion egg white omelette.

When we returned to the table, Joan said that she had called Meggie and invited her to join us for breakfast, but Meggie said she was too busy getting ready for our dinner this afternoon.

"I asked her if she needed any help, but she said for us to relax, enjoy our visit together, and not eat too much. We are to be at her house by two P.M. with big appetites."

"Is there anything special you'd like to do till then?" I asked them.

"As a matter of fact, we'd like to walk the beach on Padre Island," Angela said.

After breakfast they put on jeans and tennis shoes, more appropriate dress for beachcombing. I waited in the lobby while they changed their clothes. I found a comfortable deep sofa to settle into and watched a family of four getting ready to venture out on Ocean Drive to visit the marina. The children were prevailing upon their parents to let them ride the small boats docked on one of the piers. After much cajoling the parents gave in to the request, and off they went. Restless, I decided to wait outside the entrance for Joan and Angela, where I could still watch for them through the large glass doors.

Across the street the bay looked its darkest blue except where the sun was spraying it with ribbons of gold. This is the part of Corpus that impresses not only visitors but also the locals. It is this site of the city that gives it its epithet, the Sparkling City by the Sea. A splendid location for bird watchers, the gulls en masse were fishing for their breakfasts. Different groups of gulls find their way to their favorite daytime locations. Some follow the shrimp and fishing boats. Others prefer the tourists who are always feeding them parts of their own meals. These gulls hardly ever miss catching in midair what is thrown to them. They are quite competitive with each other and provide continuous entertainment. Unafraid of people milling around them, they come quite close to the visitors. Looking around I noticed several brown pelicans perched on pilings placidly observing the human comedy as if they were above such undignified behavior as begging food from tourists. They appeared as interested in the tourists as the tourists were in them. Then to add to the activity, a couple of terns began diving into the cool water. As soon as they rose to the surface, they flew upward until they were high enough to plummet into the water again.

"I don't suppose we need to drive by your apartment and let you change too?" That was Joan who found me before I knew they had come down.

"It's not necessary. I come prepared for any contingency." I said leading them to the Honda.

The drive to Padre Island took about half an hour. I took the scenic route on Ocean Drive. We passed several other hotels, and I noticed that they had changed their names again. The Regis has had five different names in the last seven years. It is constantly being sold, and every time someone else purchases it, the name changes. So much for name recognition. Visitors are always surprised that the natives do not know the names of the city's most popular bayfront hotels. After we left the downtown area, we drove by the apartment buildings and condos that line the avenue. These come in all sizes and price ranges, but because they are located on the most expensive real estate in the city, they are all overpriced. We passed my apartment building, one of the more modest edifices on this grand boulevard.

"How lucky you are to live so close to the water," Angela said.

"I know. The apartment is small, but I would hate to give it up." Finally we drove by the residential section of Ocean Drive with its large houses and estates. We passed by Harvey Stone's Mediterranean-style mansion, but I didn't comment. I have told Joan about Sharon Ames but decided not to bring the subject up right now. We made the turn onto Snake Road and soon connected with the freeway that would take us to Padre Island.

The ride was pleasant with Joan and Angela talking about their work, what was going on in Dallas, and the news and gossip about mutual friends. Finally I pulled into a parking lot near one of the more popular public beaches. This cold November day it was almost empty, being too late in the year for swimmers and surfers. Angela, a shell collector, went her own way, deliberately not keeping up with us. It was obvious that she was giving us a few minutes alone to talk. At first we walked in silence close to the edge of the water. It had been a couple of years since we had seen each other, but being together was as natural as if there had been no separation at all. Joan is more sentimental about our childhood than I am. She is the family historian. Much of what she recalls is not always clear in my own memory. She began to reminisce about the times we spent in Corpus as children. It was always during the first part of our summer holidays, and our parents rented a condo on the beach.

"We used to dream about living here when we were young. Do you remember?" Joan asked.

"I remember everything," I exaggerated.

"Even the times you swam out too far, and I had to rescue you?" she laughed.

"Wait a minute. It happened only once, and I was just three years old."

"More like six years old. I can still see Mother asleep on the sand. She never even noticed that you almost drowned."

"It was typical of her parenting skills."

"She wasn't a bad parent — just different from all our friends' mothers, but she did make us independent and able to take care of ourselves."

"Is that what she was doing. I thought she just didn't enjoy being around young children."

"She liked us."

"How could you tell?"

"Jeremy, did you feel the lack of love and nurturing when you were a kid?"

"I've never required a lot of nurturing. Anyway I always had you hovering around."

"I think Mother's lack of intimacy made us closer."

"I like the spin you put on things."

"Not to change the subject, but there is something I'd like to talk to you about before we go back to Corpus."

"Sounds ominous."

"It's about Angel and me."

"So, that's why Angel's over there looking for shells."

"I've decided to move into Angel's house with her and the children."

"Do you think that's wise?"

"Angel has just been diagnosed with breast cancer. She's going to need a lot of assistance and support. There are major decisions that she has to make regarding treatment. I think I can help her."

"Have you thought about what her ex-husband is going to say about that?"

"Of course, we have. We know that Jack's not going to like it."

"I thought you both had made a decision about that years ago."

"Angel's sick, Jeremy. I'm not going to let her down no matter who doesn't like it."

"I understand how you feel, but are you ready for all the trouble that Jack will start? He's a lawyer. The cards are stacked in his favor. And what about the children? They're teenagers now. Shouldn't Tim and Carolyn have some voice in the matter?"

"Of course, they should. And we want them to stay with

us, but we both know that they're old enough to make up their own minds whom they want to live with."

"Have you told them yet?"

"They know about the cancer. We haven't told them anything else, but we'll talk to them as soon as we go home. They're with Jack for Thanksgiving."

Joan and I stood on the wet sand looking out at the water. All the years had dropped away, and we were kids again, ready to stand up together against the world and all its outsiders. I could see the determination in her eyes, and I knew that she had already made up her mind. She wasn't asking for my opinion.

"How bad is it?" I asked.

"The cancer? It's very bad, but, of course, we're hopeful."

"Is there anything I can do to help?"

"I know we can count on your support. That's all for now."

With that Joan turned away and called to Angela, who came toward us holding some perfectly shaped sand dollars.

"They're lovely," I said.

"Today's my lucky day," she said, showing them off to us.

When I dropped them back at the Regis, I suggested picking them up around two to go to Meggie's, but they had leased a car and wanted to drive themselves.

❦ 11 ❦

When I entered my apartment, I noticed there was a call on the answering machine. I didn't need the introduction because I recognized Ted Ames' voice immediately: "Jeremy, I won't be able to meet with you before I return to Houston 'cause I'm leaving directly from the ranch. Maybe next time I'm in Corpus. After I left you, I remembered the name of that professor Sharon used to talk about. It's Randy Thorpe in the Kinesiology Department. I think he was her personal trainer. Sharon always liked working out. From what she said they became pretty good friends. I'm sure he's not the one you're looking for."

I don't know Randy Thorpe very well, although I see him occasionally at faculty meetings. I remember that there had been some gossip about his leaving his wife a few years ago for a student with whom he got involved. It was a bit of a scandal. He married the student, and I think they have a child. I never heard the whole story, but it seems unlikely that he would be pursuing another student again. I decided I'd talk with him next week after we returned to school.

It was nearly two o'clock when I stood on Meggie's front porch listening to Harold bark his announcement that another guest had arrived. Sarah answered the door and led the way to the living room. Joan and Angela were already there, seated together on a white sofa. Jim Butler, his wife Lynn, and their sons were clustered around them, asking Joan questions about her travels and her teaching English in foreign countries. Sarah excused herself and returned to the kitchen to help Meggie slice the turkey. A few minutes later Bill Walker, Royall's friend from the History Department, and two more faculty members from the Business Department, Phillip Jones and Ron Harris, and their wives appeared to complete the group.

The table was set with Meggie's best china, silver, and crystal. There were a large arrangement of autumn flowers and candles on the table. The napkin holders were porcelain turkeys. Meggie sat at one end of the table and asked me to sit at the other. The dinner was worthy of the setting. It was the traditional holiday feast, and I could see that Meggie had spent many hours in the kitchen, probably with very little help except for Sarah. I glanced over at Meggie as she talked to Joan and was amazed at how relaxed and fresh she looked after all her preparations. Bill was sitting near enough for me to ask him where Royall was spending Thanksgiving.

"He's gone home to Los Angeles to spend the holidays with his family," he said.

After dinner when everyone who wanted to watch football had congregated in the large family room, I had a chance to talk to Jim alone for a few minutes. I told him that I had heard from Ted and that he mentioned Randy Thorpe as the teacher that Sharon had been friends with.

"Are you suggesting what I think you are?" Jim asked.

"Do you think it's likely that Thorpe could be the one who was harassing her?"

"I used to hear some pretty wild stories about him, but that was a while back — before he married Cindy."

"Maybe he's still getting involved with students."

"I don't think so. Cindy is not the kind of young woman who'd let that happen. Remember that's how she got him. No, I don't think so. I hear she keeps him on a short leash."

"I think I'm going to have a few words with him anyway."

"What if he won't talk to you?"

"Talking to me is better than talking to the police."

Just then Lynn Butler found us and asked us to join her and the others who were watching the game. Texas was playing A&M. It was going to be an animated afternoon since the group was made up of graduates from both universities. There were plenty of comfortable chairs to sink into, along with beer and mixed nuts for those who still had room to continue eating and drinking. As the game got into the second quarter, Sarah came over and whispered that she was leaving.

"Where's your boyfriend today?" I asked her.

"Maybe he's having dinner with his family since I'm not free."

"I hope one of these days you're going to let us meet him."

"What are you always telling me? Have patience."

After the game the others slowly took their leave. Joan and Angel wanted to go back to the hotel and let Angela get some much needed rest. I could see her getting more tired as the afternoon wore on. Finally there was no one left but Meggie and me. We were standing by the door, having just said goodbye to the Butlers and the Joneses.

"Is there anything I can do to help you clean up?"

"A nice offer, but a little late."

"You can't tell me that you're so efficient that you've already cleaned the kitchen."

"I had plenty of help from Sarah, Joan, Lynn, and Jenny Jones. You were so busy talking to Jim and watching the game that you didn't even notice."

"And you've put everything away already?"

"You'd make a good supervisor."

"How can I thank you. The dinner, the table, everyone had such a good time, and it was all the things you did that made it so perfect. I could tell that Joan and Angela were comfortable with you and happy to be here."

"They're delightful. They'd have had a good time anywhere just being together and being with you too. But now let's sit down a minute. I think it's time that we have our talk."

"Not now. Aren't you tired after all that work?"

"We have to settle some things now. We're near the end of the semester, and I have to make some plans."

"Are you still thinking about taking that position in Austin with Frank Garza?"

"You asked me to wait before I gave him my answer, and I did. But I'm not able to postpone it any longer. Frank's been patient, but he deserves to know whether I'm going to accept the job or not. I've been patient too, Jeremy, but now it's time."

The time had come that I had been dreading for the last few weeks, and there was no way to respond that would soften my answer.

"I'm sorry, Meggie. I can't tell you what you'd like to hear."

She looked surprised for an instant, but then I saw her suppress her reaction.

"Then there's nothing more to say," she said, rising to look out the window.

"Believe me. It's not you, it's me. Nothing for me has changed. I'm just not able to make a commitment. I don't mean to hurt you, but . . ."

"But, of course, you do."

"Time and time again I've told you how much I care for you. If you look at me, you'll see every word I've been saying is true."

She turned to face me then. "I know you "care," as you put it. No further explanations are necessary. It's quite clear. You choose your freedom."

"I kept my promise. I thought about it. I made this decision not just for myself; it's for both of us."

"That's an illusion, though I'm sure you think it sounds nice to hear. But that's unimportant now."

"So where do we go from here?" I asked.

"I've thought about this moment too, many times. Please forgive me if I seem naive, but aren't we finally saying goodbye?"

"Nothing has to change. Even if you move to Austin, it's only a four-hour drive. We can still see each other as often as we like."

"Now that's a solution. You don't want me out of your life, but you don't want me in it too deeply either. I'm a simple person, Jeremy, not nearly as complicated as you. But I won't continue our present modus operandi — a hurried weekend, a frantic tumble, and a shy goodbye until next time."

"So what happens now? You always say that no one else can give you what I can."

"It won't be easy putting you out of my life, but I'll survive."

"When are you leaving?"

"In two weeks."

"Can I call you?"

"No, not for a while. Maybe in a few months, just to say hello. I'll be in the directory."

"You're really trying to force my hand."

"Not at all. I used to be convinced that someday you would see that I'd be too good for you to miss, but I was wrong. So go home to your little apartment and your cats, Jeremy. They're all you really need."

With that she turned and left the room in the direction of her bedroom with Harold right behind her. I put the spare key she had given me on the table in the entry and left. All the way home I kept thinking that she would change her mind, that there would be a call waiting for me on my answering machine when I arrived home, but, of course, there wasn't. The next move was up to me, and I wasn't ready to make it yet.

❀ 12 ❀

The next morning at nine o'clock I called the hotel. Joan answered the phone and asked me to join her for breakfast. When I walked into the dining room, I noticed that she was alone at the table.

"Angela is having breakfast in the room. She isn't well enough to come downstairs this morning," Joan said.

"What are you planning to do for the rest of the weekend?"

"We had been hoping to remain here and visit with you, Meggie, and Sarah, but now our plans have changed. We need to get back to Dallas as soon as possible. Angela must see her doctor. She may even have to be hospitalized."

"You really have let yourself in for something. Are you sure you want to take all this on?"

"I know it won't be an easy ride, but Angela is not going to make this journey alone."

"But she's not alone. She has the children, and they're almost grown."

"They're still children, Jeremy. We need to get back to talk to them. They know their mother is sick; they just don't know how sick."

"Angel's lucky to have you. Why are we so different? You're willing to take such chances and not be concerned about what happens to you. Obstacles don't deter you. It's not that you don't see them, but you go on. You have so much more courage and ability to love than I do."

Just then the waiter came to the table holding two pots of coffee. We both took decaf and ordered the continental breakfast. He was back in a few minutes with a tray filled with bagels, various breads, and Danish, along with two large glasses of fresh squeezed orange juice. Joan took a sweet roll and put it on her plate. I wasn't hungry.

"What's the matter, Jeremy? I noticed something was wrong as soon as you walked into the room."

"Yesterday after everyone had gone home, I told Meggie that I was unable to make the commitment she wanted. She told me we were through, and she didn't want to see me anymore."

"I'm so sorry, Jeremy. But not seeing each other will be hard to do with both of you teaching at the same college. You'll be running into each other all the time, won't you?"

"She decided to take another job at an accounting firm in Austin. She'll be gone in two weeks."

"I know how much you're going to miss her. Isn't there something you can do to change her mind?"

"I could ask her to marry me. But that would be unfair to both of us."

"Why would that be so unfair? You love her. She loves you. It seems perfectly clear to me."

"You're capable of making this kind of a commitment. You've already done so, but I can't. I need space. I can't imagine what it would be like being with someone all the time."

"Nobody can tell you what to do at a time like this. I just hope you won't regret your choice."

"I'm sure given a little time I will. Then again Meggie's probably right about me. She thinks all I need are my cats."

Joan shook her head sadly, "What did Grace do to you?"

"What did we do to each other? I can't stand the thought of marriage, and she's been divorced three times already. Enough. Let's talk about something else."

95

"I am curious about something. What's happening on the student's case you were telling me about? I think her name was Sharon something."

"The police have stopped working on it since the results of the coroner's report stated that she committed suicide. I'm thinking of conducting my own investigation."

"Why?"

"One reason is Sarah's going after the story. I don't want her out on a limb by herself."

"You don't think it's a suicide?"

"No. I'm not sure. I want to talk to some people before I make up my mind."

"And who would they be?"

"There's a short list: her mother, her stepfather, her boyfriend, a teacher who might have been harassing her, to name a few."

"Haven't the police questioned all these people already?"

"I'm not sure how earnestly they interrogated them."

"Why should all these strangers talk to you and answer your questions?"

"I'm going to tell them the truth, that Sharon came by my office asking me to help her, and before I could, she disappeared. I'm going to tell them that I won't rest until I know exactly what happened to her."

"I can see they might understand Sarah's getting involved. Some people who like to see themselves on television might talk to her since she is a reporter. I just don't think you're going to get the same cooperation."

"Maybe not, but I'm not giving up until I have some answers."

"And when you're satisfied that you have the whole story, then what?"

"Then I won't stop until there is some justice. It's all I can do now for Sharon."

"Justice? Isn't that up to her family to pursue?"

"Do you remember Frost's lines?

. . . from the time when one is sick to death,
One is alone, and he dies more alone.
Friends make pretense of following to the grave.
But before one is in it, their minds are turned
And making the best of their way back to life
And living people, and things they understand."

"That's from 'Home Burial,' isn't it?" she said. Then a few seconds later, she added, "I see."

After we finished breakfast, I went upstairs to see Angela before they caught their plane back to Dallas. They told me they hated long goodbyes, so I was not to follow them to the airport. I did stay long enough to help them get their bags into the car and watch them drive away. In spite of Angela's illness, they seemed to be at such peace with each other. I wished that I could have felt so right about a relationship. I thought about how I would like to talk to Meggie about Joan and Angela's situation. I wanted to call her, but I knew that it wouldn't be fair. I missed her already, and I wondered if she were thinking about me. For a few minutes I wished I could turn the clock back, but then I realized that no matter how the conversation had gone yesterday, it would have ended up with the same results.

❀ I 3 ❀

On Monday morning I called Randy Thorpe's office and left a message on his answering machine asking him to call me. I told him it wasn't urgent. Just as I put the phone down, Royall arrived and dropped an armful of students' papers and books on his desk.

"You'll probably never find those again," I said glaring at the clutter surrounding him.

"If that's one of your not too subtle hints that I need to clean my desk, it won't work. I'm going to wait until after final exams."

"You mean during the same time you've promised to unpack all those boxes of books from publishers stacked on the floor?"

"They're not in your way. They're on my side of the room. I told you I have to go through my bookshelves and get rid of some of my old books before I put the new ones away."

"How fastidious of you. But the mess does bother me. I have to look at it. One day I'd like to have a few words with your mother. She probably picked up after you all your life."

"Don't blame her. She's extremely neat and well organized. When you meet, you'll probably adore each other."

"I'd like you a lot better if you took after her."

"Aren't we the odd couple."

"How was your trip to L.A.?"

"It was great, although it went by too fast. I called some old friends, and we went to some of my favorite night spots. Saw some celebrities. I'd tell you who, but you probably wouldn't know them."

"I'll take that as a compliment. Did you take Marian home with you?"

"I'm not seeing her anymore. There's someone else, and no, I didn't take her home with me either. She had to work."

It was almost time for the bell, and I picked up my books and papers and left for class. Later that afternoon after I got back from lunch, there was a message on my answering machine. I immediately thought it might be Meggie, but when I played it, an unfamiliar voice said he was Randy Thorpe. He said that he would be in his office this afternoon, and I could either call him or come by. Luckily none of my committees was meeting today, so I had time to go by his office. When I called to see if he was in, he answered and invited me to come right over. His office was on the second floor of the gymnasium.

The door to his office was open, and he was sitting at his desk reading the newspaper. He looked like a physical trainer, wearing blue shorts and a matching knit shirt with the college logo on it. High top Reeboks completed the uniform. I guessed he was in his middle thirties, muscular, with a broad open face, dark brown hair, and green eyes. He did not look like a man who needed to harrass young women to get their attention. He invited me to sit down and looked at me curiously.

"Are you here to invite me to join some committee? If so, I must tell you that I don't have time for one more project this school year," he said.

"I'm here to talk to you about a student we've both taught."

"And who would that be?" he asked cautiously.

"Sharon Ames." I looked to see what kind of reaction he had to her name, but there was none. He looked at me for a few seconds without saying anything. "She was your student too, wasn't she?" I said.

"I was just surprised," he answered. And then he added, "Since her death nobody has mentioned her name to me."

"Then you did know her?"

"She was in my body conditioning class last year. She liked working out so much and was such a natural that I gave her private training sessions to make sure she used the machines and the weights correctly."

"Did she pay you for the private sessions?"

"No, of course not. I don't charge anyone here. If I were working at a private club, that would be different."

"Do you give many students training sessions?"

"Just a minute. What is this all about? What business do you have asking me all these questions? Aren't you an English teacher? What did you say your connection was to Sharon Ames?"

"Sharon came to me before she disappeared and told me she had been good friends with a faculty member. She said that he wanted to help her, that he even gave her some books. Could she have been talking about you?"

"Look, I don't know you. I don't see why I should tell you anything. If you have questions about her, you ought to talk to her stepfather or her boyfriend."

"Sharon's brother is the one who gave me your name."

"I see. I'm sorry about what happened to Sharon. For a while we did see a lot of each other. We worked out, we jogged, and we talked."

"She said the relationship changed after a while," I said.

"It's not unusual for people to get close to their trainers. She was a good listener. We started really talking to each other. We were spending several hours a week together. I talked to her about my wife, who was about her age. At the time Cindy and I were expecting our second child, and she was giving me a pretty hard time. I know I shouldn't have unloaded all that on Sharon, but, like I said, she was willing to listen. And I thought her input might clear some things up for me"

"Did she help you understand your wife better?"

"Let's say she tried."

"I hope you don't mind my asking these questions."

"I guess not. She was a nice person, but she was very confused."

"In what way confused?"

"I suppose it doesn't matter any more. She confided in me that she had been abused for years, ever since she was a child, by her stepfather."

"In what way abused?"

"Look, do I have to paint you a picture? She told me that she had never told anybody else about it before and swore me to secrecy."

"What about her mother? Couldn't she go to her for help?" I asked.

"She said that she had tried when she was very young, when it first started, but her mother didn't believe her. Of course, her stepfather denied everything. After that Sharon was never close to her mother. They just couldn't talk to each other."

"What about her brother? I know they were close. Did he know what was going on at home?"

"I don't think so. She said she wanted to protect him. He's younger, you know."

"What did she want you to do?"

"Here's where everything got confused between us. I thought she wanted my help, at least some advice, but she obviously didn't like whatever I had to say."

"And what was that?"

"I told her that she had to go to the authorities and report him. That what he did to her was a crime."

"Maybe she didn't think it would do any good. Harvey Stone is a powerful man with friends in high places."

"You're right. She said she couldn't go to the police and reminded me that I had promised I wouldn't tell anybody either. She told me that it would only make matters worse."

"If she wasn't going to file a complaint, what could you do?"

"Nothing at all. I told her she had done nothing to be

ashamed of, but I could tell that she had stopped listening. She made it clear that she was sorry that she had talked to me. All she wanted now was to get away. When she did leave, I knew she would not be back again for more training sessions."

"Was that the end of the relationship?"

"No, I'm sorry to say that it was the beginning of a change in our relationship."

Just then the phone rang, and Randy answered it, almost relieved for a break in the conversation. I could tell that he was talking to his wife. She wanted to know when to expect him at home. He promised to stop by the supermarket for the short list of items she requested. Then I saw what Jim was referring to about the short leash when she must have asked him who was in the office with him. He answered all her questions with more patience than I would've had. After he hung up, he just said, "Cindy. Are you married, Jeremy?"

I thought about Meggie, but just answered, "Not any more." I suggested that we go across the street to the student center and finish our conversation over a cup of coffee. He said he preferred to go down the block to a small Mexican restaurant for a beer. I thought that was an excellent idea, so we walked the short distance to the café.

When we were seated at a corner table in the back and had ordered two Coronas, I asked him what he meant when he said that after Sharon had left it was only the beginning.

"I'm not trying to make any excuses for myself, Jeremy. Sharon was a beautiful girl. I have to admit I was very attracted. Not that I would have acted on it. I had already paid a big price for doing something like that."

I didn't know what to say, so I just nodded.

"Cindy was giving me a lot of trouble about that time. Like I said before, Sharon was a good listener. And then, my sister had been raped by some college student at the university and had never reported it. That really bothered me. All these ideas were going through my mind."

"So what did you do?"

"When Sharon did not return for our next training session, I went looking for her. I got her schedule from the registrar's office, so I knew if I waited till she got out of class, I could talk to her."

"What did she say when she saw you waiting for her?"

"She was surprised or should I say shocked that I had tracked her down. She said that she was sorry she had said anything and for me to forget what she told me."

"I said that I thought we were friends and that I just wanted to help her, but she said that I should just go away. That I didn't know what I was asking of her."

"What did you do then?"

"I left, but I couldn't get her or what she had told me out of my mind. I called her at the house where she was living. I think it was her boyfriend who answered the phone. When she got on, she said she couldn't talk at that time and that she'd call me at my office tomorrow."

"Did she call?"

"No. Somehow I didn't expect her to. I then thought that this was none of my business, and I'd just do what she asked me to do and forget it."

"And that's all that happened?"

"For a while that's all. I would see her around the campus, but she would always walk quickly in another direction. I tried to get her off my mind. Then about two weeks later my sister called. We had lunch and I asked her if she were ever sorry that she hadn't reported the guy who raped her. She said she was sorry every day. That her worst fear was that he had gone on to do the same thing to other naive young women and girls. She said she should have stopped him."

"What happened next?"

"I had given Sharon books that I thought she would like on different occasions, but now I decided to give her some college catalogs I had collected for my advisees. I thought it might be a good way for her to get away from South Texas and her stepfather. I knew she had a class in the history building the next day, so I took the catalogs and met her as she was entering the building."

"How did she react when she saw you?"

"She wanted to know why I was following her. I told her I just wanted to give her the catalogs. Before all this started, we used to talk about her going away somewhere to finish her degree. She took the catalogs from me and then asked me not to give her any more books."

"She must have thought that you were harassing her."

"I don't know what she thought. The worst is that I don't know what I was thinking either or why I was doing all this. I thought we were friends, but I guess I was wrong."

"Did you see her again?"

"Yes. I realized how upset she was the day I gave her the catalogs, and I didn't want to leave it like that. She had never worn a watch when she and I worked out together. Sometimes she had arrived at the training sessions late, and I used to tease her about it. I decided to give her a gift to remember me by. Maybe it would erase all the bad memories of the last few months."

"Randy, after all the times she asked you to leave her alone, why couldn't you do it?"

"Jeremy, I know now it was a crazy thing to do, but at the time . . ."

"So you bought her a watch. Then what?"

"I called her house to ask her to meet me one more time. I could tell by the way she talked that her boyfriend was there. At first she said no, but I told her that it was important and that it would be the last time."

"So did she meet you?"

"We met the next day at the track. She had been missing her training sessions and wanted to run. I asked her if she wanted me to jog with her, but she said no. Then I gave her the watch. At first she didn't want to take it, but when I told her that it was a goodbye gift and that I would never call her again, she finally took it."

"And did you keep your word? Was that the last time you ever talked to her?" I asked. He was silent for a minute, and then he answered, "Yes, I never called her again."

❊ 14 ❊

One morning two weeks later I awoke in agony. Perhaps I haven't been clear, even to myself, about my feelings for Meggie. I was in love, and I had let her go. School was out for Christmas break. All of a sudden it hit me that I was not going to see her anymore and that she didn't even want me to call. As the ancients used to say, love is a form of madness. Now that she was out of my life, I longed to be with her. It was not enough just to know that she existed. I wanted to talk to her, to touch her, to hear her voice. I wanted things to be back the way they were before Thanksgiving.

By the next day I really needed to see her. There were so many things I had to catch up with now that I wasn't teaching, but I couldn't think about anything but my longing for Meggie. I would have to figure out some strategy to approach her. If she hadn't left for Austin already, she would be gone soon. She could be in Austin by now setting up her new living quarters. I wondered if her house here was on the market yet. I could drive by to see if there was a "For Sale" sign in the front yard. Then I realized that was a bad idea because she might see my car. I knew she liked to take Harold for a walk in the evening. Maybe I could be sitting on a bench when she got to the park to let him run, and we could accidentally meet. No, she'd see right through that.

The transformation of my feelings surprised me, but physical desire had been part of our relationship from the first. Sex had always been a connection between us, and I missed the intimacy of our lovemaking. But most of all, I missed the one person whom I could always count on to be there for me. Tony and Cleo acted restless too, following me from room to room. Every time the phone rang, I hoped it was Meggie calling to tell me she changed her mind, that she needed to see me too. Of course, it was always somebody else, and so I was left in deep anxiety and yearned for her even more.

I went to the refrigerator and found a beer and decided to use it as a temporary liberation from pain, determined to stop thinking about her for a while. Then I saw packages of Swiss cheese and rye bread and made a sandwich, although I wasn't sure I could eat it. I brought the tray of food into the living room and turned on the television to watch the news. There was Sarah in front of the camera, talking about a small explosion at one of the refineries on the west side of the city. She looked very professional as she interviewed two refinery workers, who had been lucky to get out of the building without injuries. I'd have to call her later to tell her what a credible job of reporting she had done and how great she looked in front of the camera.

Sometime in the middle of the evening, Joan called. She said that Angela was feeling better and that Tim and Carolyn now know that Joan will be living at the house with them. They seem relieved that there will be someone to help their mother go through her treatments. Angel has decided that if the chemo goes well, she will teach in the spring. Jack hasn't said anything yet about the new living arrangements, but that could change at anytime. I said that it all sounded like a good plan to me.

Then she asked, "What's the matter, Jeremy?"

"Nothing."

"Don't give me that. I can tell by your voice."

"I don't feel like going into it right now."

"If you want to suffer alone, that's your affair."

"What makes you think I'm suffering?"

"Is it Meggie? You know you can talk to me."

"Yes, it's Meggie."

"Call her. Go to her house and see her."

"Never. I promised her I wouldn't do that."

"Write her a letter. Tell her how you feel."

"It would only upset her or make her angry."

"If you could do it without sounding — overemotional . . ."

"No matter how I'd try, I'd still sound desperate. At least I'll maintain some dignity in remaining silent."

"You're going to have to talk to her sooner or later."

"I know you mean well, Joan, but can we talk about something else?"

"I'm sure Meggie is miserable too."

"Enough."

"Are you coming to Dallas over the break?"

"I'll be there as soon as I finish writing the conference paper. It has to be submitted in a couple of weeks if I'm going to present it in March."

Later on I sat down and thought over what Joan had said to me. Maybe she was right. I decided that I would find a way to talk to Meggie. I would call her and ask her to have dinner with me. After all these years she could hardly reject the idea. What I would say to her, I still wasn't sure. It would come to me when we were together. She didn't pick up the phone, and I noticed that she had reset the answering machine to connect on the second ring. I left a message and asked her to return my call as soon as she came in. I didn't hear from her that evening. The next day I drove by her house. Everything looked the same. There was no sign in the yard, but I noticed a key box attached to her door. I wasn't sure whether this meant she was out of town or not. When I got home, I tried her number again, but the answering machine turned on, and she never picked up the phone. Was she screening her calls? I decided to leave one more message, asking her to return my call. Again I didn't hear from her. I could have called one of her friends in the Business Administration Department, but I didn't want anybody to ask questions about why Meggie didn't say goodbye when she left. If she were still here, I didn't want them to think I was going behind her back trying to get information about her. Whether she were in Austin or Corpus, I knew that she would get my messages, and if she wanted to, she would call.

The following morning I called Sarah to tell her that I watched her on the news last night. She was pleased and said that her work at the station was progressing well. Betsy's father had taken an interest in her and was acting as her mentor. He was encouraging the station manager to use her as much as possible in front of the camera. Mr. O'Ryan told her she had a lot of potential and could go as far as she wanted to in television news. I said that mine was not a professional opinion, but as a member of the viewing audience, I had to agree with him. Sarah said she was off this afternoon and asked me if I would like to meet her somewhere for lunch. I immediately accepted, and we made a date at noon at the Seafood Market, a popular downtown restaurant.

Sarah was studying the menu with Buddhist concentration. "I guess I'll have the blackened redfish and a dinner salad," she finally said, handing the menu back to the waiter. After I ordered the broiled trout, Sarah turned her full attention on me.

"You look terrible, Jeremy, like you haven't slept in days."

"I'm sleeping just fine. I've been trying to get my conference paper completed, and I have a little eyestrain from sitting in front of the computer all day."

"Have you been doing any investigating of the Sharon Ames case?"

"I've been wanting to talk to you about that. One of my colleagues told me something about Sharon that you're going to find interesting."

"Are you talking about Jim Butler? What did he say?"

"No, not Jim. Someone in the Kinesiology Department. His name is Randy Thorpe, and he was Sharon's trainer. From what he told me, they developed a very close friendship. He said that Sharon told him that her stepfather sexually abused her for a number of years."

"Really. I find that hard to believe."

"Why is it so hard to believe? Because you know Harvey Stone so well? Because he's such a nice guy?"

"I don't know how nice a guy he is, but I don't think he's capable of that. I've talked to Harvey quite a bit since I moved into the apartment. He's really devastated by Sharon's death. He's told me many times that he considered her his daughter."

"Then you tell me why Sharon would make up such a story and then tell it to Randy Thorpe."

"I wouldn't know, Jeremy, but you'd better check it out before you tell anyone else, or you might be in for a lawsuit."

"Check it out? Sharon is dead, and you can be sure that her stepfather isn't going to admit it."

"In that case you may never be able to prove it happened."

"But she told some other people about it. She hinted something to Jim, though she never came right out and said it."

"Sounds ambiguous to me. How long did she say this had been going on?"

"Years. Since she was a kid."

"Then why all of a sudden was she talking about it, and why to her men teachers? Whom else did she tell — her boyfriend? Did she tell any women that she'd been abused?"

"I don't know. She tried to tell her mother, but Linda didn't want to believe her."

"If it were true, it must have been awful for Sharon," Sarah said.

"I'm not sure whether she told her boyfriend or not. I haven't spoken to him yet."

"Would you like me to go with you when you do?" Even though she had always been sympathetic to Sharon, she was still a reporter after a good story and wanted to be part of the investigation.

"No. I think I'd better talk to him myself," I said.

Just then the waiter arrived with our dinners, and for the next few minutes, our interest was focused on the fish. Then

Sarah put down her fork and looked as if she were assessing me.

"What? Do I have something on my chin?"

"No. I just wanted to say how sorry I am about you and Meggie. Is there anything I can do to help?"

"Thanks, probably not. How is Meggie these days? I tried to call her and left a message, but she never returned my call."

"She feels that a clean break is best for both of you."

"Has she left for Austin yet?"

"She's in the process of moving. She's found a townhouse she likes. She's going to rent it for a while and then decide if she wants to buy something. It's in a beautiful part of Austin, I hear, on the side of a hill."

"Is she selling the house here?"

"It's on the market. I wish I could buy it. She says she may have a serious buyer already, though I don't know the details."

"I'm surprised that she wouldn't call to say goodbye."

"Have you changed your mind about what you told her?"

"Perhaps. I do miss her. I need to talk to her. I believe we can straighten all this out."

"That would be wonderful. I feel like the child of a divorce. I love you both, but I have no power to change anything."

"I know and I'm sorry."

"She'll be at her house this weekend. There's a moving truck coming on Saturday. Why don't you go by and talk to her some time Saturday morning?"

"She'll probably be too busy to talk then, but I'll try. Thanks for the information. I wasn't up to calling any of her other friends."

After we finished the main course, the waiter came by to ask us if we wanted anything else — more coffee or a dessert. We both wanted a refill of coffee. Then Sarah ordered a slice of turtle cheesecake, which I agreed to split with her. The waiter was back immediately with the coffee, dessert, and two small plates. Sarah divided the cheesecake and passed my share over to me. Half a piece was sufficient with its rich topping of carmel, chocolate, and nuts. Then I took the opportunity to ask Sarah a few questions, mainly about what she had been doing lately. She answered that she had been working mostly. When she got home at night, she was usually too tired to do anything but read and go to bed.

"Then when do you see Harvey Stone?"

"He's taken me to lunch a few times. We just talk. He's lonely now that Sharon is gone and Ted is away at school. He doesn't have much of a relationship with Linda because she spends most of her time just sitting at home drinking. There's no way to have a social life with an alcoholic wife. His friends no longer want to come to his house because it's so unpleasant, and who can blame them?"

"Does he ever say anything about Sharon?"

"All the time. He talks about what she and Ted were like as children. He has dozens of funny stories about them. He tells how he had to take them to their school functions, games, and other activities because their mother couldn't. He's the one who took them to their dentist and doctors' appointments. He taught Sharon how to drive. When Sharon was going through the usual teenage girl problems, he's the one who tried to deal with them."

"That's funny. The last time we talked you said that Harvey told you that Sharon was a real problem."

"That's true, but now he blames most of that on Ben Haynes. He said that he didn't mind Sharon having a boyfriend, but there was something about Haynes that he never trusted. He said that Sharon changed after she started seeing him."

"Why did he stop paying for her education?"

"He never wanted to do that, but he thought that by putting pressure on Sharon, she would break off the relationship. She was an excellent student. He knew how much she wanted to complete her education."

"That strategy obviously didn't work."

"He wasn't so sure that it wasn't working. Remember

Sharon had told him that she didn't want to give up her apartment. He felt sure that things weren't as good between Sharon and Haynes as she tried to make him think."

"He still sounds like he was trying to control her to me, and she obviously resented it."

"Of course, Harvey doesn't see it that way. He feels he was just acting like a father protecting his daughter. I'm not so sure that my father wouldn't have done the same thing."

"If the father-daughter relationship had been so close, why would Sharon accuse him of incest?"

"Careful, Jeremy. All your information is second hand and very questionable."

"You've become pretty supportive of Harvey Stone."

"Not entirely. But I don't think he would have killed her. If you still believe Sharon was murdered, maybe you should be looking somewhere else for the killer."

"I'm keeping all the possibilities open, which means I'm not ruling him out either. Now can we change the subject a minute?"

"I have a feeling I know where you're going."

"Are you still dating your mystery man?"

"We're taking things slowly. Both of us agree that we've never felt this way about anyone before. Now don't look so disturbed; we aren't rushing into anything yet."

"So why the secrecy?"

"As soon as we're sure we know where this is going, we'll let the whole world know."

Sarah looked at her watch then, and we agreed it was time to go. As I walked her to her car, I told her I would call her after I talked to Ben Haynes.

❧ 15 ❧

I was living two lives now. The first I showed to the world was the one in which I conducted the ordinary business of my life. I took care of my household needs and the cats and tried to work on my conference paper. I also occupied myself with the mystery of Sharon Ames, determined to bring it to some resolution. My second life was the condition of insanity that I now found myself in because of my lost love. Love had dimmed the purpose of my public self and made it secondary. It was time to find Ben Haynes and discover what he knew about Sharon and perhaps bring the mystery to its conclusion, but I was too paralyzed with longing for Meggie to undertake the meeting with Ben at this time. I needed my head to be clear when I talked to him.

The lunch with Sarah had helped me formulate a plan. I would go by Meggie's house on Saturday, we would talk, and she would realize that she could not turn her back on our love. We would then spend the rest of the morning figuring out a graceful way for her to cancel her Austin plans.

Just as I was leaving the house on Saturday, the phone rang. When I picked it up, I heard Joan's voice.

"Jeremy, I've been thinking about you."

"That's nice, but you needn't worry about me. You have enough on your mind."

"You sounded so strange the other day."

"I'm taking your advice. I was just leaving the house to go see Meggie."

"Did she ask you to come over?"

"No. But after she hears me out, everything will be fine."

"But what if it isn't? Will you be all right?"

"You don't have to be concerned about me, Joan. How's Angela?"

"She's having a difficult time with the chemo. She's sick all the time. I only hope it's helping her."

"How are you holding up? I know it's not easy for you either."

"It's hard on all of us. The children are acting very strangely. Angela is so sick that we haven't much time or strength left for them. They're away from the house all the time now. They practically live at their friends' houses."

"Aren't they going to spend some of their school break with their father?"

"They don't seem to want to do that either."

"They probably understand more than you think."

"We'll figure it out."

"Maybe this isn't a good time for me to come to Dallas."

"Oh, Jeremy, if you can stand the chaos, please come. Angela is so fond of you. I know she'd like to see you, and your being here even a few days would be good for me."

Before we hung up, I told her I'd try to make it for Christmas and would let her know more in the next few days. Before going by Meggie's house, I stopped at the bakery and picked up her favorite butter pecan coffee cake and two large coffees. I guessed that she probably had all her kitchen things packed and ready for the movers.

When I arrived at the house, the door was open, and two men were already moving furniture into a large van. She looked surprised when I walked through the door. Harold was unhappy, wearing his leash, which was secured to the doorknob of the pantry. He jumped up and tried to come to me, but the leash restrained him.

"Why haven't you ever thought of tying Harold up before?" I asked holding out a cup of coffee.

"I just don't have time to run after him today. What are you doing here? And don't say you just came to bring me a cup of coffee."

"I brought your favorite coffee cake too." I handed the box to her. "Have a piece."

She opened it and admired it for a minute, then laid it on the counter.

"Weren't you even going to call to say goodbye?" I asked.

"I hadn't decided yet."

"Don't you think you owe me that much after all these years?"

"Is that what you came here to say? If so, goodbye, Jeremy. Have a nice life."

The moving men were going in and out of the house, and I realized this was a bad time to try to talk. "Can I take you to lunch?" I asked.

She thought about it, but before she could turn me down, I added, "It's just a lunch."

She finally agreed, and I told her that I would be back for her around noon when the movers would be taking their lunch break.

We were seated at a table in the corner of the small restaurant in the art center on Ocean Drive. Meggie had ordered a soup and salad, and I chose a bacon cheeseburger with home cooked fries. The waiter had just brought us a basket of assorted breads and two glasses of raspberry tea, two of the house specialties.

"Why haven't you returned my calls?"

"I didn't see any point right now. You'd just confuse me."

"I've really missed you."

"Like a comfortable old sweater?"

"I realize that I said some things Thanksgiving that changed the course of both our lives."

"You told the truth about how you feel and what you want, or should I say what you don't want. I can't fault you for that."

"You took me by surprise that evening. We should have had that talk later. It had been a long day for both of us, and I had so many other things on my mind — Joan, Angela. I realize I didn't explain myself well to you that night."

"You explained yourself very well. I just hadn't been listening well until then."

"I realize that if we do get back together, things can't be the same as they once were."

"Jeremy, I don't see us ever getting back together. And you're right; we can never go back to the way we once were."

"I thought we had a pretty good time together."

"We did — most of the time."

"Then how can you throw all those years away so easily?"

"So that's what you think I've done? Thrown it all away and you had no part in it at all?"

The waiter arrived just then with our lunches and asked if we needed more tea and bread. We did and he quickly filled our glasses and left with the bread basket.

"Would it change your mind if I asked you to marry me right now?"

"No. I'm not marrying anyone who asks me because he feels he's being pressured into it."

"You know how much I care for you. I can't imagine a world without you in it. Marry me, Meggie."

"I'm sorry, Jeremy, but I've accepted the job in Austin. I gave my word to Frank. I'm not going to let him down again."

"He'd understand if you told him you were getting married."

"I can't marry you now. I'm going to Austin. I have a buyer for my house. I rented a townhouse. My moving wasn't a ploy to get you to marry me. It's time we both got on with our lives."

The waiter returned with the bread, and noticing our untouched plates, he asked if there was something wrong with the lunches. We assured him that they were fine, and he left.

When we finished eating, I drove Meggie back to her

house. The movers were still at lunch, so we had a little time alone. Harold was in the backyard. I put my arm around Meggie's shoulders, and for a few seconds I felt her lean against me. Then she stiffened and moved away.

"What's the matter?"

"We're not going to do that anymore."

"Just once more to say goodbye?"

"What are you suggesting — a quick tumble on the living room carpet for old times? No thank you."

"There was a time when you wouldn't have thought that was a bad idea."

"Now I do. It's taken me a long time to come to this, but whatever we had together, Jeremy, is over."

"I don't believe you. You can't look me in the eyes and tell me that you no longer love me."

"Like you said to me at the restaurant, I'll always care about you, and I'll always wish you well."

"Isn't there anything I can say to change your mind?"

"Nothing. I'm glad I'm moving. I'm looking forward to making a fresh start."

"But what about me?"

"You'll be fine. You're fine already, although you don't know it yet."

"You're wrong, Meggie. You may think that moving to Austin will erase me from your life, but it won't. It's not over between us yet."

"We'll just have to wait and see," she said softly.

Somehow I got home, but I had the strangest feeling — as if the whole world had to be reconfigured. For some foolish reason I had never expected Meggie to respond to my arguments so vigorously and say with such assurance that it was over between us. We had had disagreements in the past, but I was always able to convince her to be reasonable. Together we would think our differences through rationally and straighten them out. As far as I was concerned, nothing had changed between us. I had never lied to her. I had always told her how I felt about commitment. She had said she would be patient, and I counted on that. She had never given me an ultimatum before. For her to change the rules now without letting me know was unfair.

There was no use sitting at home and feeling sorry for myself; in self-preservation I decided to work on my usual Saturday agenda of chores. Before the crowds at the stores became too large, I felt this was a good time to do some Christmas shopping. My list was short, but I wanted to bring presents to Dallas for Joan, Angela, Tim, and Carolyn. I thought that one of the malls would offer me the most choice with the least effort.

I never go to a mall that I don't find myself in a bookstore. Since I was in no hurry to return to the apartment, I spent an hour browsing through the new releases, picking which ones I wanted to read immediately and which could wait for summer reading. While I looked through the shelves, I found several books I thought would interest Joan and Angela. I would look elsewhere for the children's gifts. I finally settled on six books, a combination of fiction and nonfiction, and took them to the front to pay for them. The woman standing in line in front of me moved to the side so that I could pile the books on the counter while I waited to check out. She had a store discount card, and when the clerk finished her transaction, he thanked her, using her name, Mrs. Stone.

She took her package, and I wanted to speak to her, but just then the clerk asked me how I wanted to pay for the books. When I turned to answer him, Mrs. Stone had disappeared from the store. I wasn't sure that this was Linda Stone, but I had a strong feeling that it was. I remembered that in my office at school, I still had an excellent paper and an exam that Sharon had written, which I'd saved to send to her parents. Monday I would go to the college and get the papers. I'd write a short note about Sharon and send her mother her work.

Back in the apartment that evening, I started thinking about Meggie and the mistake I'd made trying to convince her to come back to me and not move to Austin. I couldn't believe that I'd been so wrong about her. I'd thought she would've been as anxious as I to put the relationship back together. An appalling sadness overwhelmed me when I realized that the affair was over. She was ready, even eager, to go on to a new life in a new place. It was just beginning to reach me that I had no power to change her mind. But even though she'd said that it was finished between us, it wasn't over for me. Exhausted, I sat down in my large chair by the window to read one of my new books, *The Dark Glass,* and fell instantly asleep.

I was walking down a long hall with many strange men and women hurrying along side me. I was not sure what I was doing there or where I was going, but I walked very fast, almost running. Many of the others in the hall were carrying suitcases, so I realized that I must be at an airport. Then I noticed that I was carrying an envelope. It was a round-trip ticket to Dallas. I must have been on my way to visit Joan, but where were my suitcase and packages? We finally arrived in a large public room with many counters, indicating the gates for the various planes.

All of a sudden I saw Meggie, standing in line at one of the gates. I rushed over to her, but she turned her back to me as if she didn't know me. I touched her shoulder and she responded immediately, saying, "Go away." She said she was just about to board the plane to Austin. I tried to talk her into coming with me, but she just laughed and shook her head. Then I had a brilliant idea. I would board her plane and sit down in the seat next to her. The trip would give us time for an uninterrupted conversation, and I could convince her to come with me to Dallas. When I climbed over her to get to my seat, she was not pleased. I looked around and noticed several people whom I knew. A few seats behind us sat Bill Walker, Royall's good friend. I'm sure when he returned to Corpus from his trip, he not only spread the news to Royall but also told everyone on the campus that Meggie and I had parted. Then I looked beside us in the same row on the other side of the aisle and saw the Walterses, two of the biggest gossips in my apartment building. They were staring at me and whispering.

A few minutes later a passenger stopped by our row and asked me to move, saying that I was in his seat. When I refused to get up, he quickly got one of the flight attendants, who asked to see my ticket. When I showed her my ticket, she told me that I had made a mistake and that I was on the wrong flight. She asked me to get off the plane. I said I would leave if Meggie got off with me. Meggie refused, and while I sat in disbelief, she told the flight attendant that she didn't even know me. She said that she wanted another seat because she didn't want to sit by me. The flight attendant told her there were no other seats; the plane was filled to capacity.

The man whose seat I was in was demanding to sit down. Since the flight attendant was powerless to make me leave, she called for help from the cockpit. Before long the captain came to talk to me. I told him I was going to remain on this flight. He said firmly that he'd see to it that I wasn't and asked me to leave the plane at once or he would be forced to take stronger measures. I said I wasn't moving and gripped the arms of the seat, holding on firmly. He tried to remove my seatbelt, but I twisted away from him so that he couldn't reach it.

The rest of the passengers were becoming restless. Several of them stood up and crowded into the aisle yelling obscenities at me. It was time for the plane to take off. Passengers began shrieking that they would miss their connections. A few started reaching for me and pulling at my shirt, my jacket, or whatever they could grab. One told the captain to hit me over the head with a blunt object and drag me off the plane. I heard the murmuring of several voices in agreement. The captain returned to the cockpit, I was sure, to get a weapon, though I never saw him again. The faces around me had puffed up and looked like angry balloons of various shades of red, orange, and yellow and were bobbing up and down in my face.

The flight attendant attempted to reason with me once more. When she was unable to convince me to move, she asked Meggie to tell me to be rational, to appeal to my sense of logic. She told her to promise me whatever I wanted. Then

Bill Walker pushed forward and grabbed my arm and started pulling me, trying to get me out of the seat. Mr. Walters started hitting me on the head with a rolled up newspaper. Meggie tried to get out of her seat, but there were too many angry people milling around.

"I'm going to be sick," she said, reaching for the white bag in the pouch on the back of the seat in front of her.

"Please don't," I told her softly, "or I'll be sick too."

She asked again if she could move to another seat, but nobody could hear her in the din. I was still determined not to get off the plane without her.

Somebody must have come up with a plan, for suddenly the entire aisle was full of angry passengers. One of them told me that I could either leave on my own feet or they would carry me off. I began yelling to Meggie for her not to let them do this to me. My state of mind is hard for me to explain. A part of me knew that Meggie still loved me and that she alone could put a stop to this deplorable harassment. Another part of me realized that I was alone, without any support, and if I didn't do what this mob demanded, they would humiliate me by forcibly removing me from the plane.

I was about to answer when suddenly several of them grabbed me from behind and lifted me out of the seat. I yelled, "Wait, wait. I'll go on my own." But nobody listened to me. I tried to pull away, but there were too many of them. I could see the other passengers' faces as I was carried down the aisle and out the door. Their expressions were contemptuous, some were laughing, some were yelling, but there was so much noise that I couldn't hear any words. They dropped me in the jetway and started dragging me toward the gate area. I looked up to see if Meggie was following us off the plane, but she was nowhere to be seen. Then they picked me up again and threw me out of the jetway.

I sat up and began to check to see if anything was broken, but I was still in one piece. It was suddenly much quieter. Then I realized that I was still in my own chair, and my book had dropped to the floor. It was past midnight, and the cats were soundly asleep on their backs on the sofa. I tried to remember if I had heard someone say before they all turned and walked back on the plane,

"Well, we're finally rid of him. Now we can get on with our lives."

❧ 16 ❧

The sky was overcast when I awoke Monday morning. I was feeling weak and tired from not eating much in the last few days. I wondered if Meggie was missing any meals. Probably not. Looking out the window, I decided just to lie in bed all day, but the cats wouldn't let me. Cleo kept climbing on my chest until she decided to pursue one of her more unpleasant habits of chewing on my hair. Tony was busy bringing his toys on the bed, so I could play with him. It was easier to get up and start the day.

I remembered that I was going to my office this morning to retrieve Sharon's test and essay so that I could mail them to her mother. I called the college security to let them know that I would be at the office around ten, so they would turn off the burglar alarm. Then I tried to eat a small breakfast of cereal and coffee, but I still wasn't hungry.

After I shaved, showered, and dressed in a pair of jeans and a sweater, I sat down in the living room. I couldn't get motivated to do anything except sit in my chair and think. Nothing had gone the way I had expected it would, and now here I was alone — right in the middle of the holiday season when everyone else was with family and friends, all enjoying themselves and going to parties. And I'd probably be alone for the rest of my life.

I finally got up and made the short drive to the office around ten. Driving down Ocean Drive always lifted my spirits, but today my mood was like the black clouds hovering overhead. When I arrived at the campus, it was deserted. Nobody was around except the security guard parked in front of the building. It was not too cold — in the forties — and the guard told me that he couldn't turn any heat on in the office. I assured him that I was not staying very long.

The office looked the same as it did after final exams except that Royall's mess seemed to have increased and was creeping closer to my side of the room. He had promised to do something about it as soon as the semester was over, but I realized that as long as I shared an office with him, I would be surrounded by clutter. I knew exactly where to find Sharon's papers, so I grabbed them and left the room, locking the door behind me.

When I got back home, I wrote and mailed this note to Linda Stone:

Dear Mrs. Stone,

You have probably never heard of me, but I was Sharon's English teacher this past semester. I can't tell you how sorry I was to hear about her death. We talked briefly in my office once, and so I did not know her very well personally, but she was a pleasure to have as a student. She was an excellent writer, and so I thought you might enjoy having the last two papers she wrote for the class. One of them is a major exam on which she did especially well. The other is a fifteen page research paper. You will be able to see for yourself how good it is.

If you have any questions that I might answer for you, feel free to call.

Sincerely yours,
Jeremy Greystone

PS. If you call my office at school, I'll get the
message as I check my calls regularly.

The following Wednesday morning the phone rang, but I
no longer even hoped it would be Meggie. The woman's voice
on the other end was unfamiliar:

"Mr. Greystone? This is Linda Stone. I got your number
from the telephone directory. I hope it's all right to call you at
home."

"Of course, it is Mrs. Stone."

"First, let me thank you for sending me Sharon's work.
You may not believe this, but it is the first time I've ever read
something she wrote for school."

"It's very good, as I said in my note, don't you think?"

"Very good. But I also wanted to tell you how considerate
I thought you were to send it."

"I'd like to say again how sorry . . ."

"I know, Mr. Greystone, we're all sorry. In your note you
kindly offered to answer any of my questions. Are you still
willing to do that?"

"I'll certainly try. What questions do you want me to answer?"

""Oh, no, not over the phone. I'd like you to come by the
house, if it wouldn't be too much trouble."

"It depends. When do you want me to come?"

"How about this afternoon around three P.M.?" she said,
sounding pleased by my acceptance.

I arrived at the house on the east side of Ocean Drive
around three o'clock. The first thing I noticed were the beautiful palm trees blowing gently in the wind. I turned into the
wide circular driveway and saw what looked like visitors'
parking on the left front side. I pulled my Honda into a space
next to a shiny black Jaguar. The landscaping looked almost
too perfect to be real — like the setting of a movie filmed on
an exotic Caribbean Island. I walked up the tiled walkway

lined with large clay pots filled with plants and colorful flowers toward the large, two-story Mediterranean-style off-white
house with its red shingled tile roof. Then I rang the doorbell,
and moments later an attractive Hispanic woman opened the
door and led me through a long entrance hall into a beautiful
room looking out on a garden at the back of the house facing
the bay. This view was even more beautiful than the entrance
with its large terraced garden, pool that seemed to flow into
the bay, and another large and elegant structure, which could
have been a pool house, guest house, or party rooms. After
she announced me, her housekeeper stood there a minute to
see if Linda Stone wanted something else. Mrs. Stone nodded
slightly, and the woman disappeared. Linda Stone was wearing a long, loose lounging gown made from a colorful fabric
in a large floral pattern. Her light brown hair was pulled back
from her face, and although she was still quite attractive, at
one time she must have been beautiful. I could see the family
resemblance between her and Sharon, except for their coloring. Sharon's hair had been darker and her eyes were brown.
Mrs. Stone's eyes were blue, but still the mother and daughter
looked very much alike.

She indicated a love seat next to her chair and asked if I
would join her for a drink.

"Teresa makes an excellent Bloody Mary and margarita, or
would you prefer a glass of wine, Mr. Greystone?" she asked.

"The Bloody Mary sounds good, Mrs. Stone," I said, taking the chair.

"Teresa," she called, and the woman who had answered
the door came in and handed her a drink. "Mr. Greystone
would like a Bloody Mary." Teresa quickly left the room
again. Mrs. Stone leaned back, shifting her position to reveal
long, slender, suntanned legs. "Please call me Linda," she said
in a low, husky voice. "Do you mind if I call you Jeremy?"

"No, please do."

"How well did you know my daughter, Jeremy?"

"As I said in my note, I didn't know her very well, except I
noticed at once that she was an exceptional student. She came

to my office shortly before she disappeared to ask for my help. She was going to return the next day, but she never did. That was the last time I saw her."

"Was she looking for help with her English course?"

"No, it was of a more personal nature."

Linda leaned toward him, her gown falling open to reveal some cleavage. "Tell me, Jeremy, what did she want from you?"

"She told me someone was harassing her, and she wanted me to help her."

"And who would that be?"

I was surprised at the way she accepted the news so nonchalantly. Just then Teresa entered the room carrying a tray with two drinks, two small plates, and a platter of raw vegetables with a dip in the center. She placed it on the coffee table in front of us and left the room again.

"Please help yourself," Linda said, waving her hand toward the tray. "You haven't answered my question, Jeremy. Who was harassing my daughter?"

"I don't know. She never told me. That's what she was going to reveal to me on the following day, but she never kept her appointment."

"Sharon always had a flair for the dramatic."

"Are you saying that you don't believe her?"

Linda placed her hand on my arm and looked steadily into my eyes. "This wouldn't be the first time that she made accusations like this."

"Mrs. Stone, Linda, please explain what you mean. I've been concerned about what happened to Sharon ever since she disappeared."

She took her hand away, picked up her glass, and took a long, slow drink before she answered. "Let me just say that there have been other boys and men that she claimed were, should I say, annoying her from time to time. At first I always took these accusations seriously. But when I looked into the situations, I found that she had exaggerated and that much of what she said was sheer fabrication. Sharon liked attention, especially from men, Jeremy. And she knew how to get it. Men seem to jump at the chance of saving a beautiful young woman in distress, don't you agree?"

"I saw the pain and fear in Sharon's eyes. I don't believe she was making it up."

"I think I knew my daughter better than you did, Jeremy."

"Then what happened to her? Do you have any idea how she died?"

"The coroner said that she killed herself. I don't believe that either. Sharon was not a person who would take her own life."

"Then do you think it was murder or an accident?"

"If he hadn't had an alibi, I wouldn't be surprised if it were her boyfriend who shot her. Maybe she was finally putting an end to that relationship. They were an ill-suited pair from the beginning. We told her many times that he was all wrong for her."

"Linda, I don't know anything about Sharon's past, but I do know that she asked me for help, and that I could have done better. I can't help her now, but I made a promise to my-self that I would find out what happened to her and try to see that justice was done."

"I see. And you don't think the authorities have done a very commendable job."

"There still are a lot of unanswered questions."

"When you find the answers, I hope you will share them with me." All this time she had been sipping on her drink. Now that her glass was empty, she rose and asked me if I would like to see her garden. I went with her out the French doors, and she pointed out the various flowers blooming pro-fusely in their well tended beds. Then we walked over to the pool. It was clean and inviting.

"Would you like to go for a swim, Jeremy? The pool is heated, and there is a hot tub we can get into after our swim." She indicated a hot tub attached to the pool that seemed big enough for eight people.

"I didn't bring my bathing suit."

"Never mind. I always have extras in a variety of sizes and styles in the guest house."

"Thanks, but not today. I'm getting ready to go out of town in a few days, and I still have some errands to run and need to get someone to feed my cats before I leave."

"Then you have to promise me that you'll come back when you can stay longer."

"I've told you everything I know, Linda."

"But I haven't told you everything I know, Jeremy. I'd like to talk to you some more about Sharon. Promise me that you will come back." She smiled at me and took my hand in hers, and I thought how attractive she is.

For a minute I felt I was being unfaithful to Meggie. And then I was uneasy making a promise I knew that I would never keep, but I nodded that I would return. She walked me to the door, and just as I started to open it, the door burst open, and Harvey Stone walked in. He looked at Linda first and then at me, and his eyes narrowed. Linda introduced us, but I felt suddenly unwelcome, and so I left the house as quickly as I could.

❧ 17 ❧

The next morning I wondered if I should call Meggie in Austin to see if she had got moved in all right. Then I remembered that she asked me not to call her for a while. I wondered if I should pay attention to her request or would it be better if I let her know I was thinking about her? Just as I was about to pick up the phone, it rang. Could she be thinking about me too? When I picked the receiver up, however, I heard a low, husky voice.

"Jeremy, this is Linda. I hope I didn't call too early, but I must see you before you leave for Dallas. I may have some important information for you."

"I don't think your husband was too pleased to see me at your house yesterday."

"I'm sure he didn't care. Anyway, he's left for the ranch. He probably won't be back until tomorrow. Come around two."

When Teresa led me into the large family room, Linda was standing by the French doors, looking out on the garden. She was tall and slender, wearing red plaid shorts and a short sleeved red sweater, and looked younger than I thought she was. She immediately came toward me, took my hand, and led me to the love seat where I had sat yesterday. Then she sat down beside me.

"Jeremy, what you said yesterday about your wanting to

find out the truth about Sharon's death and see that justice was done really moved me. You so remind me of someone I used to know a long time ago."

"And who would that be?"

"Can I tell you a story? Then I think you will understand more about Sharon and me."

Teresa quietly entered with a tray with two Bloody Marys and a pitcher of refills and left the room. Linda turned toward me, put one of her knees under the other leg, leaned back on the cushions of the chair, and began to speak. "Where should I begin?" She appeared to ask that question not to me, but to herself.

"When I was sixteen, I lived with my parents and my older brother James on a small ranch, just outside the city. We didn't have very much, and my father worked hard night and day to eke out a living from the land. I can't complain about my childhood. My parents spoiled me as much as poor parents can. I did well in my classes and I was a cheerleader, but I was conscious of never having enough money for clothes and other luxuries teenaged girls want. For my sixteenth birthday I had wanted my own car like so many of my friends got, but, of course, that was out of the question.

"Of course, there were boys who liked me. I had my choice among the school athletes, and for a while I dated Ricky Warren, the captain of the football team, until he decided he'd rather be with Jennifer Holmes, another cheerleader, who came from a prominent South Texas family. I cried a lot about that, and it was the first time I realized that having lots of money can get you whatever you want.

"It wasn't too long after that when I started dating Teodoro Castillo. He came from one of the wealthiest families in South Texas and Mexico. He was good-looking in a sensitive way, not at all like the football players that I was used to dating. He was more interested in the school newspaper and debating than acting like a wild teenager. He was the president of the National Honor Society. He liked opera and plays, and he had traveled with his family all over the world.

"My parents were concerned about the relationship. They told me that Teodoro and I came from two different cultures, different religions, different economic family backgrounds. You know the pitch parents can make when they think they're saving their daughter from disaster. Teodoro's family were even more against the relationship. They talked about bigotry and racism. They didn't especially like poor Gringas and thought that I was interested in their son for his money. They were fervent Catholics and didn't approve of his dating a girl from another religion. Their reasons for disapproving went on endlessly.

"Perhaps our parents' trying to break up our relationship convinced us that we were like the Montagues and the Capulets. You're an English professor; you know all about *Romeo and Juliet*. Just like them, we ran away and got married. Our parents tried to have the marriage annulled, but we told them I was pregnant. After much cajoling we convinced them that we were serious about the marriage and would do anything it took to make it work. Ted's parents made me promise that I would convert to Catholicism and that we would both complete our education. We went back to school and graduated with our class. Teodoro went on to the University of Texas, and much later I had Maria Sharon and Teodoro the fifth.

"I don't know what happened to the marriage. We were just too young and too different in every way. Even though I became a Catholic, his family never approved of me, and I always felt like an outsider. I couldn't go to my parents for help. They would have reminded me that they had tried to warn me. When I met Harvey at a party, he was so forceful and energetic, a real take control kind of guy, and I fell for him pretty hard. I'm not making any excuses for myself. I started going behind Ted's back and meeting Harvey at different places. At first we were careful, but someone must have told Ted. One night he caught us together in Harvey's apartment. There was a terrible scene. When I continued to see Harvey, Ted finally gave me an ultimatum. Give up the relationship or give up the family. I must have been obsessed because I couldn't give Harvey up even though it might mean my losing my children. There were months of torment for all of us, but in the end it was settled by a gunshot to the head. I try not to blame myself, but I guess I do. A few drinks help sometimes. He didn't have to kill himself. Why did he do it? From the moment she was born, Sharon had been her daddy's girl. She was so young — just five years old and, even then, so smart. She must have heard all our fighting, and I know she's always blamed me entirely for her father's death. Little Ted was just a baby and didn't know what was happening until much later when Sharon told him her version of the story."

Linda stopped speaking and picked up one of the Bloody Marys. "What do you think?"

"That's quite a story," I said.

"That's just the first part of the story. After six months Harvey and I were married, and then my troubles really began."

"What could be worse than what you've already told me?"

"I married Harvey because I was madly in love with him. He married me for the challenge of the hunt. Harvey is a great hunter. Very soon after our marriage, the excitement of the chase was over for him, and he was ready to go after new game." She stopped to take another drink. "Oh yes, he said he loved me, but what attractive woman didn't he love? Of course, it took me a year to catch on to what he was doing. When he didn't come home until late at night, when there was lipstick on his shirts, when he made furtive phone calls and disappeared right afterwards, I finally caught on that he was doing to me what he had done so many times before with me and with so many other women. I don't believe he's ever been faithful to anyone for more than three months in his whole life."

"But you remained married to him all these years."

She appeared to smile to herself and said in her low, sultry voice, "It's been a rocky marriage for us both. I'm sure he thinks I drink too much. He does too. We had some good times together as well as all the bad. I don't know. I suppose I needed to prove to a lot of people that I hadn't made another terrible mistake. He said he loved the children and wanted to help me with them. I'm sure I wasn't the best mother in the world. To be honest, I don't know why we're still married."

She stopped talking and looked at me to see how I was reacting to what she had said.

"How did Sharon fit into all this?"

"Sharon was Harvey's favorite. He doted on that girl. Ted was just a baby, so he couldn't do very much with him for a long time."

"Did Sharon ever complain that Harvey abused her in any way?"

"Sharon seemed all right with Harvey when she was a child. He gave her everything she wanted before she ever asked for it. They did not begin having trouble until she started dating. He was always suspicious of the boys she went out with because she was not very discriminating in her choices."

"In what way?"

"She had the opportunity to date many young men from good families. She chose boys that—what's the use? No more need to go into that now."

"Sharon was such a good student. Why didn't she go to college right after she graduated from high school?"

"Just another one of her bad choices. When we told her that we were willing to send her to either the University of Texas or Texas A & M, she decided she wanted to go to some small private college in northern California. Probably because a boy she was interested in at the time was going to attend there. We argued about that for a while; then Harvey told her to pick any school she wanted to attend in the state, but she refused. By that time it was a real battle of wills. Neither one of them would give in, so she didn't enroll anywhere. That was typical of Sharon. She had always been headstrong and stubborn."

"So what did she do for the next couple of years?"

"Very little. To embarrass us she got a few inconsequential jobs around town. She waited tables for a while and then did some hostessing at a dinner club. I think that's where she met most of her boyfriends before she got mixed up with that last one." The look on her face revealed the contempt she felt for Ben Haynes. "Why are we spending so much time talking about Sharon when what I'd really like is to get to know you better."

"There's not much about me to know."

"Let me be the judge of that. You're not wearing a ring; does that mean you're not married?"

"I haven't been married for a long time."

"I'm sure someone like you is tied up with a woman friend."

"Actually right now I'm quite unattached."

"Last time you were here I invited you for a swim. The pool is heated. Would you like to try it?"

"Not today. Maybe next spring or summer."

She stood up, walked toward the French doors, and turned back to me and smiled. "Let me show you the guest house. It has a wonderful exercise room, steam room, and sauna. We even have our own massage room."

I put down the glass and followed her out the door onto a brick path that snaked through the garden, past the pool, to the large Mediterranean-style guest house near the seawall. The house was large and elegantly furnished with a glass wall facing the bay. It had two large bedrooms, each with its own bath, a modern kitchen, and a formal dining room. I could see that the Stones were collectors of art, and the lighted rooms with their high ceilings were the perfect setting for the large paintings, tapestries, and sculptures. The inlaid wooden floors reminded me of the pictures of Italian palaces I had seen in travel magazines. The exercise room was filled with every piece of equipment that anyone could ever expect to use.

"I have a trainer who comes three times a week, but I only let him give me massages. Harvey likes to work out. He thinks it keeps him young."

"This place is amazing. Do you spend much time here?"

"I think of it as my," she paused for a few seconds and laughed to herself, "my sanctuary."

She then led me around to the rest of the rooms — to the sauna, the steam room, the massage room, and then back to the large living room. "This is a perfect party house, but we don't give parties anymore."

She led me to a large, white, overstuffed sofa and asked me to sit down and enjoy the view for a few minutes. She then sat down beside me and rested her hand on my leg. I felt uncomfortable, but I didn't move for a minute. Then she said, "Harvey and I have gone our own ways with our personal lives for a long time, Jeremy."

"I'm sure you know what you're doing, Linda, but I think this is a little dangerous. What if he comes home again?"

"He's at the ranch. He probably won't be home until tomorrow some time. Relax, Jeremy; I just want you to know how attractive I find you. You remind me so much of someone I used to know a long time ago, except in some ways different too."

"I really don't think this is a very good idea."

"You don't find me attractive?"

"It's not that, Linda. I find you very attractive, but I have a rule about married women."

"Forget the rule for now, Jeremy. Let's just concentrate on getting to know each other better."

"I don't think so." But even as I protested, she began unbuttoning my shirt. Her hands were all over me, and she pulled me toward her and began kissing me. Before I realized it, I was helping her undress too. She led the way to one of the bedrooms and closed the door, and for the next hour we were lost in our lovemaking. Then I came to my senses and thought of Meggie. I felt like I was being unfaithful to her, as ridiculous as that sounds. I sat on the side of the bed, wondering how I could gracefully extricate myself from the situation.

"How about a shower together and a steam bath?" Linda asked stretching her long, slender legs and then grabbing her terry cloth robe that had been lying on a chair by the bed. She put it on and then got back into bed and drew her legs up, folding her arms around them. She looked like an older version of her daughter.

Just as I was about to decline the offer, the phone by the bed rang. From her conversation I could tell that it was Teresa, telling Linda that Harvey had just arrived unexpectedly. I had to get out of there immediately. I quickly pulled my pants on, then my shirt, and tried to stuff my underwear and socks in my pockets.

"I thought you said he wouldn't be back today."

"I guess I was wrong."

"Is there a way out of here where he won't see me?" I asked, fumbling to get my shoes on without the socks.

"That just depends on where he is."

I started out the door, still trying to stuff my shorts into my pocket. It didn't work, so I put them inside the front of my shirt.

"Wait, Jeremy, there's a locked gate around the side of the house. I'll take you out that way, and if we hurry, he probably won't see us." She didn't even bother to get her shoes, and we rushed out down the path toward the side of the house.

As I drove back to the apartment, I thought about how lucky I was to get away from that house without a confrontation with Linda's husband. What would Harvey Stone have thought if he had caught me with his wife in the middle of the day, and all she was wearing was a white terry cloth robe? Then all he had to do was enter the guest house and find her clothes scattered all over the living room and bedroom. Everyone says that he has an uncontrollable temper. That and his large gun collection could mean more trouble for both of us than a love affair was worth. I wondered why I had allowed myself to get into such a mess. Well, it wouldn't happen again. Next time Linda Stone called me, I wouldn't be available. The only reason I had got in touch with her in the first place was to obtain information to help solve the mystery of Sharon's death. She's probably told me everything she knows about that already.

As I walked through the door to my apartment, the phone was ringing. I rushed to answer it before the machine answered the call. The voice on the other side was soft and husky. I recognized Linda immediately.

"Are you all right? I thought you were going to have a heart attack when Teresa called."

"I'm fine. I just don't like close calls like that."

"I found one of your socks in the living room when I returned to the guest house. Don't worry, Harvey didn't see you."

"Just throw it away. One sock isn't good for anything."

"No, Jeremy, I'm going to return it to you. How about later this evening at your place?"

"That won't work. Besides, I have plenty of socks. Just get rid of it."

"I have to see you. If not at your place, where?

I felt trapped and yet a little intrigued. I don't remember how long it had been since any woman had made me feel that it was urgent that she should see me. "What about your spouse?"

"He's out for the evening with one of his women friends. He says it's a business meeting, but I know better than that. Come back over here."

"Absolutely not. There's a small, dark dinner club called Nexis on Santa Fe in the shopping center not too far from the hospital. Do you know where it is?"

"I've never been there, but I know which one it is."

"It is mostly frequented by the younger crowd. I doubt that it's your husband's style. They have entertainment and great Mexican food. I'm going there for dinner tonight. Would you like to accidentally bump into me just inside the entrance around seven?"

"That sounds intriguing. And don't worry about Harvey. You're right; it's not his style."

After she hung up, I was sorry that I had asked her to meet me. But after thinking it over, I realized that it might not be such a bad idea. Tonight after dinner over a drink, when everyone was calm, I would make it absolutely clear to her that I was not going to embark on an affair. As tempting as it was, I had enough complications in my life at the present without getting enmeshed in another one.

At seven o'clock I was standing in the entrance after just giving my name to the hostess. I could hear the rock group playing loudly and remembered why I always hated to come to this restaurant. The only reason I ever came was that they made the best bean nachos and green enchilladas this side of the border. I hadn't been hungry in a long time, but tonight I was just in the mood to order them both, along with a few margaritas. Maybe I was beginning to forget Meggie at last.

About 7:15 the hostess called my name, and I was wondering what to do when I saw Linda walk through the door. She was wearing a tight, short black dress that showed off her long, slim body. The hostess escorted us to a booth in the corner that was dimly lit by a candle. After the waitress took our order, Linda pulled out a familiar sock from her small black bag, and put it on the table.

"Thanks for remembering." The music was playing so loudly I could hardly hear her reply as I stuffed the sock into my pocket. "Is there anything else you can tell me that might help unravel the truth about Sharon's death?"

Just then the drinks arrived, and we waited for the waitress to leave. Then she answered, "I've thought about it a lot, and I can't think of anything else except that it was probably an accident. The coroner said that she had traces of gunpowder on her hands, so she must have shot the gun herself. But I know my daughter, Jeremy. She would never have deliberately killed herself."

"May I ask a personal question?"

"Ask anything you like." Then she smiled and added, "I may not answer it."

"Why did you and Harvey have such large insurance policies on the lives of Sharon and Ted?"

"How did you know that?"

"I can understand parents taking out a small policy to help

pay for a burial, if needed, but I hear that these policies are extremely large in multiples of six digits. Is that right?"

"You're perfectly right, but they were Harvey's idea. I'm not a businesswoman. All of us have large policies on our lives. We can afford them, so we have them."

"Another personal question?"

"Ask away."

"You say that Harvey has been unfaithful. Do you think that he was ever abusive to Sharon when she was a child?"

"Now you are striking a nerve. Do you think I would ever allow my husband to be sexually abusive to my daughter?"

"I never mentioned sexually, but is there even the remotest possibility, Linda?"

"I used to feel very sure about the answer to that question. Now I don't know. Sharon came to me once and hinted at something, but I couldn't understand what she was saying. She was so vague, and when I tried to question her, she wouldn't speak. I'm sure I could have handled the whole incident better, but I was preoccupied at the time, and she never approached me with it again. I thought there was nothing to it, or she would have been more persistent about telling me."

"Now do you think that it might have been possible?"

"I'm not sure I know all that Harvey Stone is capable of. He's proved to be quite capable of cruelty to me, but I always thought he loved the children."

"Would he have threatened Sharon if he thought she was going to expose him as an abuser?"

"If he felt threatened, even by the children, Harvey Stone would be a very dangerous man. He's hurt a lot of people who've crossed him. He always gets what he wants, and I've never seen anyone get the best of him."

At this time the waitress arrived with a large plate of nachos and a pitcher of margarita refills.

I asked her how much money it would take for her to tell the musicians to play quietly, or better yet, to get them to stop playing at all. She laughed and said I'd have to take that matter up with the owner. After she walked away, I looked at

Linda and asked, "Aren't you taking a big chance meeting me here tonight?"

"Not as big a chance as you're taking, my friend. Are you frightened?"

"I'm more driven than frightened. Now more than ever, I'm determined to learn the truth about Sharon's death."

"Have I mentioned how attractive you are when you're so intense?"

"You just like me because I remind you of someone. May I ask who that might be?"

Just then a waiter arrived holding a tray over his head with our main courses. It took a minute to set the hot plates before us, along with a basket of hot flour tortillas. For a few minutes we concentrated on our food. Then I looked up and saw a familiar young woman being seated by her date on the other side of the room. It was Sarah. I recognized her even in the dim light, but could not make out whom was she with? Then my eyes focused, and I saw him more clearly. It was Royall Phillips, and they were holding hands and intimately leaning toward each other across the table. I felt betrayed. How could she be involved with Royall when she knew how I felt about him? I had told her that he was a self-absorbed womanizer. From all that I knew of his past relationships, he would break her heart like he had done to so many before her. It finally made sense. Now I understood why she had kept her boyfriend's name a secret from me all this time. I wanted to jump up from my chair and cross the room to where they were sitting and confront them both. How could they have been so devious and betray my trust?

"Who are you staring at?"

"I'm not staring. I just thought I saw my niece across the room."

"Has she seen us?"

"I don't think so. She's too engrossed in the man she's with."

"Then you can take a lesson from her. I was just about to tell you whom you reminded me of before our dinners arrived."

I tried to make myself concentrate on Linda, telling myself that I would talk to Sarah later, but I couldn't keep my eyes from returning to the table across the room. "Tell me whom I remind you of," I said.

"You remind me of Ted, my first husband, Sharon's father," she said looking deeply into my eyes.

For a minute I couldn't speak. Then I asked her how I reminded her of Teodoro Castillo.

"You're good-looking in the same way he was. You're intellectual, interested in books. Oh, I'm not sure how to describe it, but you have some qualities that bring back memories."

"And the differences?"

She poured us each another drink, and then said, "You're stronger than Ted. I feel like I can depend on you — that you won't fall apart in a crisis."

"You mean like this afternoon?" And we both laughed. I felt like this was the time to tell her that she could not depend on a relationship with me. I wanted her to know that besides her being a married woman that I was still in love with someone else. But before I could begin my speech, she continued telling me how important to her a relationship with me was at this time.

"Jeremy, I'm completely alone in the world. My parents are dead. I have no other family except my son, and he's away most of the time. Even when there are no classes, he lives and works in Houston. I've never wanted to be a burden to my children. After Sharon's death I promised myself I wouldn't do this to Teddy."

"I commend you for letting your son live his own life, Linda. Many mothers are unwilling to do that. But what about your friends? You've lived in South Texas all your life. Surely you have many friends you can rely on."

"I know this sounds cliche, Jeremy, but I've never enjoyed women friends. The women I know are always tied up with their husbands, children, and grandchildren. I never felt that I could really talk to them like I talk to you. It's not that they're not good, remarkable women. Many of them do good works in the community through all kinds of organizations. I tried to be like that too for a time, but I'm just not fit for all the meetings and the small talk. Jeremy, I need a real friend. Don't you desert me too."

I decided to wait to have the talk with her. It was not the right time to tell Linda how I felt. I just wouldn't get any more involved than we already were. I was leaving for Dallas tomorrow and would be gone a few days, so that would cool things off a bit. When I got back, I just wouldn't call her. The rest of the evening went well with both of us having our share of two more pitchers of margaritas.

Finally it was time to walk Linda to her car. As we were leaving Nexis, I had to guide her by the arm as she seemed shaky on her feet. When we got nearer to the table where Sarah and Royall were sitting, I saw the surprise on their faces when they recognized me. I looked back at them so they would know that I saw them, and then I continued steering Linda through the door to the entrance. It was a cold night for Corpus, and as soon as we got outside, I felt clearheaded again.

"I don't think you should drive yourself home. You've had too much to drink," I said.

"Nonsense. As soon as I felt the cold air, I was fine."

"If you're not sure, I'll be glad to drive you in your car."

"Then how will you get home? No thanks. I'm fine," and with that she got into her Jaguar, put on her seat belt, waved, and was gone.

For just a minute I thought of going back into Nexis to confront Sarah and Royall, but even in my half inebriated state, it was clear that this wasn't the right time. They had watched while I escorted Linda Stone out of the club and would probably challenge anything I told them right now because I was standing on slippery moral ground. This matter could wait until I returned from Dallas. Besides, I had packing to do to get ready for my flight in the morning.

❧ 18 ❧

The next morning as I was stuffing my shaving kit into the suitcase, I thought about Meggie. I missed her, and, as strange as it seems, being with Linda yesterday only made me miss Meggie more. I would have liked to talk to her about Joan and Angela and get her advice on how to handle my visit with them. Joan had told me that Angela was now going through a difficult series of treatments, and I wondered if my coming would help them or if I'd just be in the way. I picked up the phone and called information in Austin, and asked for a listing for a Margaret Ryan. There was no listing for a Margaret or Meggie, but the operator found an M. A. Ryan. Before I lost my courage, I dialed the number. An answering machine picked up on the second ring, and I recognized Meggie's voice, asking the caller to leave a message. I left a short message, telling Meggie that I was thinking of her and that I hoped she was adjusting to her new house and job, as well as to all the other changes in her life. I asked her about Harold and told her to call me when she could just to let me know she was all right.

The doorbell rang, and I assumed it was my neighbor who was going to look after the cats while I was gone, checking with me one last time before I left. Jeanne was an animal lover who was active in the local humane society, so I knew Tony and Cleo would be in good hands. Without asking who was there, I opened the door, and in walked Linda Stone.

"What are you doing here? You know I have a plane to catch."

"Jeremy, you can't leave now. My whole life is ruined." And with this tears started streaming down her face.

"What do you mean your life is ruined. Did he find out? Does he know about me?"

"We had an enormous fight when I got home last night. He'd been drinking. He said awful things to me, so I hit him. Then he went into my closet, took out some of my clothes, and started throwing them at me. He told me to get out of his house." She looked like she was going to collapse, so I led her to the sofa. She turned away from me and covered her face with her hands. "Don't look at me. I look terrible. I don't have any makeup on."

"Where did you sleep last night?"

"I didn't sleep. I was so frightened I locked myself in the bathroom and waited until early this morning when I knew he would be asleep. Then I grabbed my purse and rushed out of the house. I came straight to you."

"Linda, you can't stay here. I'm about to leave for the airport."

"I have nowhere else to go. I can't go to a hotel. Jeremy, you've got to help me."

"You must have someone else. Don't you have a friend who can help you?"

"No, Harvey has turned everybody against me. He's told everyone lies about me. You're the only one I have."

"What about Teresa?"

"She's not my friend. She's my maid. I pay her to take care of me."

"Does Harvey know about — yesterday?"

"Not exactly."

"What do you mean 'not exactly'?"

"He knows I was with someone yesterday."

"What do you mean, 'with someone'? Do you mean he knows about me? Is that why he's angry? What do you think he'll do next?"

"He told me if he didn't kill me first that he was going to divorce me as soon as he could." She sobbed and took a breath. "He's going to marry that cheap secretary of his. She's going to have his baby. He said I was no use to him or anyone else anymore. He said nobody would ever want me again. He called me a drunken . . ." She stopped and pulled a handkerchief out of her purse and blew her nose. "I don't even want to repeat what he called me."

"For that reason, Linda, you definitely need another place to stay. He might find you here, and then what? He'll kill both of us."

"I'm not leaving. I can't leave. He'll find me if I check into a hotel. Please, Jeremy, just let me stay for a few days until I figure out what to do next."

"You can stay till I get back from Dallas. Then you'll have to leave."

"I knew I could count on you."

"A neighbor of mine will be in to take care of the cats. Don't tell her any of this."

"I'll probably be in the bedroom when she comes. I'm sick. I have a migraine from all this."

"And one more thing, don't answer the telephone. I don't want anyone to know you're here."

"I'm parked in front of the building."

"Give me your keys and I'll put your car in the back in my parking place."

"Can I have a set of your keys in case I have to leave the apartment for something?"

I went to my desk and got the spare keys and put them on the coffee table in front of her.

She looked like she had slept in her clothes. She had come without a suitcase, so I asked, "Won't you need some things?"

"Teresa will bring them to me."

"No, then she'll know where I live."

"Don't worry, Jeremy, we can trust her." With that she walked into my bedroom and got into the bed.

After I had moved her car, I returned to the apartment and

sat in the living room, stunned, and thought desperately about what I could do now. I had only an hour to catch my plane, so I could do nothing but hope that by the time I returned from Dallas, she would be gone. I picked up my suitcase and looked into the darkened room. She was lying with her back to the door, so I told her goodbye softly, so I wouldn't wake her if she were asleep. Then I took the twenty-minute drive to the airport.

Throughout the hour and a half flight to Dallas, I kept wondering how I had let myself get into such a mess. Why hadn't I followed my rule of not getting involved with married women? I hated the complications that they brought with them to relationships. And this husband was violent. He might have killed his stepdaughter, and now he was threatening his wife. What would he do to the man his wife was sleeping with? I could see myself lying on the ground by my car in the parking lot one night when I returned home, shot by an angry husband. It was not a pretty picture.

The small twin engine plane was so crowded that I couldn't wait to get off at the Dallas/Fort Worth Airport. Joan was waiting to drive me to their home. I carried all my luggage and gifts with me, so we didn't have to stop at the baggage area. On the way home, Joan told me how difficult Angela's treatments were and how sick they made her. She was now on her second series of chemo, and because the lesions appeared to be shrinking, they were very hopeful. Tim and Carolyn were staying at their father's house now, but they would make an appearance on Christmas Eve.

I asked Joan how she was holding up, and she answered that this was Angel's time to have everyone's complete attention, and she would not complicate matters with any problems of her own. When we got to the house, Joan took me to the guest room, which was more than adequate with its king-sized bed and private bathroom. I dropped off my belongings and went into the family room to see if Angela was up to seeing a visitor. Joan nodded and led me into their bedroom. Angela was pale, lying in a hospital bed. She looked smaller than she had at Thanksgiving. I noticed a small cot at the end of the room, which I presumed was for Joan. The bedroom was full of paraphernalia found in hospital rooms, including a stand that held the infusions. But Angela was smiling at me, so I walked over to the bed and took the hand she extended to me.

"I'm so glad you're here, Jeremy. I want you to take Joan away from here for a while. She needs a break, and she always loves her time with you."

Joan protested and said that I had come to celebrate the holidays with them both. We visited until I could see that Angela was growing tired, and then we left the room to let her rest.

"Are you sure I'm not in the way? I could stay at a hotel."

"Nonsense. I prepared lunch. I hope you're hungry."

Joan was a gourmet cook and knew recipes from all over the world. Even her soups and sandwiches were scrumptious. The gazpacho was flavored perfectly, and on a plate in the center of the table were Italian ham sandwiches made with her own bread and special dressing.

While Angela was asleep, Joan and I took the opportunity to catch up with each other's lives. She asked about Meggie, and I told her that I was trying to give her some space. Maybe if we didn't see each other for a while, Meggie would come to her senses and see how wrong it was to throw away a relationship that had been so good for so long. Joan asked if I were seeing anyone else, and for a minute I wanted to tell her about Linda. Then I thought that she had enough to worry about without adding me to her list. Besides, I was sure she wouldn't approve of my getting involved with Linda for other reasons besides the fact that she was married.

My mind kept going back to this morning at the apartment to Linda firmly entrenched in my bed. I wondered how hard it was going to be to get her to leave. Then a frightening thought crossed my mind. What if Meggie called while I was away and Linda picked up the phone? Even though I told Linda not to answer, she might not pay any attention to me. What would Meggie think when she heard Linda's voice? What would Linda tell her? I calmed myself, remembering that Meggie hadn't made any attempt to get in touch with me since she left town and probably wouldn't return my call. For the first time since we parted, I didn't want her to call me. As soon as I got back to Corpus, I would see that Linda returned to her own house or found another place to stay. By then she would see for herself that the apartment was too small for both of us. Her closet was bigger than all my rooms put together.

Then Joan asked me if I were still investigating the death of Sharon Ames. I assured her that I wouldn't stop until I found out what happened to Sharon. She wondered what I had discovered so far. I told her that I had talked to Sharon's brother once and learned that her stepfather was a man who always got what he wanted no matter who got hurt. She wanted to know if I thought that he had shot Sharon. I answered that I was beginning to wonder about that myself.

The next couple of days passed uneventfully. Then the morning before Christmas Joan got a phone call that disturbed me. She talked for a few minutes and then knocked on my bedroom door to tell me that Grace was on the phone and wanted to talk to me.

"I don't want to talk to her," was my quick answer.

"She says it's important, and if you don't come to the phone, she's coming right over. Jeremy, she won't take no for an answer, and Angela is not feeling well enough for visitors. Please talk to her."

I grudgingly picked up the phone on the nightstand near the bed. "Hello, Grace. What is it you want?"

"It's been years, Jeremy, but your voice sounds just the same."

"I'm really tied up right now, but Joan said it's important. Why do you want to talk to me?"

"It's been such a long time. I want to see you while you're in Dallas. I've been meaning to call you in Corpus."

"Don't bother. I have no time. I'm very busy these days writing and teaching."

"The family is very concerned about Sarah. She called her mother the other day and told her that she might be getting married in the summer."

149

"She hasn't confided that to me."

"We're really concerned. She's made no attempt to bring this man to Dallas and introduce him to the family. Now she's talking about being engaged. There must be some reason she's being so vague and not introducing him to us. What do you know about him, Jeremy?"

"What makes you think I know anything about him?"

"Because Sarah mentioned that he teaches in the English department at your college, but that's all we know. How can she be serious about anyone so soon? She just ended a three-year relationship before she left for Corpus."

"I had no idea about any of this. Sarah does not confide in me either."

"She's always been headstrong and impulsive. I hate to think of her making the same mistakes you and I did when we were her age."

"So what do you want from me, Grace? Sarah has made it perfectly clear that she doesn't want any interference in her personal life, and I intend to honor that."

"Jeremy, I must see you."

"Sorry, Grace, but I don't want to see you."

"Jeremy, can't you get over those old, petty grievances? It's been over ten years since we went through our divorce."

"You might consider them petty; I don't. We got the divorce so we wouldn't have to see each other again, and that's the way I like it. So goodbye, Grace."

"All right then. I'll just have to come to Corpus and take care of this myself. Goodbye, for now, Jeremy."

"Wait — just a minute. Okay, you win; I'll see you, but it can't be here. Angela is too sick to have visitors in the house. Where and when do you want to meet?"

"I know about no visitors. Joan told me. I'm leaving for Roswell tomorrow to go skiing with some friends, so it'll have to be today. How about lunch at one P.M. at the Old Manse?"

"That's fine. I'll be there."

As soon as I had hung up, I regretted accepting the invitation. Then there was a knock on the door and Joan came in. I answered her questioning look by telling her, "Don't count on me for lunch today."

"I had a feeling you wouldn't be available after that call. Where will you two be going?"

"The Old Manse. But don't get the wrong impression. She blackmailed me into it."

"How lovely. The perfect setting for the two of you to get reacquainted."

About one o'clock I pulled up to the old European style hotel in Joan's Taurus and finally found a space in the crowded parking lot. As I approached the front door, Grace was just arriving, and I waited for her as she was helped out of her black Cadillac by a young man in a uniform from valet parking. Slender as ever, she was wearing a short, trim black wool suit, which looked as if it came from one of the designer shops in the Galleria. I looked at her face and saw that she still looked amazingly young and attractive — not a line on her face that I could see. We walked together into the restaurant and were led into an elegant dining room with dark paneling and large picture windows, looking out onto a flourishing garden filled with colorful flowers and lush greenery. The maitre d' greeted her by name, saying in his cultivated British accent, "Your table is ready, Mrs. Evans." He led us to one of the tables by the window. After we were seated, the wine steward wanted to take our order. Grace ordered for us both.

"I hope you don't mind my ordering, Jeremy, but I think I still remember your preferences, and they do have such lovely wines here."

"Not at all. So your last husband was named Evans."

"You could try to be nice, Jeremy. After all, I am buying your lunch."

"Are you going to order that for me too?"

"You needn't worry. They'll bring you your own menu, and you can order whatever you like."

"Mr. Evans must have had a lot of money. What did he do for a living?"

"He was a trial lawyer and a very good one."

"He obviously took very good care of you. You always did appreciate the finer things. So, if I'm not getting too personal, what happened to him?"

"He was a man of many appetites, one of them being women. I got tired of all the girlfriends he was supporting. Everyone in town knew about his philandering. It was very humiliating. He was always repentant when I discovered him with some little bimbo and said he would never do it again, but, like so many of his ilk, he was a liar. I didn't know what diseases he was likely to bring home, so I stopped letting him into my bed. As you can guess, after a few months when he realized I wasn't going to relent, the marriage ended."

"Well," I said, looking around at the elegant surroundings, "at least he left you well-fixed."

"Are you really that naive, Jeremy? He's a lawyer. He cheated me out of as much money as he could. If I appear prosperous, it's because of Johnny, my second husband. Now he was a real gentleman, and he adored me."

"What happened to him?"

"Hasn't Joan told you anything?"

"Not much, but that's my fault; I didn't want to know anything."

Just then our drinks arrived, and as Grace predicted, I liked her choice of wine. The waiter soon came by, and we both ordered a crabmeat salad plate.

"You haven't changed, Jeremy. You look exactly like you did when we were together."

"You may not see it, but I've changed."

"You're more attractive. I think it's terrible how men get better looking as they get older. And then, of course, they want younger women. I'm surprised you never remarried. I heard that you were involved with an instructor at your school. Marjorie, Midgie or something — what is her name?"

"It's Meggie. But right now I'm not involved, as you put it, with anyone."

"I've thought about you so many times since the divorce and what a mistake we made giving up on each other so easily. Looking at you across the table reminds me of the good times we shared together."

"That's not the way I remember it."

"Was it really that terrible?"

"Much of the time it was. I suppose you've forgotten all the fighting. It wasn't just you. I'm probably not suited for marriage to anybody."

"That's not true. You have a warm and sensitive side that you don't like to show to people."

"I think you have me confused with your second husband. You were going to tell me what happened to him."

"Johnny had a drinking problem, and his therapist said he needed to move away from Dallas and his drinking buddies. I couldn't move to the Hill Country with him. I'd have gone mad."

"You mean that you gave him up for the Galleria?"

"Don't make it sound so crass. Life is meant to be enjoyed, and I've always hated small, rural places like Kerrville, with deer and birds and possums running all over the backyard. Don't you remember, I like big cities, the bigger the better? Now if he had said we could move to New York or Los Angeles — that would have been different."

"So I take it that he moved to Kerrville without you."

"Yes, and he's been clean and sober ever since. I hear he's quite active in AA. He's married again to some woman he met at his meetings who had a couple of children. He's helping her raise them. He always did want to be a father."

"I do like happy endings."

"About Johnny, I have no complaints. He was very generous to me in the settlement. Actually, it was Michael who handled the divorce. That's how we met."

"Are you going skiing with the future husband number four?"

"There is no future husband right now. Just think, Jeremy, you and I meeting again when we're both unattached. This could be very interesting. I wish I wasn't leaving town tomorrow."

"What are we doing here, Grace? You must have had a reason why you wanted to see me today besides hashing over old times."

"That's what I've always liked about you. You don't bother with small talk but want to get right to the heart of things."

"If it's to continue our discussion about Sarah, you might as well forget it. When I told you that she doesn't confide in me, I wasn't simply putting you off. Ever since she arrived in Corpus, she's made it perfectly clear that any questions about her private life were off limits. Not that she didn't ask me plenty of questions about my own personal affairs."

"One reason I called was that my sister Sybil told me how fond of you Sarah was."

"I was beginning to think so myself before this Royall Phillips debacle."

"Jeremy, is she rushing into matrimony because she's expecting a baby?"

"How can I answer a question like that? I don't know. I don't think so."

"Why at this time when she says her TV news career is just beginning to take off? If she has nothing to hide, why isn't she more forthcoming with you and the rest of us?"

"You're going to have to talk to her yourself. I can't help you."

"You're right, Jeremy. Her mother, we're all, very worried about her. We intend to speak to her ourselves very soon. I was just hoping you could give me some insight into her strange behavior before we approached her."

The waiter arrived with our crabmeat plates and refilled our wine glasses. For the rest of the lunch we talked about other subjects. She wanted to know how Angela was doing, and I told her what I knew, that we were hopeful, but the doctors could make no promises. She then gave me the current news about each member of her family, and I was surprised to realize that I was still interested. Grace asked again what had happened with Meggie. She had heard that we had been involved in a serious relationship for the past few years. She added that Joan was very fond of Meggie too and had hoped we would marry. I told her that, by mutual consent, we had simply decided to go our separate ways for a while, that she then took the opportunity to accept a position in a large Austin accounting firm, which had been after her to work for them since she had become a CPA. But, I assured Grace, we were still close friends.

Then Grace began talking about her coming to Corpus to visit Sarah. Nothing I could say would discourage her, and so what I had dreaded when I first heard that Sarah was moving to Corpus was about to happen. The waiter, noticing that we had finished eating, took our plates and then wheeled the dessert cart to the table. He recited his detailed description of the cakes, pies, and fruits, which looked tempting but too much, following the large servings of crabmeat we had just consumed. But Grace convinced me to share a large slice of lemon meringue pie with her while we drank our coffee. She still remembered all the foods I liked best.

We left the restaurant on friendly terms, and she asked if I would like her to pick me up later in the evening for dinner. She wanted to show me the exciting Dallas nightlife as she suspected that I hadn't been out of the house since I arrived. I told her I wasn't interested. I had come to spend as much time as I could with Joan and Angela. I waited with Grace while they brought her car to the door. For a minute she looked like she was about to hug me, so I stepped back out of her reach. She then offered me her hands in a parting gesture, and when I took them, she reached up and kissed me on the cheek. Then she got into her car. As I started to walk away toward my own parking place, she rolled down her window and called to me. When I turned back, she said, "I'll call you when I get to Corpus. You owe me a lunch." Then laughing, she waved and drove off.

❧19❧

I sat in the plane, holding my book in my lap and thinking about the visit with Joan and Angela. It had gone smoothly enough. Angela's two children, Tim and Carolyn, appeared to be both grateful and relieved that Joan was there, caring for their mother. They both seemed happy to see me again. Tim and Carolyn brought laughter and music into the house, and Angela seemed to gain strength from their presence.

I hoped Grace didn't expect to see me when she came to Corpus. I planned to be very busy. I might get lucky and be at the conference while she was there. Sitting by the window, I could see the cars, like toys, speeding along the freeways as the small twin engine plane flew close to the ground. In my row by the aisle was a middle-aged woman working a crossword puzzle. I was relieved that she didn't try to engage me in some inane conversation for the ninety minutes we would be in the air. Before long the flight attendant came by with drinks and snacks. The sound and movement of the plane lulled me back into my reverie. I had mixed feelings about Grace's coming to Corpus. I didn't want her there. But I also thought that she might be able to talk some sense into Sarah, who was certainly rushing matters with her engagement to Royall. She couldn't possibly know what he was like. I had watched how cavalierly he had handled his romances with countless other young women, and I hated to think of Sarah ending up like the others.

156

My mind drifted to Meggie. When would I see her again? I'd call her as soon as I got home. How enjoyable could it be to spend the holidays alone in a new house in a strange city? Perhaps by now she realizes that she misses me as much as I miss her. Then for a minute a terrible image intruded on my thoughts, but I immediately pushed it aside. No, she couldn't have got involved with someone else already. I mustn't let my mind go there. Next week I'll drive to Austin, and the two of us will have our long overdue talk about a future together. She has had enough time to understand what a mistake she's made by selling her home, quitting her job, and leaving Corpus. I must convince her that neither one of us can be happy while we're apart. And so I continued to drift, half awake, and for a short while, I felt hopeful that everything would work out.

When I next looked at my watch, I saw that it was twenty more minutes until we landed. The flight attendant returned to ask if anyone wanted another drink. I asked her for cranberry juice without ice, and she handed it to me with a bag of pretzels. Since school was out for the holidays, I hadn't been working on the investigation of Sharon Ames' death like I should. I would begin again by interviewing her boyfriend, Ben Haynes. Sarah wanted to question him with me. Maybe our working together would give me the opportunity to talk to her about Royall. And she could be a big help with the interview. Ben might talk more easily to a reporter than to me alone. I was anxious to find out firsthand about Sharon and Ben's relationship. So often when a young woman dies an unnatural death, the police find that it is the husband or lover who is responsible. No matter what anyone said, I wasn't convinced that Sharon had died by her own hands.

I thought about everyone but Linda until the last ten minutes of the trip. I wasn't sure what I would find when I returned to the apartment. If she were still there, I'd have to come up with a plan, but I wasn't sure what I would do if she created a scene and refused to leave. I didn't want my neighbors to see me having an altercation with a married woman. Since there was no way to solve the problem until I got home, I decided to put it out of my mind for now, but, of course, that was impossible.

I've always enjoyed returning to the city. The freeway took me directly to Ocean Drive, and the azure blue sky, full of cumulus clouds, and the bright sun sparkling on the blue-green water lifted my mood. It was hard to imagine that in other parts of the country people were shoveling snow. As I pulled into the driveway, I saw the black Jaguar still parked in my place. By the time I got to my door, my mind was made up. She would have to leave. I would help her find another place to stay immediately.

I opened the door, and for a minute I thought I was in the wrong apartment. I dropped my suitcase in the middle of the room and just stood, looking at all the changes. The furniture had been moved around so that the sofa was now facing the uncovered windows, looking out onto the bay. The two easy chairs were placed on either side to form a conversation area. There were pictures of birds that looked like Audubon's *Birds of America* prints on the walls. Wood carvings and bronze statues of birds had been placed on the tables on either side of the sofa. The mini-blinds had been removed from the large windows facing the water. They had been replaced by shutters that were open and folded back on each side so the view would not be obstructed. There was nobody in the room as I stood there, aghast, deciding what to do next. I picked up my suitcase and walked to the bedroom and knocked on the open door.

"Jeremy, I'm so glad you're back. It's been so lonely here without you. But at least the cats kept me company." Wearing a bright pink and orange silk gown, Linda was propped up on several pillows with both cats on the bed. She had been watching a talk show and turned it off when I came in. There were several magazines on the bed, and Tony and Cleo had chosen to lie on them. I was the one who seemed out of place.

"I was thinking that by the time I got back, you'd have gone home or be ensconced in more comfortable quarters."

"You're right. This place is small, but it does have possibilities. How come you've done nothing with it to make it your own?"

"I liked it the way it was. It was simple and utilitarian. I don't need decorating, not from what I've seen. Wealthy people hire designers to decorate their houses so they'll look like movie settings or fancy hotels. The middle classes do a poor imitation of the wealthy, and the poor simply do an even more wretched copy of the middle classes. Of course, present company is excepted."

"Thanks for that much. You're angry with me."

She looked so disappointed that I wanted to take it all back. She had lost her daughter, and now her marriage was in shambles partly because of me.

"I was so sure that you would be pleased by the changes. I only wanted to do something nice for you to pay you back in my small way for taking me in." Tears welled in her eyes, and I felt like the villain in a melodrama. With so much sadness in the world, why did I always end up making things worse?

"I'm not angry with you. What you did was lovely. The sofa looks much better there, and the birds — how did you know I'm a birdwatcher?"

"Then you really do like it?"

"Of course, I do; I love it."

She was now smiling through her tears. "What do you like the most?"

I couldn't believe that I was taking part in this little scene. "All of it," I said thinking that this was not the way to get rid of her. "What have you been doing besides decorating since I left town?"

"I had Teresa bring over some of my things. I talked to my lawyer. I thought about you."

"Did Teresa help you move the furniture?"

"Yes, it wasn't so hard to do working together. I had the prints in the attic. Nobody was using them, and I thought they would look nice here."

"And they do. Have you talked to Harvey?"

"Not yet. I don't know if I ever want to talk to him again

after the terrible things he said to me," and with that tears began to stream down her face.

"I know he's hurt you, but nothing can be resolved unless the two of you talk. I know that from personal experience."

"You're right. That's what Tom told me. He's my lawyer and has been a friend of the family for many years."

"What else did Tom tell you?"

"He said that I need to go home. He says that if I don't, I am just letting Harvey have the house that I should be living in. If anyone should get out, it's Harvey. But I can't go home now."

"Why not? Because you don't feel safe?"

"I'm not afraid of him. Except for that one night he's never physically hurt me."

"Then maybe you should follow your lawyer's advice."

"I just might do that, but before I leave, come join me in bed."

"Where are you going to tell Harvey you've been for the past few days?"

"I'm going to tell him that he's not the only one who is attractive to the opposite sex."

"You can't do that. It will only cause more trouble — for you."

"Jeremy, are you worried about me or yourself? Don't tell me that you're afraid of him."

"Of course not, but you and everyone else tell me that he has a violent temper and that he's killed someone before and got away with it. I don't especially want to become one of his targets."

"Come sit down by me for a few minutes. You've just come home, and I want to give you a proper welcome."

I walked over and sat on the side of the bed, and in an instant she was on her knees, throwing herself into my arms.

"Wait a minute. I don't think this is the right time for this."

"Why not? We're all alone where nobody can interrupt us." She was running her fingers through my hair. "We need to take advantage of the little time we have together."

"But there is so much to think about right now." I tried gently to move away from her, but she grabbed my hands and tried to pull me closer. "We have to decide what you're going to say to your husband about your whereabouts for the last few days. He can't know that you've been with someone or even that you've stayed in my apartment. It wouldn't be to your advantage; that is if you're still planning on going through with the divorce."

"Do you want me to go through with the divorce?"

"That has to be your choice. Don't do it for me. I have nothing to offer you. I don't believe in marriage, at least for me."

"Not now, Jeremy. We'll talk later. Now show me how much you missed me while you were away." She put her hand on the back of my head and pulled me toward her, kissing me. Her perfume smelled intoxicating, and her nightgown was the smoothest silk. She pushed me down on the bed and began to undress me, fumbling with the buttons on my shirt.

Before she could tear one off, I said, "I can do that myself."

"Then while you do, I'll light the candles and put on some music. Have you ever made love to a trumpet concerto? You had it in your CD player, and I've been listening to it over and over while I waited for you to come back to me. Making love to it could be very erotic." She got out of the bed, and walked over to the CD player and turned it on. Haydn's Trumpet Concerto filled the room as she went from nightstand to dresser to nightstand, lighting the scented candles she had brought. Then she pulled the gown off over her head and crawled back into bed. Although I kept my shorts on, I had drawn the sheet over me, but she grabbed it with expertise and flipped it over the foot of the bed.

"We won't be needing that," she said as she lay down next to me. Then turning on her side so that she could face me, she propped her head on one hand and let her other hand slide gently from my chest to my abdomen. "Let's not rush," she said. We have all afternoon."

Much later I still wondered how I was going to get her out of my bed and out of the apartment. She seemed in no hurry to get dressed. "I'm going to take a shower."

"Do you want company?"

"Not this time," I called back and rushed into the bathroom and locked the door. I noticed a bright new shower curtain with a matching curtain on the window and a basket of small, colorful soaps that had not been there before.

When I had dressed, I stood over the bed and told Linda it was time to get up. We needed to go to some out-of-the-way restaurant to get something to eat. After that she had to go home. I told her that the trip to Dallas had been stressful, and I was tired. I wanted to get to bed early and sleep late in the morning.

While she showered and dressed, I blew out the candles and fed the cats. Then I called Jeanne, the neighbor who fed the cats, to tell her I was home. She told me that my friend had relieved her of all responsibilities for them. I listened to the messages on the answering machine and was relieved that there were none from Meggie — just a few invitations from some of my tennis friends to get together for some matches before school started again. Then I unpacked and looked around to see what other changes Linda had made. I wasn't sure how to handle her redecorating after the earlier scene we had when I first arrived. I decided that I would simply offer to pay for all the items she had bought. The kitchen held more surprises. She had replaced my odd dinnerware with a matching set. The same with the glasses. This was going to be expensive, but I was not going to permit her to pay for any of my household things. She was to have no rights of ownership around here. I was still irritated. I couldn't imagine what made her think that she was doing me a favor by coming into my home and, without permission, making all these "improvements." I hadn't asked for them. I'd never wanted them. I hadn't even allowed Meggie to redo the place, although she had offered more than once.

Just then Linda came out of the bedroom and informed me

that she wasn't hungry. She had decided to go home instead of going out to eat and had packed what she was taking back to the house with her. Relieved, I didn't try to persuade her to change her mind. I went into the bedroom to get her suitcases to carry them out to her car. When I returned, I asked her if she had checked all the rooms to be sure she had retrieved all her belongings.

"Everything I'm taking now," she said.

"This is a small apartment, Linda. Take all your stuff with you now."

"I didn't leave very much, Jeremy, just a gown and tooth brush and stuff like that. I'll certainly be back, won't I?"

"Do you have your story straight that you're going to tell Harvey?"

"I'm going to play that by ear. Don't worry. I won't involve you in anything I say."

"Before you leave, Linda, I'd like to give you a check for what I owe you for fixing this place up. It was quite a surprise, and I hope you don't think I was ungracious. I'm aware of all the trouble you've gone to and how much you've accomplished. What you've done is amazing."

"That's all right. I did it for myself as much as for you. I needed something to take my mind off my problems, and I've always loved decorating. Everyone says I have a talent for it."

"You do, but I won't feel right about it unless you let me pay you what I owe you."

"I'll figure up the bill later. Maybe I can take it out in trade."

"This is not a joke to me. You've done all this hard work for me. You shouldn't be out any money at least."

"If you insist," she said and picked up her purse to leave. I started to walk toward the door with her, but she put her hand out in a motion to stop me.

"Let's kiss goodbye here. I don't think we should take any chances of the wrong person seeing us together." I put my arms around her and we kissed. "Will you call me later?"

I assured her that I would call her some time tomorrow.

We kissed again passionately, and as I opened the door for her, I said, "Just one more thing."

She turned and smiled. "Yes?"

"Could you give me back my keys?"

"Now that's what I call showing a lack of appreciation," she said, fishing in her purse.

"I don't mean to sound ungrateful," I said, smiling as I took them from her hand.

"Well, you do. Just a little. Remember, part of the difficulties I'm going through have to do with my feelings for . . ." She stopped and then added, "We won't go into that now. *Hasta mañana, mi amor,*" she added as she went out the door.

I locked the door and leaned against it, thinking aloud, What have I got myself into now?

❦ 20 ❦

When I awoke the next morning, I opened the shutters in the bedroom and looked between the buildings on the east side of Ocean Drive to claim my small view of the bay. The sun was glistening on the water, and the walkers and joggers were trailing each other in large numbers. I stood by the window for a moment, wondering whether I should join them. I decided instead to call Sarah and invite her to have brunch with me. I told her that we needed to talk about getting more active again in the Sharon Ames' investigation before all the trails got too cold. She agreed but said she had an early call at the TV station. She added that she might be able to meet me for lunch around one o'clock. We agreed on the White Kitchen.

I arrived first and had the hostess show me to a booth. I asked her to bring a couple of glasses of water and two menus. She returned immediately and also set a basket of small slices of garlic toast on the table. Sarah ran in breathless ten minutes later.

"I'm sorry I'm late. I was covering a meeting of one of the school boards that was supposed to be over by eleven, but the members kept talking an extra hour. They were trying to decide what to do about their superintendent's contract. I'm not even sure the news team will use the story."

"I haven't been waiting long."

"So how was your Christmas?"

"I spent it in Dallas with Joan and Angela. It was good. How about you?"

"I'm still low man on the totem pole, so I worked. It wasn't too bad. The producers had some fabulous food brought in from a couple of restaurants for us to munch on all day. I think I gained ten pounds."

"You certainly don't look it."

"That may be so, but you can't fool the camera."

"I saw your aunt while I was in Dallas. She asked about you."

"So that's what this is all about. It's not the Sharon Ames' investigation at all you wanted to talk about. Why don't we cut the small talk, and you tell me exactly what's on your mind."

"Sharon is on my mind, but can't we clear the air a little before we begin?"

The waitress came to take our order, and we both ordered chicken Caesar salads.

"So begin, Jeremy. Clear the air."

"All right, I'll start. I want to tell you that you've really hurt my feelings by going behind my back and dating Royall. Don't you think you owed me a little honesty? I work in the same office with him. How do you think it felt when I saw the two of you in Nexis the other night? I felt like a fool."

"You know perfectly well why I've never told you we were seeing each other. Would you have approved? I don't think so. Every time I've ever mentioned his name, you've had something negative to say about him."

"Only because I know him a lot better than you."

"You've known him longer, not better. There's a side of Royall you've obviously never seen."

"Are you referring to the side who thinks he's in love for two weeks and then drops the poor, lovesick woman for his next conquest?"

"You see. That's the type of comment I'm talking about.

What's clear to me is that he's kind and considerate and that he's more fun to be with than anyone I've ever known before."

"If he's such a paragon, why haven't you taken him home to meet your family? Why have the two of you become engaged before any of them have ever laid eyes on him?"

"I've wanted to invite him to Dallas with me, but the timing hasn't been right. We're planning to go as soon as we both get some free time. There's no rush; he'll meet the whole family very soon."

"Your aunt doesn't feel very good about your engagement either. She's talking about making a trip to Corpus to see for herself what's going on."

"Aunt Grace can come any time she wishes. We'll be glad to have her here. I suppose you didn't bother to reassure her that she had nothing to worry about, did you, Jeremy?"

"How could I do that with a clear conscience?"

"What were the two of you doing together anyway? I thought you both disliked each other, or is there something more I should know about your getting together?"

"She wanted me to tell her what I knew about Royall."

"And, of course, you gave her your opinion about him."

"I said she'd have to talk to you herself about him. You don't confide in me."

"Nor do you confide in me."

I was about to ask her if she had something particular in mind when the waitress brought our Caesar salads to the table and refilled our water glasses. She asked us if we wanted anything else, and Sarah ordered a large glass of buttermilk. After she brought it, Sarah looked at me enigmatically and said, "Now it's my turn to clear the air."

"I suppose you're alluding to the other night at Nexis."

"I saw you there sitting in a dark corner with Mrs. Stone, your heads together."

"We were talking about Sharon. I was trying to find out what she knew about her death."

"And so you found it necessary to be together at a trendy night spot?"

"We both decided that it would be nice to talk over dinner. There was no more to it than that."

"I couldn't help but notice the trouble you had escorting her out of the restaurant. She looked a little wobbly to me, like she had had a little too much to drink."

"What is this — an official interview for one of your news broadcasts? She may have had a couple of margaritas. I didn't notice that she had any trouble walking out the door. If she had had too much to drink, I can assure you, I'd never have let her drive herself home."

"You are aware of her drinking problem, Jeremy. I told you what her husband said about it."

"Check your sources, Sarah. Disgruntled husbands are not always to be believed."

"And did she tell you anything that could help solve the mystery of Sharon's death?"

"Not exactly. But she did give me some background information about Sharon, herself, and other members of the family that could be helpful."

"I'll ask you the same question you asked me about her husband. Are you going to see her again?"

"I'll give you the same answer you gave me back then. If she has more to tell me about the case, then I probably will."

"And you're being perfectly honest with me now?"

"As honest as I can be. I'm not under oath."

"I didn't think I'd ever use these words on you, Jeremy, but you're a hypocrite and a liar."

"Just a minute, young woman. What are you talking about?"

"I think you know exactly what I mean, but I'll explain it so there won't be any confusion. You judge my relationship with Royall as wrong or at least terribly flawed, even though we're both unattached, of age, and free to make any choice we want. While, on the other hand, you are having an affair with a married woman, probably an alcoholic, someone who is vulnerable because she's just gone through another terrible tragedy in her life. I'd say that's being a hypocrite."

"How did you ever jump to the faulty conclusion that Linda and I are having an affair?"

"Now for the second term. Are you going to deny that you're seeing Linda Stone?"

"You met with Harvey. I was just getting information about Sharon. You know how committed I am to finding out what happened to her."

"Now you're lying to me or, at the very least, not telling the whole truth. And by the way, you don't make real commitments, Jeremy. You avoid them."

"What is that supposed to mean? Then let me say it again. I'm not stopping my own investigation into Sharon's death until I know the truth. I'd say that was a real commitment."

"To you words like "truth" and "commitment" are abstract concepts. You're not interested in real commitments. You probably prefer the company of a married woman because you don't have to get permanently involved."

"That's pretty far from the truth. I thought you knew me better than that. How did we get started on all this?"

"I don't know. I guess I'm disappointed, Jeremy. I thought you were serious when you said that you were going to win Meggie back."

"I am serious. I want that too. You know that."

"I thought I did. Then why was Linda staying over at your apartment?"

"How could you possibly know that? Are you spying on me now?"

"Of course not. Meggie told me. She said that you left a message on her answering machine, and on an impulse, she returned the call. An inebriated woman answered the phone. She asked Meggie what her name was and if she wanted to leave a message."

"Oh, no," I groaned. The worst possible thing had happened. I got a sinking feeling in my stomach. I had told her not to answer my phone. She just couldn't keep her hands off my phone or my apartment. There's no telling what Linda said to Meggie, especially if she had been drinking. And Meggie — what must she be thinking now?

"What did you say?"

"Nothing. I never got the message that Meggie called."

"Linda told Meggie that she was staying at your place for a few days."

"So you've known this all along. You've been setting me up. I would never have done that to you. I've always tried to protect you, even from your aunt's questions."

"If you and Linda are not involved, what's going on? She wouldn't admit this, but I believe Meggie's hurt that you've already found someone else, and you've even let her move into your apartment."

"You've both misunderstood the entire situation."

"What have we misunderstood? After I talked to Meggie, I called the Stone house, and the maid told me that Mrs. Stone was away for a few days. Of course, she wouldn't say any more than that."

"Did you also check to find out that I was out of town while she was staying at my apartment?"

"Linda told Meggie you were in Dallas for a few days. If you don't mind my asking, What is going on between you and Linda Stone?"

"After all the secrets you've kept lately, you have a lot of nerve asking me anything about my personal life. But the answer is nothing. Linda had a fight with her husband and just needed a place to be alone and think." I felt guilty not being completely honest with Sarah about Linda, but for the present, the truth would only muddle matters more and help nobody. I needed time to think before I said anything to anyone, and, for now, I wasn't sure what I was going to do about Linda. To end the discussion, I finally said, "I think we've both said what we came here to say. Now can we talk about the case?"

Sarah said that she hadn't heard any new information about the Ames case in a long time. I reminded her that we still needed to talk to Ben Haynes. We weren't sure if he would talk to both of us at the same time, but we thought I should try to set up a meeting with him as soon as possible.

When I got back to the apartment after running a few errands, I checked my answering machine. There was a message from Linda asking me to call. I dialed her number, and Teresa answered. I was relieved to hear that Mrs. Stone was out. I didn't want to speak to her right then anyway. Then I called the Haynes house. A young woman's voice answered and asked who I was and if she could help me. I asked if I could speak to Ben Haynes, and she said she was his wife and would be glad to take a message. I told her I taught at the college that Ben attended and needed to speak to him. She said that Ben was at work, but that he would be home in the evening. I could reach him after seven o'clock. In the background I could hear a child's voice.

After I fed the cats and made a tuna salad for sandwiches, I was about to sit down for supper when the phone rang. I recognized the voice immediately even though she didn't identify herself.

"You said you were going to call me, Jeremy."

"I did call this afternoon, but Teresa said you were out."

"You should have tried me again. I really needed to talk to you."

"What's going on?"

"Harvey is acting so strange. He never even asked where I'd been. It's as if he knows. He's planning something, Jeremy, and I don't like it."

"Is he home now?"

"As a matter of fact he just came in. I'd better get off the line. Call me tomorrow."

I didn't like being tied to these phone calls. I would have to tell Linda that this wouldn't work. I was beginning to feel trapped in a way that I never had with Meggie. Besides it would be very unwise for both of us if I were to get involved in her marital difficulties. It would also inhibit my investigation. I knew what I had to do about Linda, and I hoped it wasn't going to be too difficult to disengage myself from her. I still felt both anger and guilt about how she had invaded my apartment and redecorated it without ever asking me what I'd have liked. Even after I pay her for everything she's brought over, she'll still feel that she's done me an enormous favor, which I never fully appreciated.

About a quarter after seven, I called the Haynes house again. Mrs. Haynes recognized my voice immediately and called her husband to the phone. He acted as if I was disturbing him while he was eating dinner, so I offered to call back. He said to just make the conversation brief and explain to him what I wanted. I told him that I was Sharon's English teacher and that she had come by my office to talk to me right before she had disappeared. I said that Sharon had said some very disturbing things. I needed to talk to him to clarify what she told me, or I would have to go to the police with my story. He was not happy to hear from me. I said that our conversation should not take too long, but there were some vital questions that I needed to ask him. He paused for a few seconds as if he were weighing what he should do. When he finally answered, he said that I couldn't come to his house. He didn't want to upset his wife and daughter by talking about Sharon in front of them. I asked him when and where he would like to meet. I said that if he wanted privacy, he could come to my office. He said he was off the next day, and we arranged to meet in my office at the college around eleven o'clock. Remembering Sarah, I asked him if it would be all right if a young woman who also had a few questions about Sharon could join us. I told him that he had met her at Sharon's funeral. He was reluctant to have anyone else join us; so fearing he would call the meeting off, I made no further attempt to persuade him. He then lowered his voice and told me he was cutting the conversation short because his wife and daughter were within hearing distance. We signed off, agreeing that we would meet tomorrow.

I called Sarah and told her about my talk with Ben and that he wanted to meet with me alone. She understood but made me promise that I would call her as soon as the interview was over. Then I called the security office at the college to tell them I needed to use the English Building the following day at eleven. Even though classes were still out for the winter break, they were happy to accommodate me and said that someone would be around at 10:45 to turn off the alarm. When the arrangements were completed, I called Meggie, to see how she was and, if she were in the mood to listen, to explain about Linda's staying at the apartment. The phone rang several times, and then her answering machine went on. I didn't leave a message. She was probably at work. I would try again tomorrow evening. Perhaps over the weekend, I could drive to Austin to see her. But I knew I had better let her approve my plans. The days of the drop-in visit were over for us. As I thought about the weekend, I remained hopeful. I remembered the days when I had been able to persuade her to understand my point of view on most any subject. But, of course, now everything was different. I wondered after our last conversation if I were up to asking her again to come back to me. She seemed set on making me suffer, and yet I was convinced more strongly than ever that we belonged together. I was determined to make it happen.

❧ 21 ❧

The next morning I awoke with Tony lying on my stomach and Cleo chewing on my hair. I put the coffee on and took a quick shower. I was going to have to do something about those two cats. They were getting into a lot of mischief lately — missing the litter box and digging around the philodendron that Linda had brought over. They always misbehaved when they thought they were not getting enough attention. From their point of reference, I had been gone too often lately and was much too preoccupied when I was at home. I filled their dishes and watched while they crunched on their breakfast. Then we all went into the living room, where I pulled the shutters aside, opened the window, and looked toward the bay. It was a brisk morning, and the water rolled in on small whitecaps. The sun was shining on the blue-green water, making it glitter like aquamarines on jeweler's velvet. It was a brilliant South Texas day and easy to see why so many snowbirds from the North arrived each year to become winter Texans. Then I sat on the sofa and brushed each cat for several minutes. They purred, letting me know that I was finally tending to the real business of the day.

After a quick breakfast of a bagel and coffee, I left the apartment. On my way to my car, I passed Clyde Walters carrying a bag of groceries into the building. He had a strange expression on his face as we greeted each other. I wondered if he knew that Linda had been staying at the apartment and if he and his wife had spread the news to the rest of our neighbors. I couldn't worry about that now. I pulled into my parking space in the faculty lot around 10:30, just as a man in a security uniform was leaving the building. I went into my office and looked around. All I could see was the mess on Royall's side of the room. It was obvious that he hadn't been around since final exams. When I had come to pick up Sharon's papers, I had grabbed them and run. Now I looked more carefully at his half of the office. His exams were piled on his bookcase, his boxes were still unpacked, and there were several stacks of unfiled papers and unopened mail on his desk. I wondered how Sarah was going to like living with his messes when they got married. He had even let some of his clutter creep onto my reading chair. Now he had passed the boundary that we had agreed on, and I scooped up his books and papers, lying in my chair, and, with relish, dumped them on top of everything else on his desk. I then did some filing of my own while I waited for Ben Haynes to arrive.

At eleven o'clock there was a knock on my open door, and I turned from my filing cabinet to see a tall, muscular young man with sandy colored hair and green eyes. He was wearing khaki pants and a green pullover sweater.

"You're Ben?" He nodded without smiling, and I extended my hand. "I'm Jeremy Greystone." I motioned at my upholstered chair, and he sat down.

"You said you wanted to speak to me. That Sharon had been talking about me to you. What's all this about?" he said.

I could see through his bravado that he was nervous. "I don't know if you realize this, but I was Sharon's English instructor this fall."

He nodded. "I know who you are. I used to hear her talk about you. She liked your class. Sharon was good in English. I'm not."

"Sharon came to see me right before she disappeared, probably the same day. She said she was being harassed by someone and needed my help. She was going to come to my office the next morning, and we were going to try to work on the problem, but she vanished. I knew something was wrong when she didn't come back to take a major exam. That wasn't like her."

"I had no idea that she had gone to you for help."

"And I promised her I would do what I could for her."

"I've told the police everything I know. What do you want from me?"

"I wasn't able to save her life, but I've promised myself and her that I would not stop until I found out what happened to her. I'm not letting this go until I can find some closure, not only because she was my student, but because she came to me for help. So you see, for me it's not over because she died. That's when my obligation and my resolve really began."

"I've been sick myself about what happened to her, but why should I talk to you? You're not the police. Like I already said, I told them everything I know."

"Not everything. You and I know there's a whole lot more you didn't tell them."

"What did she tell you about me?"

"Look, Ben, we both need to exchange information. As I said over the phone, I haven't been to the police with my story."

"The police." I could see that he was trying to remain calm, all the while trying to size me up. "Okay, what do you want to know?"

"I know that the two of you were living together."

"Just a minute. Sharon and I had already decided to call it quits before this happened. My wife and I had been separated, but we were getting back together again. We have a kid to think about."

"How did Sharon feel about that?"

"She didn't like it too much, but she understood my little girl needed me."

"Were the two of you still living together at the time of her disappearance?"

"She still had some of her things at my house, but she was moving back to her apartment."

"Do you know who could possibly have shot her?"

"From what the police said after their investigation, Sharon shot herself with her own gun."

"Then how did her body get moved to Padre Island?"

"I guess that's where she killed herself."

"The coroner believes that she might have been moved to Padre Island after she was dead."

"I wouldn't know anything about that."

"When is the last time you saw Sharon alive?"

"I told the police that I saw her alive the day she disappeared. I told her I was going over to my mother-in-law's house to see Clair and my daughter. I told her to be gone by the time I got back."

"And was she gone when you got back?"

"When I took off that night, that was the last time I ever spoke to her. I assumed she had done what I said and gone back to her own place."

Ben leaned back in the chair and closed his eyes for a few seconds. When he opened them, he looked directly into my eyes and said, "It's true. Sharon and I had been having lots of fights around that time, and I'm sure plenty of people can testify to that. I had had as much as I could take of it. I was anxious to see her gone, but I never wanted anything bad to happen to her. You do believe me, don't you, Mr. Greystone?"

"I sure want to believe you, Ben. Would you do me a favor? It might help me understand what you're telling me."

"What kind of a favor?"

"Would you tell me what you can about Sharon, how the two of you met, what your life was like together, and what made it all finally go sour?"

"I don't know. Do you really have the time to listen to this? I'm not much for talking about personal things. Except for the questions the police asked, I've never told anyone about Sharon and me before. I'm not sure I can talk about it now too good."

"Try. I have the time, and I promise I'll try not to interrupt you. Just tell me what you remember in your own words."

"We met in a freshman English class. I was taking the first part in night school. You know the class where they make you write an essay every week. I wasn't doing too good. I'd make a 'D' on a paper, and then the following week I'd try to elimi-nate all the errors I'd made before, so the new paper would be better, you know by proofreading it, but I'd come up with even worse errors and made an 'F.' I hated that class and the teacher too until one night, she asked me and some girl to come up to her desk after class. That's how Sharon and I met. The teacher had this idea to pair us up for the next two papers, just to see if that would help me improve my writing. Sharon had been making an 'A' on every paper, and the teacher said she had a real talent for writing. At first I wasn't too happy about it. I worked during the day for an oil company, and I didn't have much time at night cause my wife Clair — you talked to her on the phone — was bitching; I mean she was complaining constantly, because I was gone too much already. She saw no purpose in my going to night school. But I had got my GED, and I wanted to make something of my life. After all, I had a wife and little girl to support.

"After Sharon started helping me, I began to catch on. And my grades did improve. She didn't write my papers for me, but after class we'd talk about each assignment and what I was going to write. After I finished a first draft, she would look at it, and point out the mistakes. I had never been too good at grammar, but she was a wiz, so she taught me enough to help me get better grades. I owed her for that. She was a good listener too. I was having troubles at home, and she would pay attention to what I had to say. Clair has never been too good at that. Sharon was also having trouble with her par-ents. Her stepfather was always trying to control her life and telling her who she could go out with. Her mother was no help either and nagged her all the time about her waitress job. She didn't like her waiting tables, thought it was beneath the family. Sharon was getting pretty sick of living at home.

"We started seeing each other about then. We hung out on campus, and people were beginning to treat us like a couple. I asked her why she didn't move out of her parents' home so we could see each other more often, but she said that she couldn't afford to live on her own and go to school on her salary. At the restaurant where she was working at that time, the tips weren't too good. At first I thought that we had a lot in common, but later I discovered that she lived in that big house on Ocean Drive. According to Sharon, her mother was this society broad who drank too much. Meanwhile at home things kept getting worse between Clair and me. Now we began fighting all the time about everything, and sometimes she could get pretty physical — you know, like throw things and all? When she said she was going to take the baby and move back to her mother's house for a while, I was relieved. She never suggested getting a job. Clair doesn't have much education. We both had had rough childhoods with abusive fathers, so we didn't want Nancy — that's my daughter — to see us fighting all the time. She was only four years old, but I could tell we scared her sometimes. She'd run out of the room and hide under her bed till we stopped yelling.

"About that time Sharon's stepfather found out about me and really raised hell with her. He ordered her to stop seeing me and threatened to stop paying for her college. She was upset all the time now. I didn't know what I could do to help her, so I told her again to move out of their house. She could move in with me. Then she got the idea of moving into one of her parents' apartment buildings. They had a vacancy in one of their furnished apartments, though it wasn't in such a good location, but she was so anxious to get out of the house that she decided to take it. Her parents were still giving her trouble about me, so we decided that she shouldn't tell them that I was married. I was thinking of getting a divorce at that time anyway. Clair had found out about Sharon and me, and she was threatening to go to the college about it. She said she would tell everyone — the teachers, the deans, financial aid, and who knows who else. I knew that wouldn't matter, but she was so mad, I didn't know what else she was capable of doing.

"At first when Sharon moved into the apartment, things got better. She complained a little that it wasn't as comfortable as her parents' house, and, of course, there was no maid service, but she liked being on her own. We both did. We got to be with each other a lot without worrying that anybody would disturb us. Sharon's family still objected to her being with me, but that didn't bother us a bit. Her stepfather tried everything he could to break us up, but Sharon laughed about it. She liked getting under his skin. Her mother kept wanting to arrange dates with other guys for her, but Sharon refused to let her meddle in our lives. She told her that we were planning to try living together, and her mother got so upset, she took to her bed for a week. We both got a good laugh out of that.

"Then there was some trouble in the building. A few of the apartments had break-ins, and Sharon got scared. Her stepfather often used to drop by to see her and give her some money. One day he came over and brought her one of his guns, so she could protect herself if anyone tried to break in while she was at home. It was a Smith and Wesson .38 Special. I never saw a more beautiful handgun. He wanted to take her out shooting, but she said that I could take her to the indoor shooting range and let her practice. Actually Sharon knew a lot about guns. Her parents had a ranch, and she had started shooting at an early age.

"Things quieted down for a while, and then some guy chased her one night from the apartment parking lot to her apartment. She had been at my place and had gone home around midnight. She called me as soon as she got in the apartment, and I came and got her. After that night we decided that she should move in with me. You can imagine how mad Clair got when she found out about it. She refused to let me take Nancy home with me after that. I had to visit with her either at her mother's or in the park near their house. I didn't like that one bit.

"It wasn't easy living with Sharon. She never stopped complaining. She hated my green carpet all over the house. She called it avocado or something. She didn't like my old brown couch. She said it smelled like a baby's diaper. She never wanted to help around the house. She said she couldn't cook, and she had too much studying to do to even make me a sandwich and open a bag of chips. She didn't do any laundry. She took hers to the big house and let the servants do it. While she lived at my house, it was always a mess. At least Clair had kept it clean, and there was always food on the table and beer in the icebox. Sharon hated to go to the grocery store. Now I had to vacuum when I couldn't stand the dirt any longer. She expected me to take her out all the time and tell her how good she looked. She expected me to buy her flowers all the time, and she demanded the most expensive kind — yellow roses. One day I got home around supper time, and she had some guy over. They were sitting on the couch working on some school project. I didn't like that one bit. Hey, that's how it all got started between her and me. Then she started inviting her friends to the house without even asking. She said they needed a place to study. Isn't that what the library's for? I hated having so many strangers around all the time, acting like they belonged there. When I go home at night, I want to eat, have a beer, and watch TV.

"By that time we were fighting all the time. Every time I told her to get out, she'd push all the right buttons, and we'd end up in bed. Then I'd take it all back and let her stay. But things between us kept getting worse all the time. She was jealous when I went over to see Nancy cause Clair was there. She said Clair was trying to get back with me. That was true. Clair didn't really like living with her mother. Her mother had this live-in boyfriend who was bad news. Clair said that he kept putting the make on her, and when she refused, he told her mother to kick her and the kid out. He was tired of their eating his food. That made me mad, and I was worried about Nancy being in that house with him there. I was ready to try again with Clair, but it was not easy to get Sharon to go back to the apartment. It's funny; she didn't want to live there, but she didn't want to give it up either. Her stepfather said if she wasn't going to live in it, he wanted to rent it. But since it didn't cost her nothing, she held onto it, and her stepfather let her.

"What I soon realized about her was that she didn't know what she wanted. She saw how I had acted when I got worried about Clair living around that bozo, so she tried to make me jealous. She told me that one of her professors was chasing after her. I asked her who it was, but she refused to give me his name. At first I didn't believe her, but then she started showing me the gifts and books he was giving her. I was mixed up. I guess I didn't know for sure what I wanted either. Sometimes it was Clair, and then at other times it was Sharon. I told her to tell this creep of a professor that if he didn't leave her alone, I'd kill him. I guess I scared her; then she really didn't want me to find out who he was. I thought I could uncover the professor's name without her help, so I started following her at school. As soon as she noticed me, she told me I'd better stop or she'd call security. I told her to call them. I'd tell them we were living together, and one of her professors was harassing her. She said I was jealous, and worse than that, embarrassing her. Now we were arguing at the college too. Lots of people saw us. Our lives were such a mess that I thought about running away, leaving Corpus and the whole bloody mess. Then I'd think about my little girl, and I knew I couldn't do it. Sometimes Sharon would get so upset with me she said she was going to kill herself. Of course, I never believed her then. Once I said, 'Go ahead and do it, for all I care. It would solve all our problems.' Mr. Greystone, I never thought she meant it. She was high maintenance and wanted too much attention from me all the time.

"Meanwhile Clair was putting me under a lot of pressure to get rid of Sharon and make her move out of our house. Nancy kept asking when she could come home too, so I finally made up my mind. I told Sharon I was going back to Clair for Nancy's sake. She threw a huge fit when I told her. And then she tried to talk me out of it. She said Clair and me would just separate again after a few weeks, and then it would be twice as hard on Nancy. That last night we fought over Sharon moving out of the house. I told her I didn't care where she went, but I wanted her out immediately. She started screaming and threatening me. She had her loaded gun at my house, and she said she was going to kill herself. I was scared she'd shoot me first. I'm sure we both were yelling at each other pretty loud. I was worried the gun might go off or the neighbors would call the police, so I left. As I rushed out the door, I said that I expected her and all her things to be gone when I got back. She yelled back at me, 'Don't count on it.' And, Mr. Greystone, I swear that was the last time I saw her."

He stopped speaking, and we both sat for a moment in silence. Then he said again how sorry he was that he hadn't taken Sharon's threats of suicide more seriously. He blamed himself for that, but he didn't shoot her. I asked him what more he knew about her relationship with Harvey Stone.

"I never could figure that one out. She complained about him all the time, but when he came around her apartment, she seemed glad to see him. Sometimes they fought when I wasn't there, but as soon as I walked in the door, they would stop, so I never heard what they argued about. When Sharon moved to my place, he stopped coming to visit her and giving her money. I know that she still saw him once in a while, but I'm not sure where they met or how often. I think they sometimes got together in his office, and he may have taken her out to eat at some of his fancy clubs. I can't say for sure. They never invited me along."

"And the professor? You never found out his name?" I said.

"I guess I didn't try that hard. Too many other things got in the way."

"Do you think he might have had anything to do with her disappearance?"

"I couldn't say."

"Is there anything else you can tell me?"

"I can't think of anything now. How about you? Do you have any idea what might have happened?" he asked.

"Not yet, but I promise you, I'll figure it out. And I'll let you know when I do."

"Just don't bother my family. They've been through enough." With that he rose, looked at his watch, and said he was late. He had promised to throw a few baskets with someone. We shook hands, and he started out the door. Then he turned and said, "Remember, don't call my house. I'll check back with you."

After he left, I called Sarah on her cell phone to let her know that the interview was over in case she was ready to come by. She wanted me to tell her over the phone what Ben had said, but I said we'd talk about it when I saw her. She asked if today at four P.M. at my apartment would be all right with me. I had some errands to run during the early afternoon, so we agreed to meet at four o'clock. Before we hung up, she said she had a surprise for me. I told her I hated surprises, but she said I'd have to wait. She wanted to do this in person.

❦ 22 ❦

When I got home, I checked my messages. There were two from Linda and one from Joan, saying that Angela's chemo treatments had helped, and she was feeling better. Linda said that it was urgent that I call her as soon as I got in. When I dialed her number, she picked up the phone on the first ring and asked me if I could come to her house at once. She was slurring some of her words, and I guessed that she had been drinking. I answered that I didn't think coming to her house again was a good idea. She then said that Harvey had flown to Houston for the day on business and wouldn't be back until 11 P.M. I needn't worry about his surprising us like last time. She said again quite firmly that she needed to see me now. If she hadn't had too much to drink, I thought, this might be the right time to tell her that she and I were through carrying on a sexual relationship. We could remain friends, if she wished and I hoped we would, but that's all. I'd told her before that I had strong feelings about not sleeping with other men's wives, and I would not do it again with her or anyone else. I hated to imagine what this confrontation was going to be like, but I knew it had to be face to face. Only a coward would tell a woman something like this over the phone. Besides, I didn't know whether or not she taped her calls or if someone in the house might pick up a receiver and listen. I didn't want to give Harvey Stone a reason to be violent with either one of us.

I agreed to be at her house in an hour. It was around 1:30, time for lunch, and I needed to sort through my mail to check my bills and see if the letter that had arrived from the teaching conference held good news. A couple of weeks ago, I had sent the paper I hoped to present to the chairs of the conference, and I was anxious to see if it had been accepted. It had been — without any changes. I wanted to call someone to help me celebrate, but I didn't know whom to share the news with. In the old days Meggie would have been as excited as I was. I placed the conference dates and time I would present it on my calendar.

I looked in the refrigerator to see what there was to eat. I found a package of Swiss cheese, a loaf of rye bread, and my special horseradish mustard. I sliced some tomatoes and cucumbers for a salad. Then I looked for something to drink. I usually don't have beer for lunch, but today the idea of facing an angry Linda and telling her that our affair was over made me think I needed one.

I drove slowly, but it only took five minutes to arrive at her house. After I pulled my Honda into the space next to Linda's black Jaguar, I walked with trepidation to the front door. I had brought my checkbook to reimburse her for the items she had bought for the apartment. That should show her that I wasn't taking advantage of her. When I knocked on the door, Teresa opened it and looked at me with a troubled expression.

"What's wrong, Teresa?" I asked, as she led me into the large family room facing the bay.

"I'm sorry, Mr. Greystone, but Mrs. Stone won't be able to see you right now."

"But I just talked to her. She said that it was urgent that I come."

"She's in bed. She has a terrible headache. She told me to tell you she was sorry."

"She never mentioned a headache when I talked to her."

"It came on rather suddenly. I'm sure you will hear from her when she's feeling better."

I turned to leave, but then I changed my mind. "Teresa,

you've worked for the family for a long time, haven't you? I'd like to talk to you for a few minutes."

"Mr. Greystone, I don't know. What do you want to talk about?"

"I was Sharon's English teacher. I'm trying to find out what really happened to her."

"I know. Mrs. Stone told me. But I don't know how I can help you."

"I'd like to know more about Sharon. According to Linda, you helped raise her. You probably knew her better than anyone."

"I know both my children. I was their nanny. Yes, Mrs. Stone is right. I raised both of them. When I first came here, Sharon was just a baby, and Ted wasn't even born yet."

"Can you tell me about Sharon? I knew her as a student, but I think it would help if I could see her the way you did."

"I'm sorry, Mr. Greystone, but they wouldn't like me talking to you about the family."

"Teresa, the police have stopped investigating Sharon's death. I'm not satisfied that they found out the truth about what happened to her. I'm not going to stop looking until I do. Won't you help me?"

"I'd like to help you. I want to know what happened too. I never married and had children of my own. Sharon and Ted — they've been like my own children."

"Have the police talked to you?"

"No. They probably know I don't know anything to tell them."

"I don't think Linda would mind your telling me about what Sharon was like as a little girl."

"Maybe not." She told me to wait a minute and then returned with a photo album and handed it to me. "She was such a beautiful little girl and so smart," she said with pride.

I looked through the album and saw Sharon as a baby being pushed in her stroller by a much younger Teresa. After several pages of baby pictures, she was a toddler playing on the beach at Padre Island with a man that must have been her father. There were the many school pictures including her graduation from high school. I saw her change from an innocent to a nymphet to the beautiful young woman I knew. I looked at pictures of her alone, with her dogs and horses, and with her brother.

"This is my album," Teresa said. "Mr. and Mrs. Stone have many albums and videos too of both the children. Maybe she'll show them to you."

"Her father's death must have been a big blow to her."

"It was terrible. She wouldn't speak for months. Up to that time she had been such a happy child. She was her daddy's girl, you know. Mr. Ted loved the baby, but Sharon was his special girl. When he was around, she was always following him about. I used to tell him I'd take her, but he said, 'No, I want her to be with me.' I used to call her 'his little shadow.'"

"And then to die like he did."

"That's not true, Mr. Greystone. They say that Mr. Ted shot himself. I'll never believe that. You see, I saw him that morning before he left to go check on the horses. He greeted me with his usual smile and said he'd be back for lunch. He didn't look like a man who was going out to shoot himself."

"Then how did he die?"

"Oh, he died of a gunshot wound, all right. Of course, I wasn't there, but I know what I think."

"But I can see by your expression that you're not going to tell me what you think. Mrs. Stone must have been overwhelmed being so young and having two small children to look after."

"She never drank much until Mr. Ted died. That's when she started. She never liked taking care of her children, so when I told her I was leaving, she persuaded me to stay on. I said I would for a while until she could find someone else. That was over twenty-two years ago."

"Did she get any support from the Castillo family?"

His parents always blamed her for what happened, and after she married Mr. Stone, they and their friends wouldn't have anything to do with her."

"I'm sure that was very painful. But what about Sharon and little Ted? Didn't the grandparents want to see their grandchildren?"

"Of course, they did, but Mrs. Stone wouldn't let them go to the the Castillo's ranch since she wasn't welcome there. The children lost out on having good grandparents in their lives. The Castillos are a proud family, Mr. Greystone. I'm almost related to them. That's how I first came to work for Mrs. Stone and Mr. Ted."

"How are you almost related, Teresa?"

"I came from the poor side of the family. I think they call it very distant cousins. The Castillos took me in and gave me work. Then when Sharon was a baby, they brought me to the younger Castillo house, so I could be the nanny. After Mr. Ted died, I thought I'd go back, but the senora told me to stay with the children."

"How come you call Ted 'Mr. Ted' and Linda 'Mrs. Stone'?"

"When Mrs. Stone married Mr. Stone, he said it didn't look right, me calling her by her first name. He insisted that I call her Mrs. Stone."

"What about Linda's parents? Weren't they around to help her?"

"Mr. and Mrs. Ames? No, they were long gone. You know Linda took back her family name after all the trouble with the Castillo family about their son's death. Mr. and Mrs. Ames had moved away right after Mr. Ted and Miss Linda got married. They'd visit once in a while, like on Christmas. They're both gone now. They died in a terrible car accident on their way home from a visit many years ago."

"That's too bad. How did Sharon get along with her new stepfather?"

"In the beginning she was angry at everyone. She didn't have much to do with either her mother or her stepfather. Linda loved the children, but she was never good at nurturing them like most mothers. She was more interested in being with her husband than with her kids. It had always been Mr.

Ted who paid attention to Sharon. Of course, little Ted was just a baby then and was left for me to raise."

"But some time later didn't Sharon get closer to Mr. Stone?"

"After a while Mr. Stone won Sharon over. He put her on his lap and hugged her a lot. He spoiled her. He gave her presents all the time and played games with her. She had more dolls than any child could play with. Through the years he helped a lot. When Mrs. Stone slept late, Mr. Stone drove the children to school and took them to their appointments, like to the dentist."

"He sounds to me like he was trying to do right by the children."

Teresa looked uncomfortable as though she wanted to bring the conversation to an end, but she said grudgingly, "I'd guess you might say he was trying. Mrs. Stone didn't like him paying so much attention to Sharon and Ted and giving them everything before they even asked. She said that Mr. Stone spoiled them and that someday he'd be sorry. Sharon was such a sweet girl back then. She wasn't demanding or wild like some girls are. What she loved most was being at the ranch with her brother Ted, both of them riding their horses. Mr. Stone demanded that she come home right after school. He didn't want her hanging around other kids or the other kids hanging out around here. Later when Ted was older, he gave him more freedom. I guess 'cause he was a boy. Sometimes I could see that she felt very much alone in the world except for her brother. She was hardly that much older than he was, but she became very protective of him, almost like a mother."

"Was there a time when things changed?"

"I shouldn't be talking to you about any of this, Mr. Greystone. It's too late to help Sharon now."

"Don't worry, Teresa, I'm not going to mention our talk to Mrs. Stone. I promise you that."

"I didn't think you would, Mr. Greystone, but there are some family secrets that aren't meant for outsiders."

Just then I looked up and saw Linda walk haltingly into

the room. She was wearing a brightly colored lounging gown and had no makeup on. Her eyes looked red and swollen, and she stood for a minute, looking unsure what to do next. I ran to help her, and she grabbed hold of my arm and swayed a little. I led her to the sofa, and she sat down heavily.

"Have you been here long, darling?" she asked.

"Just a few minutes. You look like you're not well. Teresa says you have a headache."

"I have a terrible headache, but lying in bed isn't helping it."

"Can I get you something, Mrs. Stone?" Teresa asked. Then she looked at me and added, "Would you like something to drink, Mr. Greystone?"

"I'd like a Bloody Mary, Teresa," Linda said.

"Nothing for me," I said.

"Have something, Jeremy. I hate to drink alone. I do too much of that around here."

"No thanks. What was so urgent that I had to drop everything and run over here?"

"I'm so confused, Jeremy. I don't know what to do. Harvey and I talked, and he said he doesn't want a divorce; neither do I for that matter. I know it's all about money and property, but separating wouldn't be good for either of us. You understand that, don't you darling?"

"But what about his secretary and the baby?"

"He's going to take care of that. You needn't worry. It's not the first time someone has told him she's pregnant to get something from him. He's letting her go. She won't bother him much longer."

"You mean he's going to pay her off? You told me he wanted to marry her."

"That was in the heat of the argument. Yes, money will exchange hands, but Jeremy, if you're upset about what's going to happen to us, don't be; nothing's changed."

"You're wrong; everything's changed. You don't expect me to keep sneaking around behind Harvey's back with you, I hope."

"You don't have to put it in such ugly terms. You know that we've both enjoyed our little meetings; you have just as much as I."

"That's over now. There aren't going to be any more meetings. I'm glad you and Harvey have decided to stay together. But count me out of this little ménage à trois."

Just then Teresa came in holding a Bloody Mary with a stick of celery sticking out of the glass. She asked if there was anything else we wanted and made a hasty exit. I didn't like the idea of her overhearing our conversation.

"Let's go into the bedroom, darling. I can lie down again and you can keep me company."

I took her arm and she led the way to her bedroom. It actually was a suite of rooms with two huge walk-in closets, built in drawers, and a spa.

"I can see why you don't want to give this life up," I said.

"I knew you'd understand." She got into her bed and patted the place beside her. "Come here, my love, and lie down with me."

"I told you already, Linda, and I meant it. We're not going to do that anymore."

"Don't say no to me. Please." She stretched her arms toward me invitingly.

"I'm leaving, but before I do, I'm going to pay you the money I owe you."

"Just like that? You think you're going to get rid of me that easily?" Her cloying voice now changed to anger, and I could tell she was not going to let me go without a quarrel. I was determined not to fight with her and to simply let her say whatever she wanted and leave.

"Let's not do this. You've got a headache, and I have someone to meet in a few minutes."

"Who is she, Jeremy? Are you saying that I have competition?"

"You have no competition. It's a business meeting, and I have to go."

"Listen to me, Little Dick; you're not going to make a fool of me."

"I think you're mixing me up with your husband now." I took out my checkbook and a pen. "What do I owe you for the apartment?"

"Probably more than you have in that paltry checking account, Little Dick."

"Look, names aren't going to make the situation any better. Give me a figure and let me go. I'm almost late already."

"All right. If that's how it's going to be, you owe me $2,368. That covers the shutters, the dishes, the picture frames, and all the rest of the stuff. Go ahead, write me a check if you think that's going to make you feel less guilty about the way you've treated me."

I gasped when I heard the amount, but I had just about what I needed to cover it. I wrote it quickly and placed it on the foot of the bed. "I'm sorry, Linda. I know it sounds like a cliche, but I really wanted to end this as friends."

"You're so damned civilized, aren't you, teacher boy? I should have guessed you didn't have the *cojones* for a relationship with a real woman. Now get out of here before I do something to make you really sorry."

As I closed the bedroom door behind me, she continued calling me vicious names and shouting obscenities, which the solid oak door muffled sufficiently so that I didn't fully understand them. I walked quickly to the front door and let myself out. For a few seconds I leaned against the closed door. That didn't go too badly, I said to myself with great relief and a smile that I couldn't contain. Then I rushed down the driveway toward my car to make my escape before she changed her mind and followed me.

❧ 23 ❧

When I reached my apartment about 4:10 P.M., I saw Sarah parked in front of the building, sitting in her white Ford Explorer. As we entered the apartment, I apologized for being late and told her that she could spread the news to anyone who might be interested (of course, I meant Meggie) that I wouldn't be seeing Linda Stone again. Whatever small friendship there had been between us was now severed for good. Sarah, who couldn't mask her curiosity, wanted the details, but the look I gave her stopped any further inquiry.

After I served us each a glass of iced tea, I recited for her a shortened version of Ben Haynes' story. She wondered if I believed him, and I told her that I believed much of what he said, and the rest I had some doubts about. I asked for her response.

Sarah didn't speak for a minute. Cleo and Tony had jumped on the sofa and were asking to be scratched. "I believe him when he told you how they got involved and what their lives were like together, but I'm not sure that he's told you everything about that last night together when she disappeared."

"Are you referring to something in particular?"

"I'm not convinced about what he said about Sharon's threatening to commit suicide. You told me her brother said

194

that after her father killed himself, she had said that she would never take her own life."

"Others have said that before and gone back on their word."

She stopped petting the cats and looked at me. "They act like they're hungry to me."

"I think I'll feed them." She followed me into the kitchen while I opened a can of their favorite tuna and mixed it with some dry food.

When we returned to the living room, she sat down again on the sofa. "I like your new pictures and shutters. You have a much better view of the bay. Who's your decorator?"

"Never mind. You were giving me your response to Ben's story."

"I don't know how to judge whether or not their quarreling led to his murdering her. Maybe he is telling the truth. I suppose he could have left the house, and then feeling totally devastated, she committed suicide. You say he's convincing, but if he was trying to convince you that he had nothing to do with shooting her and taking her body to the beach, who does he think moved her and her car to Padre Island, and why did they do it?"

"He says she probably went to Padre alone and shot herself there. He thinks someone may have seen her car where she parked it with the keys left inside and driven it off. Then when the person heard that it was connected to a murder, he left it in front of the apartment complex where it was found."

Sarah looked doubtful. "Even though he says that he walked out on her and she was gone when he returned, how come he never checked to see if she was all right? After all, she had been threatening to kill herself?"

"He said he was relieved that she was finally gone."

"Did he mention whether she had moved all her personal belongings out of his house?"

"He said clothes and books were all she had there, and when he got back, they were gone."

Sarah sighed, shook her head, and said, "He does have an answer for everything, but remember we're only hearing one side of the story."

"I wonder how different Sharon's version would have been."

"And who knows what effect Ben's wife and daughter had on him when they were putting on all that pressure."

"True, but let's not forget there were others — Harvey Stone, for example, who had their own motives. Sharon hinted to Jim that she could tell some damaging stories about him, which she said would ruin him if they ever got out. He may have felt he needed to shut her up."

"No, I'm sure he wouldn't hurt someone he loved like his own daughter. I know him, Jeremy; you don't."

"Then where was he that night?"

"That's what I came over to tell you." She picked up her empty glass and started to stand up. "But first, that tea was so good. Do you mind if I get some more?"

I took the glass from her hand and got us both refills. "So you found out where Harvey Stone was that night. I'm going to bet he has a nice airtight alibi."

"Then you'd lose that bet. Someone saw him with Sharon about 9:30. That would be after Ben said he'd left her at his house."

"Someone saw the two of them together that night? Who was it, and where did he see them? Why would they be meeting at that time of night?"

"Do you remember my mentioning Annie Clark when I first moved into the apartment?"

"The older woman who lives in your building?"

She nodded. "We've had some wonderful conversations, Jeremy. She lives on the first floor and is very observant about what goes on around there. She's our best neighborhood watch."

"She saw Harvey with Sharon? How can she be sure that it was that Thursday night?"

Sarah got up and walked to the window and looked out. "Would you like to talk to her yourself?"

"Yes, I would. You can arrange it for me, and, of course, I'd like you there too."

Sarah walked back and picked up the phone sitting on one of the end tables and dialed the number. After a short conversation, she looked over at me. "Annie isn't busy at the moment. Can we go over there right now?"

The drive across town was slow as it was one of the busier times of the day when people were leaving their jobs for home or making their way to restaurants and malls. Corpus has a long and narrow shape along the bay, with too few thoroughfares on which traffic can move to handle the burgeoning population in the city. While we drove we compared notes on the information we had gathered so far and decided to do more brainstorming after our meeting with Mrs. Clark. The remainder of the ride took on a lighter note. Sarah related some funny experiences at the TV station. She wondered if viewers were aware of all the bloopers. Although the going was slow, we still arrived in twenty-five minutes.

A petite, slender, gray-haired woman wearing a trim blue pantsuit opened the door and led us into the living room. Sarah and I sat together on the sofa, and she asked if we would like a cup of tea. We both thanked her but refused the offer. We had drunk too much tea already to fall asleep easily that night. Mrs. Clark sat down across from us, and what struck me first were her eyes, how blue they were and how they sparkled. It was clear that she was delighted to have company and to share the information she had about Sharon. "How tragic it was," she said, "what happened to that beautiful young woman."

"Mrs. Clark, did you know Sharon well?" I asked when we finally were past the small talk.

"Please call me Annie. I knew her as well as I've known any of my neighbors in the building. I've lived here twenty years, and there have been a lot of changes. Because her father owned the buildings, we talked about what was happening around here all the time."

"Where was Sharon's apartment?" I asked. Sarah had decided that because of Annie's hearing problem (she wore two hearing aids), it would be too confusing if both of us talked at the same time, so I asked all the questions.

"It was right across the hall there. Of course, when she got scared that time in the parking lot when someone chased her, she moved out for a while. But that last night I saw her she was bringing in clothes. I asked her if she were moving back, and she said she was."

"What time did you see her?"

"I believe it was some time after 9 P.M. I remember I had just watched one of my favorite TV shows, and I heard some racket by the front door. I looked through the peephole — I don't open the door unless I look first — and she had dropped some boxes of shoes."

"Did you open the door and talk to her?"

"Yes, I did. I asked her if she needed any help. She said she could handle it."

"Did she look upset to you?"

"She seemed preoccupied, like she was trying to get her things in the apartment fast. Her car was parked out front to make it easier to bring her stuff in. After she unloaded her car, she said she was going back to get another load of her things."

"Was that the last time you talked to her?"

"Yes, but when she started out to her car — now you think I'm a busybody, but my drapes weren't closed, so I could see what was happening in the front of the building."

"I don't think you're a busybody at all. I'm glad that you can tell us what you saw that night." She smiled, so I gently persisted, "What did you see when you looked out the window?"

She leaned toward me and spoke in a low voice. "I saw Mr. Stone. He drove up in that big foreign car of his and got out to talk to her. At first it looked like they were just talking, but then I saw Sharon try to get into her car. That's when he grabbed her arm and tried to stop her. She looked like she was trying to shake loose of him, but he was too strong for her."

"Then what happened? Did they continue arguing in front of the building?"

"I couldn't hear what they were saying, but from their body language, they were having one doozie of a fight. When you're hard of hearing like I am, you learn to read body language pretty good. I thought about calling the law, but then I have to live here, so I thought better of it."

"Were they out there very long?"

"No, just a few minutes. Sharon finally got loose from him and ran back into the building with him following her. They went inside her apartment and slammed the door. I don't know what happened while they were in there, but about twenty minutes later Mr. Stone left."

"Did you ever see Sharon again?"

"No, I didn't, but a little later some young man came by her door and kept banging on it until she let him in."

"Did you know Sharon's boyfriend?"

"Of course, I did. Didn't like him too much. I don't approve of young folks spending nights together and not being married."

"Was it her boyfriend who was banging on her door that night?"

"It could have been, but I don't think so. Her boyfriend drove an old pickup. I remember I had to tell him several times not to park it in front of the building. He said he parked there to keep an eye on it. There are too many robberies and break-ins around here. This place has changed. It's not like it used to be even ten years ago."

"Did you see the car the man was driving?"

"It was one of those bugs, a white one. You used to see them all the time, but not so much any more. You know one of those German cars."

"Had you ever seen that car parked here before?"

"I don't know if I ever did. So many cars stop in front of this building; it's hard to keep track of them all."

"Did this young man stay very long?"

"I'm not sure when he left because it was time for me to take my pills. I got a new prescription that day and it was confusing. Then it was time for me to go to bed. All I know is that when I got up the next morning that white car was gone."

"What makes you so sure that this happened on the Thursday before Sharon's disappearance? Couldn't it have been on some other day?"

"I remember when it happened because I had had a doctor's appointment on Thursday with a new doctor. I put it on my calendar. I had new pills to take that night, and like I told you, I always watch my favorite TV programs Thursday night between eight and nine o'clock."

"Did the police ever talk to you?"

"They sure did, and I told them what I could remember. After they left I remembered a whole lot more, but they never came back."

We thanked her and got up to leave. She asked if she had been some help to us. I told her that Sharon's death was still a puzzle to the police, and to us too, but when we figured it out, it would be because she helped us fit in some of the important missing pieces.

When we arrived at my apartment building, I asked Sarah to come in so we could talk. She begged off, saying tomorrow morning around ten o'clock would be better for her. Tonight she had a dinner and movie date she was going to keep. I knew better than to ask any questions, so we left it at that. I watched her drive off and then went up to my apartment and the cats.

Later that evening after dinner, I dutifully brushed Tony and Cleo, putting off my call to Meggie. I would have to get her consent before I could drive to Austin to see her. When she first recognized my voice, I thought she sounded more distant than I'd ever heard her before. I told her that I was sorry to have missed her call when I was in Dallas. She said Linda had told her all about my visiting Joan. I decided I'd better explain about Linda's being just a friend who needed a place to stay.

Since I was out of town anyway, she used the apartment. I assured Meggie that Linda meant nothing to me. In fact, we were not even friends any longer. She answered that it was really none of her business. When I asked her about my driving to Austin, she said that it wouldn't be a good idea for me to come at this time. My heart stopped at those words. She went on to say she would be in Corpus in two weeks to check on her house. If she had time, she would see me then.

For a minute after she hung up, I sat staring out the window unable to move. There was a time when I needed nobody. In fact, I had preferred to be alone. But hearing her voice again struck a cord deep inside me. Not just her voice, but the memory of her, the memories of us together seduced me in spite of her coldness. I blamed myself entirely for the aloofness in her voice. But in spite of the mistakes I had made in the past, I was ready to go on and forget what had happened between us. All I wanted was another chance for us to be together again and to know there would be a tomorrow for the two of us. I didn't want to be alone any longer.

❀ 24 ❀

The next morning promptly at ten o'clock, Sarah arrived. Dressed in pressed jeans and a white buttoned shirt, her hair pulled off her face and no makeup, she looked like she was sixteen years old. I was about to offer her a cup of coffee, but she looked more like I should be serving her a glass of milk.

"I thought by now your training in literature might have cautioned you about measuring people by appearances." She followed me into the kitchen while I poured two cups. "Let me prepare my own. I like cream and sugar," she said. After putting a heaping teaspoon of sugar in her cup, she opened the refrigerator and took out a quart of milk. Before she poured it, she examined the date. When she had finished stirring the milky concoction, she took it into the living room and sat on the sofa, waiting for me.

In a minute I joined her with my coffee and a yellow legal pad.

"Last night while you were dining out and watching a movie, I worked up a list of possible scenarios that we could consider this morning. Are you ready to hear them?" I sat in one of the chairs near the sofa, drank some coffee, and was about to begin reading when she remarked, "How efficient you are, which is especially nice since I can't stay long today. I have to be at the port by noon. A Russian freighter has just arrived, and I'm interviewing the captain." She looked over at the pad filled with my scribbling, resting on my lap, and added, "Just like an English professor, you put a title on everything, even your notes." Then she leaned closer to read the word scrawled on the top line. "What does it say?"

"It says 'Conundrum,' which defines this whole enigma to me. Let's go over the list first, and then we can go back and discuss the pros and cons of each one. It shouldn't take us that long.

1. Sharon might have committed suicide because of her depression over her breakup with Ben, her problems with Harvey, and/or her harassment by Randy Thorpe. Or she simply might have got tired of the life she was leading.
2. She could have died in Ben's house, her apartment, on Padre Island, or somewhere we don't know about yet.
3. Her body, the gun, and her automobile could have been moved from where she died for reasons unknown.
4. She may have been murdered by one of the three named above.
5. Someone who drives a white Volkswagen bug might have been involved in her death.
6. A person entirely unknown to us may have been responsible, perhaps someone from her past.
7. It may have been an accident. The gun could have gone off, and she shot herself.
8. The night she disappeared she was with three men that we know of and had serious arguments with at least two of them.
9. The gun found near her body had been wiped clean of fingerprints, but there were traces of gun powder on her hands, indicating she had shot a gun.

10. We need to question Harvey Stone about what he was doing at Sharon's apartment the night she disappeared and what they were arguing about.

11. We need to talk to Randy Thorpe about where he was that night. He said he didn't see her alone again after he gave her the watch at the jogging track, but can we believe him?

12. We need to locate the owner of the white Volkswagen bug and find out what he was doing at her apartment that night. Maybe he's a disgruntled ex-boyfriend.

13. The police have closed the case because of the powder traces on her hands, the angle of the bullet entering her body, the closeness of the shot, and the lack of new evidence pointing to any suspect. Is there any other explanation of the evidence besides suicide?

"I can't think of anything you've left off your list right now," she said.

"Now I'd like to think about the arguments for and against Sharon's committing suicide."

"For one thing, Jeremy, women usually find a different way to do it. I can't imagine why she would use a gun."

"Maybe she didn't think it through and acted on impulse. She had just been told by Ben to get out. She hinted that something was wrong between her and her stepfather. What if Randy Thorpe was still putting pressure on her? Maybe it all got too much for her, and she just wanted out."

"I'm still not convinced," Sarah said. "If she killed herself, where did she do it? Why would she go all the way to Padre Island late at night? Annie said she saw her around 9:30 P.M. at the apartment. It makes no sense that she would drive out so late at night to such a secluded place to shoot herself."

"What if she shot herself somewhere else, and someone moved her body to Padre Island in order to hide it. A body might never be found out there."

"At this time we have more questions than answers. We need to go through your list and answer those questions if we are ever going to find the truth about what happened."

"You're right, Sarah. Do you think that you can get some answers from Harvey now that you know which questions to ask?"

"He'll answer my questions much sooner than he'd answer any from you. Leave it to me, Jeremy. I'm sure I can get him to talk."

"I'm going to go back to Randy Thorpe and see if he will tell me more about him and Sharon. I'm sure I haven't heard the whole story yet."

"What about the white Volkswagen?"

"That's going to be a little harder. Annie didn't get the license plate number, and she didn't notice any distinguishing characteristics on the car, so identifying it is going to be a challenge."

"I'll get back to you as soon as I have something to report, but I'd better go now and get ready for my interview."

"Be careful with Harvey, Sarah. Remember not to take any chances. If he begins to suspect what you're doing, stop immediately. And don't meet him in a place by yourself. Be sure that there are other people around."

"Jeremy, you act like I'm still a child. I know what I'm doing. Be careful yourself." She got up and took her cup into the kitchen and picked up her purse. I walked her to the door and came back into the living room and looked out at the bay. It was a dark grayish-blue day, and I wondered if I had done the right thing by encouraging Sarah to talk to Harvey about his encounter with Sharon on that Thursday night.

The following week the college reopened to the faculty and staff with the usual convocation, division and departmental meetings, and workshops. Thursday and Friday would be devoted to registration on campus, although most students had already been advised and had preregistered by phone last semester. This gave the faculty extra time to work in their offices, preparing for the onslaught of students, arriving at the beginning of the following week when classes began.

I called Randy at his office to ask him to meet with me. When he answered, I could hear the reluctance in his voice. He said he had too much paperwork to do, getting ready for his classes, to spend time with me. "It won't take long," I assured him.

When I got to his office, he was leaning back, his feet on his desk, to feign casualness, but I could tell he was nervous.

"You knew Sharon better than almost anyone. Can you answer a question for me? I don't understand why she went to the beach alone so late on the Thursday night after she moved."

Randy sat up and leaned toward me, nervously tapping his fingers on his desk. "That's bothered me too. She hated the beach. I used to suggest that she and I run on the beach, but she always said no. She complained about the wind, the sand, and especially the salt water messing up her hair, her clothes, and her running shoes. She told me once that she had problems with that boyfriend of hers because she refused to go watch him surf. She said he wasted too much time at the beach and didn't spend enough time studying. He wanted her to write his themes for him while he was out surfing, but, of course, she refused."

"I'm glad she didn't do anything that foolish. The surfing, however, seems like a harmless enough pastime. Lots of young men in this part of the country do it."

"Not only did she dislike spending time at the beach, but she resented the time he spent there with his friends and the money he wasted on boards. I believe that if she had gone somewhere to be alone that night, it would have been to the family ranch in Live Oak County."

The tapping was bothering me, but I didn't want him to stop talking, so I tried to ignore it.

"You mean she preferred being out in the country to being on the beach." I said.

"The family ranch, that's where I think she would have gone. She talked about it all the time. She said if it had been closer to the college, she'd have moved out there."

"Then what was she doing on Padre Island that night? Whom was she with?"

"I can't figure it out. Maybe she did go out there to kill herself. Sharon had a tendency to get very depressed. I thought it was due to her family problems, and I told her she needed to get away from both her parents just like her brother did."

"Did you have contact with her after the time at the track when you gave her the watch?"

Randy paused and looked at me as if he were weighing how much he wanted to tell me.

"You know Cindy. She doesn't give me much breathing space. But even so, I was deeply concerned about Sharon. She sounded to me like she was getting worse all the time. I'd call her once in a while, just to check up on her. Our conversations were always brief because neither one of us wanted to be caught talking to the other. Ben was as jealous and unreasonable as Cindy."

"You spoke to her on the phone, but are you sure you never saw her again before she disappeared?"

"I did see her on campus a few times, but we didn't speak. After the time I gave her the watch, we never were alone again." He stretched his arms and looked as though he was ready for the interview to be over. Then he looked at his watch and reminded me that he had work to do before he went home for lunch. We both stood at the same time, and I thanked him and left the office.

On my way back to my own building, I thought I'd try a shortcut and left the gym by a different door. Distracted by what Randy had said about Sharon's attitude about Padre Island, I started to cross the parking lot where the kinesiology faculty kept their cars without paying attention to the traffic.

Someone honked, and I stepped out of the way as the car passed. Then I saw it; parked in front of me was a white Volkswagen bug that I had never noticed before. I was so startled that I hardly remember rushing back into the building and flying up the stairs. When I reached his office, Randy was still there. Breathing heavily, I asked him who owned the white VW parked in the lot. He seemed surprised by the question and said that he had borrowed Cindy's car while his Buick was in the shop. He asked me why I wanted to know and was the car the reason I had come back. I asked him to sit down again. I had some information he'd be interested in.

Randy hesitated but then took his seat behind his desk. "What's all this about, Jeremy? I'm starting to feel a bit harassed by you."

I told him that he'd been seen the night of Sharon's disappearance, parked in front of her apartment building around 9:30. He sighed heavily and said, "I thought that was possible at the time, though I didn't see anyone around when I was there. Of course, in our profession lots of people recognize us when we're not aware of it. Who told you I was there?"

"Never mind who. Why did you lie to me, Randy? It makes you look guilty of doing something wrong."

"Just a minute, Jeremy, I haven't done anything wrong. Let me assure you, I had nothing to do with Sharon's death."

"I know that you kept knocking loudly on her front door until she let you in. She hadn't been living in that apartment for quite some time. How did you know that she would be there that night?"

"I had called her at the house where she was living around eight o'clock. She told me that Ben had just walked out on her."

"You knew she didn't want you calling that house when he was there, but you did it anyway. Why? And don't say it was because you were worried about her. That dog won't hunt."

"I don't know why I'm even talking to you. I don't have to answer any of your questions. You're not a police officer."

I got up to leave. "You're going to answer somebody's questions. Maybe you'd prefer to talk to the police."

"I have nothing to hide, Jeremy, but things could get uncomfortable for me at home if Cindy knew about this."

"So why not just talk to me? I'm certainly not going to discuss any of this with your wife." I took a deep breath and plunged in again, hoping he would answer the question. "What were you doing at Sharon's apartment that night?"

"That day a couple of students came by my office to tell me that Sharon was spreading rumors about my following her around and harassing her. I was terrified that she was going to get me into trouble with the Affirmative Action Officer at the college. I knew if she kept telling those stories that my chair and dean would soon hear them. That's a serious accusation, and I'd be forced to leave my classes immediately, even before the semester was over. Then Cindy would find out, and I'd have to deal with her jealousy and accusations. I called Sharon that night to ask her to stop all the foolish, harmful talk before she ruined my life. I had always been a good friend to her. Why was she doing this to me?"

"What did she say?" I asked. So he did find out what she had been saying about him, and he was pretty upset with her — enough to confront her with it.

"What I said seemed to go right past her. She didn't hear any of it. She was too upset. By then she was crying so hard that I asked her what was wrong. She said she couldn't talk right now because she just had a fight with her boyfriend."

"So you dropped the subject of her spreading those stories about you?"

"I had no choice. She couldn't handle her own problems, let alone mine. Then she told me that Ben had got violent with her and threatened to kill her if he came back to the house and she was still there. She had to pack and leave fast. She sounded terrified."

"What did she mean when she said he'd been violent?"

"I guess she was referring to the gun. It was loaded, and he had pointed it at her and told her she'd better take all her belongings with her too, or they'd end up in the garbage. I asked her where he was now, and she said he had left to see his child."

"Did she tell you where she was going when she left the house?"

"Back to her old apartment. I knew where that was because I had driven her home a couple of times when she didn't have her car at school."

"How do people get themselves into such a muddle?" For a moment I was glad I wasn't involved in a relationship. Then an image of Meggie flitted through my mind, and I thought, she's the exception.

"I know I brought this on myself," Randy said sadly. He sighed and continued, "Then she asked me if I would lend her a few dollars until tomorrow. She said Ben had taken all her money to pay the rent and to give to his wife for child support. She was low on gas for the car and had no money to buy any. She wasn't sure she could make the move without running out."

"After all those things she had been saying about you, she still had the nerve to ask you for money?" I asked.

"She was desperate, Jeremy. I asked her why she didn't go to her parents for money. They could afford it better than I could, and they surely wouldn't turn her down at a time like this."

"Did she agree to call them?"

"She said she'd call her father. Then she said she had to hang up. I asked her if she needed any help moving her stuff."

"How could you get away from Cindy at night to go help Sharon?"

"It would have been hard. The only reason I was able to talk on the phone was that Cindy and the baby were lying on our bed watching television. But Sharon said, 'No.' If Ben returned while I was at the house, she was afraid he'd kill us both."

"But you did go to the apartment later that night."

"Sharon's call disturbed me. She always had that effect on me. She obviously had it on you too, or you wouldn't be here now talking to me."

"So you were able to put your own problems aside in order to come to her rescue?"

"You make me sound like a cowboy in a B movie. I wasn't just trying to rescue her; I had to rescue myself. I couldn't get what she was doing to me out of my mind. I thought I could talk to her better in person. I'd tell her that if she didn't stop spreading those lies about me, she'd be in for more trouble around the college than she could handle."

"You were going to threaten her to make her stop talking? Oh, Randy, not smart."

"I know, Jeremy, but I wasn't thinking clearly at that time. Remember, I was desperate too."

"So how did you get away from Cindy that night?"

"About an hour after I talked to Sharon, I looked into the bedroom and saw Cindy and the baby asleep on the bed. I put the baby in his crib and left the house, hoping Cindy wouldn't wake up while I was gone."

"Why did you drive Cindy's VW instead of your Buick?"

"She had left her car behind mine in the driveway. I didn't want to move it to get to mine. I had the key on my ring, so I took it."

"So you drove to Sharon's apartment to confront her?"

"Yes, and to give her some money. I know how it feels to be broke. In case she hadn't been able to reach her father, I was going to lend her $15 until she could get some money from him."

"Did Sharon still have her job at the restaurant?"

"She'd been out of work for some time. She was trying to get a job in the English Department, but it hadn't come through yet. She didn't qualify for a student loan because of her parents."

"What happened when you arrived at Sharon's apartment?"

"I got there about 9:30, and she refused to open the door. I was determined to talk to her, so I wouldn't leave. I made so much noise that she had to let me in."

"What happened when you went inside?"

"She was still upset — how would you say it — over-wrought? — and said she didn't want to talk to me. She had called her stepfather after we had talked to tell him she had moved back to the apartment and needed some money. He came to the building and they fought about something. I don't know what it was about, but he'd just left before I got there."

"Did you get the chance to talk to her about what she had been spreading around the college about you?"

"First, I asked her if she still needed the money, but she said no, that her stepfather had given it to her. Then I asked her about what she had been telling people. She denied every-thing and told me she wasn't going to talk about it right now. The argument quickly escalated, and soon both of us were yelling at each other. Then I lost it. I warned her that if she didn't stop slandering me, I'd do something to her to make her regret she'd ever met me. I'm sure it sounded like a threat to anyone who might have overheard us arguing."

"What did she answer you?"

"She just told me to leave. She was in a hurry to get back to the house before her boyfriend returned. I wanted to leave anyway, so I could get home before Cindy woke up."

"Why didn't you go to the police and tell them all this after they found her?"

"I was afraid they might implicate me in some way, and then Cindy would find out about Sharon and my friendship. I couldn't take that chance. Jeremy, I swear that now I'm telling you everything I know. I found out about her death just like you and everybody else did."

"Why didn't you tell me all this the first time we talked? You've told me so many lies you've made it hard for me to be-lieve you now."

"I know, and I'm sorry, but no matter what you think, I had nothing to do with the death of Sharon Ames."

"Even so, you certainly must have thought about what might have happened to her that night after you left."

"All she told me was that she was returning to the house to get the rest of her things. I don't know what happened when she got there. The police investigated. There was an autopsy, and the coroner said she killed herself. She was certainly more distraught than I'd ever seen her before. And yet she was moving back to her apartment. I thought that was positive and that she'd be all right. I still can't believe something so dreadful could have happened to her."

I returned to my office and called Sarah to tell her about my meeting with Randy. I also wanted to find out if she had made an appointment with Harvey yet. She wasn't at home, and when I tried to reach her at the station, the secretary said she was on assignment.

❦ 25 ❦

S arah was out for the evening when I called again, and I suspected she was with Royall. If Royall followed his usual
pattern, the days of their relationship were numbered. I hated
to think about how she would suffer when he left her twisting
in the wind like his previous loves. Deserted by this great love
of hers, she'll be left completely on her own to explain the
broken engagement to her family, friends, and colleagues. I'd
be there for her, of course, and I won't rub it in, but she had
been warned. The next morning I tried her at home again, but
still no answer. When I called the station, they said she was
still on assignment. I'd have to wait until I heard from her.

I spent the morning in my office getting handouts for my
classes organized, with no sign of Royall except some addi-
tional stacks of mail on his desk. I was about to leave for
lunch when the phone rang. I recognized the Dallas accent immediately. As she had promised, Grace had come to see Sarah,
and now she obviously thought I had to do something about
her presence too. Wasn't our lunch in Dallas enough to convince her that we were never going to be friends? When she reminded me that I owed her a lunch, I tried to beg off by telling
her I had too much work to do all afternoon. She told me that
she had to talk to me, and if I didn't want to meet her somewhere else, she would come by my office. There was no dis-
suading her, so I decided to get the meeting over with.

We agreed to have lunch at a new Indian restaurant just past Padre Island Drive. I had never been there before, but I had heard the food was excellent. I arrived first and took a chair facing the door, so I could see her when she walked in. Looking around the room, I noticed that most diners were making their way to a large buffet. I wondered how Grace would react to serving herself since our lunch in Dallas had been in such an elegant dining room. When I looked up, I saw Grace entering the room, dressed in a light cream-colored suit, looking like a Chanel advertisement.

"Beautiful outfit," I said rising, while a waiter helped her into her chair.

"This? Just an old suit that's been hanging in my closet for years. You don't look so bad either in those jeans and cashmere sweater. That is cashmere isn't it, darling?"

"I hadn't noticed, but I think you're right. I meant to ask you something when I was in Dallas."

"Is this a trick question?"

"Just something that crossed my mind. Why are even the fat people in Dallas thin?"

"Are you being curmudgeonly or is that just one of your astute observations?"

"Just an observation. I thought you'd know the answer."

"I never thought about it before, but you're absolutely right. People in Dallas care about eating right and exercising. They also like clothes. It's the fashion capital of the South and Southwest."

The waiter brought water, asked for our drink order, and explained about the buffet. I asked Grace if she were ready to eat since I had to get back to work as soon as we had lunch. She surprised me by liking the idea of the buffet. We looked over the fabulous selection of food with labels over all the trays to identify the dishes. When we carried our plates back to the table, they were filled with more than either of us thought we should eat. Our tea was already on the table.

While we ate she told me that she had met Royall and was impressed. He was not only gorgeous, but he was intelligent and sincere. It was clear to her that he was as much in love with Sarah as she was with him. The main problem, in Grace's mind, was that he was only a college instructor, and they were poor as mice. Royall didn't appear very ambitious. He liked his teaching position and didn't see himself as an administrator. Television reporters in small cities didn't make much money either. She was concerned about how they would manage.

"Having money does not ensure a happy marriage, as you can recall from your own experiences," I said.

"You're right, darling, and I think first marriages should be for love. Ours certainly was."

"I don't recall it like that. Must we talk about this again?"

"It's time to be honest, Jeremy. When we married, you were madly in love."

"I didn't know anything about love in those days."

"And now you do?"

"I do, but I don't intend to talk about love with you."

We reverted to small talk until the waiter removed our empty plates and refilled our tea cups.

"Have you ever thought of leaving Corpus and moving back to Dallas?"

"I think you're right about my being honest with you, Grace. I have no interest in living in Dallas again."

"Your sister's there, and she needs you now more than ever. You don't want to see her take off again for unknown places, do you? She's getting too old for that. She needs an anchor in her life."

"It's nice of you to be concerned about Joan, but she has an anchor — Angela."

"You were just in Dallas, Jeremy. Didn't you take a good look at Angela. She's getting worse every day. She hardly eats anything. She undergoes constant infusions of — I don't know what."

"I got a message from Joan that the chemo was working, and Angela was doing better. She's in remission," I said.

"Joan is too close to see things clearly. She sees what she

wants to see. Angela's cancer has metastasized. It has spread to her brain. She doesn't have much time left."

"How could you know that?"

"Her internist is married to my cousin Jane. You remember her. He suggested to Joan the other day that it was time for the hospital's hospice service to intervene, but Joan won't hear of it."

"Why wouldn't she welcome their support if Angela needed it?" I felt a knot in my stomach and began to believe that Grace did know something.

"There are many reasons she probably doesn't want the hospice involved. You'll have to ask her that yourself. One could be that they insist on telling the patient that she's dying. I don't think Joan and Angela have discussed that likelihood even with each other."

"Why didn't you tell me all this when we had lunch together in Dallas?"

"I didn't know it then. I just saw Robert and Jane the other evening at a concert. Joan discourages all their friends from going to the house to visit Angela. She says Angela's not feeling well enough to have people come over. I went anyway after I talked to Robert to see for myself what was going on. It's not good, Jeremy."

"I'll call her tonight. Thanks for telling me."

Grace reached across the table and took my hand. "I'm truly sorry," she said with more compassion than I'd ever seen her display before.

Back at the office I couldn't concentrate on my preparations for the semester. Royall came in while I was sitting at my desk, staring out the window.

"I met your ex-wife, Jeremy. She's quite a charmer."

"She thought the same about you, as you probably could tell. But one question, Royall, are you really serious about marrying my niece, or is she just another one of your temporary diversions?"

217

"Jeremy, we're engaged — ring, wedding plans, and all the rest of it. I've never given you reason to doubt my wanting to marry Sarah."

"Maybe I'm remembering all the young women who have come before her. You said you were in love with them too."

"I know I've said this before, Jeremy, but Sarah is the love of my life. I've never felt this way about a woman before. You've been in love. You know what I mean. You don't have to worry about us. I intend to do everything I can to make her happy for the rest of our lives."

That evening I called Joan to see if she needed me to fly to Dallas for the weekend. She said there was nothing I could do there. Angela slept most of the time now because of all the medication she was on. At least she was feeling very little pain now. The last chemo treatments had helped. The doctor hadn't recommended radiation, and for that they were both grateful. I asked her if she'd thought about getting help from the hospice, and she said Angela didn't need their help yet. She would consider the hospice if it became necessary. I reminded her that the hospice assisted the families too. She needed help in coping with their situation. She didn't want to remain on the phone because she had medications to prepare. I asked her if she were going to teach this semester, and she said that she had taken a temporary leave of absence. She thanked me for calling and said we would talk again soon. She'd keep me in the loop.

I sat for a long time thinking about my sister and her commitment to Angela, and I realized that there was nothing I could do to help her. This was a journey they would travel together by themselves. She never complained that it was too difficult or that it required too much sacrifice. She never gave up hope nor showed the hopelessness of the circumstances to Angela. She didn't see herself as a hero. I wondered what it was that made some people so willing to give themselves to others while so many others spent their lives in narcissistic pursuits.

I was about to get ready for bed when the phone rang. Sarah called to apologize for being so hard to reach for the last few days. She explained that all her spare time and Royall's had been spent entertaining her aunt. She would soon have more time since Grace was flying back to Dallas in the morning. If Harvey was available, she would arrange a meeting with him tomorrow. Then she asked about my chat with Randy Thorpe. She listened, asking questions, as I brought her up to date.

Sarah said, "Whether Randy admits to it or not, it sounds to me like he was pretty angry with Sharon. What if their encounter did not end with his leaving the apartment and her returning to the house? Annie never saw him leave that night."

"Wouldn't Annie have heard it if a gun had been shot in the apartment?"

"She could have taken out her hearing aids and not been able to distinguish sounds. Lots of people hear noises and think a car's backfiring or a TV is being played too loud."

"If a gunshot had gone off in that apartment, there would have been a death scene with blood and all. The manager of the apartment would have seen it."

"What if Randy followed her back to the house, and they continued their argument there?"

"Right now anything is possible. That's why so much depends on your interview with Harvey."

The next days went by quickly as I spent several hours registering students in the Student Center. When I finally returned to the office, I thought I had accidentally got into the wrong room. Royall's desk was cleaner than I had seen it since the first day he invaded my work space. The boxes of books (by that time there must have been at least fifteen) had been unpacked, and the books were standing neatly on the shelves. He had removed the outdated ones from the room and emptied his wastebasket. Papers had been filed or thrown away as they were no longer in sight. I wondered if his mother had come for a visit. The surroundings were so pleasant that I worked for a few more hours, getting ready for classes on Monday. I couldn't wait to thank the person who had taken this monumental task in hand, but nobody came by.

When it was getting dark outside, I took my briefcase and left the building. Driving home I stopped at the grocery store to pick up some essentials for dinner. When I opened the front door, Tony and Cleo greeted me to let me know it was past their regular eating time. After everyone was fed, I waited for Sarah's call.

She called around nine o'clock from the TV station and asked if it were too late for her to come over. I told her I'd put a pot of decaf on. She arrived about fifteen minutes later, and while she made herself comfortable on the sofa, I brought in the cups and handed her one.

"It's just the way you like it," I said.

"I had dinner with Harvey a couple of nights ago at the Yacht Club. We sat at a corner table near a window facing the bay, so we were alone except for the waiter who occasionally came by."

"Nice surroundings for a talk."

"At first it was just a friendly exchange about what we had been doing since the last time we met. I told him that I wanted to ask him more questions about Sharon. He became a little cooler then and said he thought that was why I called."

"So you asked him about the Thursday night before Sharon disappeared when he saw her at the apartment?"

"At first he denied that he was there, but I told him that someone saw him around nine o'clock standing in front of the building, arguing with Sharon."

"How did he respond to that?"

"He said he wasn't surprised that someone recognized him since he owns the building. He said he might as well tell me what happened that night, but it was off the record."

"Did you agree to that?"

"Of course, I did. And so he told me the following story: Sharon called him that night around eight o'clock and sounded very upset. She said that she was moving back to the apartment. She was through with Ben for good. Then she told him that she didn't have any money and wasn't sure that there was enough gas in the car to make the move. Harvey asked her where the $500 was that he had given her two days before. She told him that she'd given it to Ben. Harvey said he blew up when she said that. Before he gave her money, he always made her promise that she would not give it to that gold digging gigolo."

"So Harvey thought that Ben was with Sharon only because she came from a wealthy family?"

"For money and sex, that's what he thought. He said he and Sharon argued until he finally hung up on her. Then he went into her bedroom to talk to Linda. Linda blamed him for spoiling Sharon, but she was thrilled that Ben and Sharon were breaking up. She hated Ben as much as Harvey did. She said she had been afraid to tell Harvey something she had learned recently. Ben Haynes was married and had a child. A woman whom she didn't know called her several days ago to tell her about him."

"I can guess who did that."

"So can I. I bet it was Clair Haynes. Then Harvey told Linda that Sharon needed money to move. She didn't even have enough to buy gas. Linda said that she was going to take some money to her at once."

"Then how come it was Harvey who brought her the money?"

"Harvey looked at Linda and saw, as usual, that she had already had too much to drink to get behind the wheel. He's always feared she would get him involved in a lawsuit by driving drunk and having a wreck. He decided he'd better be the one to go."

"Did he go to Ben's house or the apartment?"

"He said he tried to reach her by phone at the house first, but nobody answered. He figured then that she was already at the apartment, so he left immediately before Linda changed her mind and decided to go herself. When he arrived at the building, Sharon was about to leave. They began arguing again, and Sharon ran into the apartment."

"So he followed her inside."

"At first he said that he just got back in his car and drove off, but I told him that someone saw him follow her back into the building."

"What were they arguing about?"

"About that he was deliberately vague. I think he was chastising her for living with a married man who had a child. He said she was criticizing him for having an affair with some young woman. Harvey said that Sharon was always imagining such things if she saw him with any attractive woman. This time she was accusing him of being sexually involved with his young secretary. Of course, he said there was no truth in her accusations."

"He's a saint."

"She explained to Harvey that Ben had told her from the beginning that his marriage was over, and he would file for divorce as soon as he could afford it. Harvey then gave her the money she asked for. Sharon told him she was returning to the house for one more carload of books and clothes. Harvey pleaded with her not to go back to the house that night by herself."

"Did he offer to go with her?"

"He did, but Sharon was afraid that Harvey and Ben would get into a fight if Ben came home and found him there. Harvey asked her to wait until the next day when Ben was at work to get the rest of her belongings. She told him she had to pick up everything that night because Ben had threatened to dispose of anything she left at the house. Besides, she had accidentally left the handgun on a table in the living room. Ben had always liked that gun, and Sharon was afraid he would not give it back to her if she left it there."

"What did Harvey say to that?"

"The handgun was his. He wanted her to get it back too. He told me he didn't want Ben to have a gun that was registered in his name. Harvey feels terrible, Jeremy, about letting Sharon go back to that house alone. He said it was the last time he saw her alive."

"What does he think happened to Sharon after he left her at the apartment?"

"He's not sure. The coroner said she had shot a gun. He said that he had never seen her so distraught as she was that night. I asked him why she would have driven to Padre Island in such a frame of mind when she didn't even like the beach, and he said he had no idea why she would go there. If Ben didn't have an alibi, Harvey says he'd be certain that he killed her. Haven't statistics shown that husbands and lovers, by far, are the most frequent murderers of women?"

"Unfortunately that's true, but, if it's a murder, this may be the exception. Did Harvey tell you if he went straight home after he left Sharon?"

"I asked him that, and you'll never believe what he said."

"You mean he too has an alibi about where he was later that night?"

"As a matter of fact, he said that his secretary had taken some contracts home to work on, and he had gone by her place. They had worked together until 3 A.M. in the morning."

"Maybe he went back to Sharon's apartment afterwards, and . . ."

"No, Jeremy, when he got home Linda was waiting up for him, and they fought about where he'd been until then. She can testify to the exact time he walked in the door, so his alibi for that night is airtight. He may never receive an award for being the best stepfather in South Texas, but I can almost swear that he didn't kill Sharon. He was disappointed in her for a number of reasons, as lots of parents are in their children, but he thought of her as his own daughter, and he did love her."

"When it comes to him, I'm still not ready to suspend my disbelief. And, Sarah, no alibi is airtight unless you check it out."

"I know that, Jeremy, so early this morning I went by his office. I pretended I was checking on vacancies in some of his other buildings in case I wanted to rent a different apartment when my lease was up. I struck up a conversation with his secretary, and we started talking about what happened to Sharon Ames. I said how sorry I was that Harvey had lost a daughter in such a violent way. She seemed willing to chat at first, but when I mentioned that I had heard that she and Harvey had been working together late that night, she stopped talking. From her expression I believe he told me the truth; they were together that night, but she definitely is hiding something. I have a feeling she's going to tell Harvey I was at his office asking questions, and he's not going to like it."

"So you didn't verify his alibi after all. Stay away from him, Sarah. He's a dangerous man."

❧ 26 ❧

The next afternoon Sarah called and wanted to come over again after dinner. She arrived around seven o'clock with a box of raspberry tea and an unopened tin box of fruitcake, which she had received for Christmas. Handing them to me, she said, "I thought I'd supply the refreshments for a change. Maybe herb tea won't keep me up all night. I didn't get to sleep till early this morning."

We both had thought of little else but Sharon since we had discussed Sarah's last interview with Harvey. We knew that the case was solvable, and the answers we were looking for were probably right in front of us, but somehow we couldn't see through the smoke yet. Something was missing in our investigation. Finally we agreed what it was. The last place that Sharon had said she was going that Thursday night was back to Ben's house to pick up her handgun and the rest of her clothes. Even though I had told Ben that I would not go to his house and disturb his family, it was time to break that promise. Maybe something in Ben's home would give us a clue to the murder. Perhaps a neighbor had heard a gunshot coming from the house that night. There could be traces of the crime left behind, maybe a bullet hole in a wall or floor. I told Sarah I was determined to go.

"You're the wrong one to go to the house. Ben's wife won't talk to you. Why should she?" Sarah said.

225

"Are you suggesting what I think you are? Why would she talk to you any more than to me?"

"Because I'm a woman, and I'm closer to her age. I don't think she would suspect me of trying to entrap her husband. She's probably heard all about you by now."

"When would you go? It would have to be when Ben is at work."

"I'll go tomorrow. And I'll talk to some of the neighbors too if anybody's around during the day."

"If you go there just to ask questions about Sharon, you won't get anywhere with Clair Haynes. You need some kind of a cover," I said.

"Maybe I can tell her that I'm researching a story."

"What story?"

"I'll tell her that I am conducting a survey for the television station."

"That might work. It would also explain why you'll be talking to some of the neighbors."

"People may be working during the day, so I might have to go back there at night."

"What will happen if they call the station to check up on you?"

"That could be a problem, but I'll tell the station that I'm working on a story about how this part of town feels about our programming. The area usually isn't too responsive to answering surveys through the mail."

"Perhaps you should tell the station that you're going to do this."

"They might say no. Then we'd have to wait for weeks while they worked up a formal survey. Some committee would have to agree to the questions. There'd be too much red tape. I'd like to ask them, Jeremy, but I think I'd better not."

"Sarah, I don't like you doing this by yourself, but I know I can't talk you out of it. Let's get together again over here tomorrow night, so you can tell me what you found out."

This time it was my turn not to sleep all night. I thought of all the things that could go wrong for Sarah and decided to call her early in the morning and talk her out of going to the Haynes' house. I knew that she woke up early, so I called her apartment about six A.M., but I got no answer. She could have been taking a shower. I tried back in half an hour, but she still didn't pick up the phone. I left her a message to call me immediately, either at my office or at home. When I arrived at school, Royall was working at his desk.

"You're here early today."

"I thought I'd get a little grading done before anyone else showed up."

"I meant to compliment you on cleaning your side of the office, or should I withhold my words of appreciation until I see your mother?"

"I thought for a minute that you would never notice. Actually, I did have some help. My future bride and I spent a day here during registration, and we didn't stop until there was a total transformation. I have to admit our doing it together made it almost fun, so if you're going to thank anyone, it ought to be Sarah."

"From my experience of sharing quarters with you, I suppose she'll have to get used to cleaning up after you regularly."

"I also came in early to ask you about this mission you sent Sarah on. It worries me that she's doing undercover work for your investigation of a possible murder. I'm afraid she could get hurt or at the least get into trouble at the station. Had the two of you considered that, Jeremy?"

"She's just going over to Ben Haynes' house and ask his wife a few questions."

"What if Haynes comes home and finds her there?"

"Not a chance. He works all day and won't be home till late afternoon. Sarah is going this morning."

"I told her to leave her cell phone on, and if she needs me to call. I'll leave class if I have to, but, Jeremy, I'd appreciate it if you would not send her on any more of these expeditions."

"Actually, I tried to call her off of it this morning, but she had already left her apartment. Don't worry, Royall, this will be the last time."

The rest of the day dragged by and I couldn't wait to get back to the apartment to see if I had a message from Sarah. She had not returned my call either at the station or the apartment. I tried her apartment again but still no answer. Before I fed the cats and thought about my own dinner, I put in a call to Joan. There was no answer, which was strange since she had to be home with Angela. Maybe she had made a quick run to the store to pick up some groceries or other supplies. I left a message for her to call me back whenever she could. I went into the kitchen to feed the cats and eat a grilled chicken sandwich while I waited for the phone to ring. Finally at 6:45 P.M. Sarah called and said that she would be at my apartment in half an hour. "Have you had supper yet?" she asked. "I could bring over some tacos."

"I just had a sandwich, but if you'd like, bring them for yourself, or else I'll be glad to make you a grilled chicken sandwich or heat up some soup."

She paused before answering. "No. I'll just pick up the tacos on my way over."

"Are you all right?" I asked her.

"I'm not sure," she said. "I'll tell you when I see you."

Thirty minutes later the doorbell rang, and I opened it to see Sarah in jeans, carrying a bag full of tacos. "Where should I put these?" she asked.

"How about on the kitchen table. We'll be informal tonight." I reached into the refrigerator and brought out two raspberry teas.

She sat down and started fumbling inside the bag. She pulled out some of the tacos and offered one to me. I sat down across from her while she ate. "How have you managed to get away from Royall these past nights?" I asked.

"He understands that I'm working on this case. He's been wonderful; he's so supportive. I've never had a relationship with anyone like him before."

I thought to myself that he might be otherwise occupied, but I didn't say anything to Sarah. I've known Royall a lot longer than she has, and I have never had any reason to trust him when it came to his relationships with women. After Sarah had finished her tacos, I offered her some of her fruit-cake, but she said that she would pass on it for now. We moved into the living room and sat facing the window, so we could enjoy the lights of the city while we talked.

"Now tell me what happened today when you went to the Haynes' house. What did you find out? Did you have any trouble?"

"Last night after I got home I worked up a survey so that I would have questions to ask when I went over there this morning. I have to admit that they sounded pretty legitimate. When I got to the house, this thin, small blond woman opened the door. I told her who I was and what I wanted, and she asked me to come in. She was alone except for her dog, which jumped on my lap the moment I sat down. She asked if I liked animals, and I assured her that I did.

I've seen you on the five o'clock news, she said. *Otherwise I would never have let you in my house.*

"I saw some Barbie dolls and clothes on the floor, so I asked her how many children she had. She told me she had only one daughter, Nancy, who had visited overnight with her grandmother and that she had to leave shortly to pick her up. For the next ten minutes we worked on the survey. She said that they didn't have cable right now until they paid off their new furniture. She said Nancy wasn't too happy about that as she missed some of her favorite programs. I told her that I thought her new black leather sofa and chair went really well with the gray carpet.

The carpet is new too, she said, *but the owner paid for that. The old one was so horrible. It was that old-fashioned pea-green shag. I hated it. Since we were such good renters and repaired and painted the whole place, he supplied the paint, the plaster, and the new carpet.*

"I looked around, and everything had been fixed up, so that it would have been impossible to tell if there had ever been any violence in that house. Then in the corner I saw a surfboard leaning against the wall. When I asked her if she

229

was a surfer, she told me that it was her Christmas present to her husband. She wanted him to put it in the garage, but he first had to build a cabinet in the garage to store it in, and he hadn't got around to it yet. I asked her where he surfed, and she told me on Padre Island, but someday he wanted to go to California and Hawaii and catch some really big waves.

"I told her that I came from Dallas and didn't know too much about Padre Island yet. I heard that it was a dangerous place for a woman to go by herself.

It depends, she said. *If a person goes swimming alone, it can be dangerous. There are places that have strong undercurrents, but they're usually marked,* NO SWIMMING HERE. *It's always better to have a buddy with you when you're in the water. There are coyotes out there too, but they don't bother people. You hardly ever see them, but if you have a small dog or cat, you'd better be careful. Lots of people live out there too. Of course, Padre Island is a wonderful place. It's a national seashore. It's clean, and it's not crowded. We take Nancy with us out there all the time.*

"I thought that this was the perfect opportunity to bring up Sharon, so I said, 'When I first arrived in town, I heard that some young woman was found shot dead out there and buried in a shallow grave.' I asked Clair if she had heard about that. Clair just looked at me with a quizzical expression, as if she now understood what I had been getting at, and she was not pleased. Without answering me, she looked at the clock on the wall and said that she had to leave now to pick up Nancy. As I was about to walk out the door, Ben walked in. I recognized him immediately from the funeral, but he didn't remember where we'd met before. He must have been too upset that day to remember me. When Clair introduced us and said that I was a reporter on the five o'clock news, he asked me what I was doing at his house, and I told him about the survey. I'm not sure he believed me because he said, *I've never heard of any TV station sending their reporters out to a neighborhood like this one to answer survey questions.*

"I told him that Clair had been able to answer all the questions, and I was going to go next door to survey his neighbors. I thanked them both and left as quickly as I could. He still looked at me suspiciously as I walked to the house next door; I could feel his eyes burning through my back. While I waited for someone to answer, I looked back and he was still watching me. Then when the door opened, he disappeared inside his own house. I was afraid that he might call the station and check to see if anyone was doing a survey in his neighborhood. While I was worrying about that, the door opened, and a man holding a can of beer stood there and rudely asked me what I wanted. I told him about the survey, but he didn't want to answer the questions. He invited me to come in, but I told him that I had to get back to the station. I asked him about the neighborhood, and he said, 'I thought you had a TV survey, not a neighborhood survey.'

"I introduced myself and asked if he ever watched the morning and evening news programs. He said just the sports news. I asked him if he had ever seen me do a spot as a reporter. He said yeah and asked if I could get him on TV. I said maybe, if he had a good story to tell. Hey, I said, I hear that a woman who lived around here recently was found dead on Padre Island. I wondered if the police had been around asking questions. He assured me that he had seen no policemen, and nobody had asked him any questions. I asked him if he had ever heard any gunshots at night. He said that he hears all kinds of noise in the neighborhood. At night he comes home from work, eats dinner, has a few beers, and watches TV. He doesn't pay any attention to the noise outside. He might have heard a gunshot or some car backfire sometime. He didn't remember when or where the noise came from, and he didn't care. He was someone who minded his own business.

"Just then Clair came out of her house and got in her car and drove off. Ben came out on the front porch and began staring at me again. I felt that I had better get out of there, so I told the man I had to go and rushed back to the station expecting the worst when I got there. But I guess Ben hadn't called to check up on me after all."

When Sarah had finished, she sat back and stretched her back as if she had had a long, hard day. "I'm sorry I didn't get very much," she said.

"I'd say you did all right. You found out that since Sharon's disappearance that the whole house has been completely redecorated and the old furniture replaced. New furniture, new carpeting, painting and plastering. Doesn't that tell you something?"

"Yes, if this is the crime scene, it has been totally destroyed. All the evidence has been removed, cleaned up, or repaired."

"I know we can't prove anything yet, Sarah, but I'm almost certain now that whatever happened to Sharon that night took place in Ben Haynes' house."

❀ 27 ❀

The next morning while I was drinking coffee and reading the paper, the phone rang. The minute I heard Joan's voice, I knew that something was wrong. She calmly gave me the bad news. Yesterday Angela had gone into convulsions and was rushed by ambulance to the nearest hospital.

"The doctors worked on her for hours and thought that they had finally stabilized her, but during the night she died quietly in her sleep. Her heart had suffered an assault that it was unable to survive."

"Oh, Joan, I'm so sorry."

"The doctors said that they couldn't believe that she had made it this long. It was her strong will to live, Jeremy. That's what kept her alive. Can you come right away? The funeral will be tomorrow."

"I'll be there as soon as I can get a flight out."

"I'm so glad. I have to hang up now and start making some other calls. There are so many people to inform and arrangements to make."

"I'll help as much as I can when I get there. Don't worry about picking me up at the airport. I'll take a taxi."

"Nonsense. Call me back when you've made your reservations, and I'll be at the airport."

I called the English Department and told them to release my classes. It was Friday, so I wouldn't have to worry about them for a couple of days. Then I called the airport and made reservations on a 10:30 A.M. flight that would get me into Dallas by noon. My neighbor Jeanne told me not to worry about the cats. She would take care of them for me as long as I needed to be away.

On the flight I could think of nothing but Angela and what she had been like when I first knew her. She had been so full of life and the promise of the future. Even before they met, I knew that she and Joan would like each other, and they had hit it off immediately. I thought about her courage throughout her illness; about my sister's devotion to her and how she had put aside all her own concerns to be there every minute so that Angela would not be alone. She asked for nothing in return. This was going to be my time to give something to Joan.

That afternoon we met with the young minister of the Presbyterian Church, who would conduct the services. He asked me how well I had known Angela, and I told him that we had been friends ever since we had begun our teaching careers together. He asked me if I would speak at the funeral. At first I said no, but then I looked at Joan, and she said, "Yes, Jeremy, please do. It would mean so much to me."

I could not say no to her, so with much reluctance, I agreed to do it. Making the rest of the arrangements made the rest of the day pass quickly. The children were with their father. He had taken Angela's death pretty hard. Joan and I stayed up until one o'clock in the morning talking. I asked her if she were going to remain in Dallas, and she said that she was not sure. I asked her to consider moving to Corpus, but she just smiled and said she'd consider it.

"We're all the family we have left, Joan. Don't you ever think that someday you'll be too old to travel all the time and will want to settle in some place you can call home?"

"My friends in Dallas tell me that all the time, but I never thought I'd get that from you too, Jeremy. I'm a long way from being too old to do anything I want to do. The only drawback is being so far away from you. It's time that you started visiting me and seeing what my life is all about. I think you'd approve."

"Why do all the women I love have to be so strong willed and independent?"

The funeral service was well attended by most of the faculty and many students whom Angela had taught through the years. Other friends outside the education community also filled the sanctuary. Joan and I sat with the family, which, along with her two children and ex-husband, included her mother, brother, and sister and their families. We remained in a small room until the service began and then were led to our seats. After the first part of the funeral service, which included the reciting of Psalms 121, 15, 100, and 23, the minister spoke about the meaning of death and life after death. He said this was not an unhappy day for Angela, but it was for those who would miss her. He spoke for several minutes about his relationship with Angela as a member of the church and how active she had been in teaching Sunday School and singing in the choir for all the years he had been there and even before he came until her illness would not permit her to continue. He spoke of her as his friend, a woman he much admired and whose conversations with him he would miss. Then as Angela requested, the string quartet from her college played several of her favorite short works by Mozart.

Finally it was time for me to stand before the congregation and speak. I stood behind the pulpit for a few seconds, hesitating, looking for the first time at the church filled with people looking back at me. Some were familiar. I had taught with several of them. I knew many of Angela's other friends from the years when I went to parties at her house. Then suddenly I saw her. Sitting halfway back in the center of the sanctuary was Meggie, looking up at me. When our eyes met, she nodded a greeting. Somehow her being there gave me the confidence I needed to begin.

"I'm thinking today about my friend, Angela McLeary, and what she'd have liked me to say about her. She was such a private person that I must not say too much. I have been fortunate for the last eighteen years to have known her, and although I now live in Corpus Christi, four hundred miles away from here, she has remained an admired friend.

"What was she like to me? Like all of us — a combination of strengths and weaknesses. Because I'm also an English teacher and must evaluate characters in my literature classes, it is not my nature to focus always on the most pleasant qualities of people, but with Angela focusing on her attributes will not be hard to do. She had a sense of style that was uniquely her own. She loved the beauty she saw around her, whether it was a flower or a bird, a young animal or a young child. She loved music and art, science and history, poetry and drama. She was a good teacher not only because she knew so much about the subject matter she taught but also because she never lost her own love of learning. I can still see her standing on the beach at Padre Island, her hands full of sand dollars and shells, watching the shore birds run along the beach. She knew the name of every bird. She used to say that teaching was sharing what she knew with others and inspiring them to want to know more. She loved being a teacher.

"But most of all, she loved Tim and Carolyn. She did not want to leave them, but then she never will entirely be gone from their lives as long as they remember their remarkable mother, whom they resemble in so many ways. She will remain in their hearts, and they will take her with them wherever they go. She will continue to watch over them in spirit. And what a spirit. Angela showed such courage throughout her illness. She wanted to live, and she struggled hard to win her battle with cancer. Although she lost that contest, she still believed like so many others who came before her — including some of her favorite writers — John Donne, Walt Whitman, and Ralph Waldo Emerson — that there is no death. There is simply a transformation, another stage in the cycle of life, which we ordinary human beings can't begin to understand. Finally, Angela loved my sister Joan, who never turned away from her during the hard times Angela went through, no matter how painful it was to watch her struggle, especially during those last months of her illness. Joan was devoted to her in a way that I shall always use as my own standard for love.

"At this moment I wish I were a poet, so I could say some words of deep consolation to those who are suffering from their loss. Perhaps a short parable I once heard a clergyman tell at another funeral of a remarkable young woman might apply here too and give us all some words of advice to serve as a beacon of light for the dark hours.

"A king once owned a large, beautiful diamond of which he was justly proud, for it had no equal anywhere. One day the diamond accidentally sustained a deep scratch. The king summoned the most skilled diamond cutters and offered them a great reward if they could remove the blemish, but none could repair the jewel. After some time, a gifted craftsman came to the king and promised to make the rare diamond even more beautiful than it had been before the mishap. The king was impressed by the jeweler's confidence and entrusted his precious stone to his care. And the man kept his word. With superb artistry he engraved a rosebud around the imperfection, using the scratch to make the stem. The clergyman said that we should emulate that craftsman. When life bruises us and wounds us, we can use even the scratches to etch a portrait of beauty. What our great religious leaders and philosophers have always taught us is that we should not fear death; we are all destined to die. We share this fate with all those who have lived and with all who will ever live. We must remember that the pain we feel today is part of the joy we have known in having loved someone. In spite of the pain, I would not have missed knowing Angela McLeary."

After the service Joan was surrounded by people, and I said a few words to some of my old colleagues and friends. Then I saw Meggie talking to a woman I didn't know, but I went up to her anyway to tell her how glad I was to see her. She introduced me to her friend, Susan Miller, whom she had known when they were both students at the University of

Texas. After the introduction Susan left to join her husband for the ride to the cemetery. I told Meggie that there was room in our car and asked her to ride with us. While we waited for Joan, she told me how Joan had called her to give her the news about Angela and to ask her to come to the funeral. At first she said that she was not going to come, but Joan told her that it would mean so much to her and the family to have her there.

"It certainly meant a lot to me," I told her. "I didn't know if I could speak today even though Joan had asked me until I saw you sitting there."

"I wondered about that myself, but when you began, I had no doubts at all. I thought I knew you so well, but today I saw a warmth — I don't know — a humility in you that I'd never seen before."

Just as I was about to ask her to tell me more about what she saw, Joan came over to let us know that it was time to go to the cemetery. As we were walking to the car, Grace joined us. After she expressed her condolences to Joan, she looked at Meggie and me and smiled, waiting for an introduction. I could see each of them measuring the other. Grace then offered to drive us to the cemetery, but we told her we already had a ride. Joan asked Grace to come by the house, and she assured Joan she would drop by later.

After the brief graveside service, we returned to the house. Some of Joan's friends had brought food and prepared a buffet. I never can eat after a funeral, and today was no exception. For a while I talked to Angela's mother and sister. They were very fond of Joan and said that they wanted her to remain part of their family. After a while I located Meggie sitting with an instructor from the college's business department. When I crossed the room to her, Meggie said that she could only stay a few minutes longer, and then she had to call a taxi to take her to the airport, so she could fly back to Austin. I told her that I would borrow Joan's car and drive her myself.

As we drove, I asked Meggie about her new job and her life in Austin.

"I think I was ready for the change, Jeremy. I liked teaching, but not the way you and Angela did. It's nice to be dealing with adults again and actually practicing accounting instead of trying to explain the concepts to students whose only reason for taking the class is that the course is required."

"I can understand that, but don't you miss anything about college life?"

"I don't miss the endless meetings and the small salary."

"How about all your friends? Don't you miss any of the people you used to work with?"

"Of course, I do. And I miss plenty of other things about Corpus too."

"Maybe we should stop dancing around, Meggie. There are so many things I want to say to you, but we're at the airport already, and there's no time. Unless you can take a later flight?"

"I can't, Jeremy. Frank is meeting my plane, and I have no way to get in touch with him."

"Frank. I see. That's how it is."

"It's not what you think. We're just friends right now. I'm not ready for another relationship yet."

"Are you saying that you really don't want to have this talk?"

"Until today I would have said that's right, but now I'm not sure how I feel. Seeing you up there, giving the eulogy for Angela, brought back old feelings that I thought were gone forever."

"Meggie, your being there made me realize even more how much I've missed you."

"Don't say any more right now, Jeremy. All our emotions are too close to the surface because of Angela's funeral and Joan's feelings of loss. We need a cooling off period, so we don't make any poor choices and end up hurting each other again."

"Then when can we get together and have that talk?"

"I'm not promising anything. It's important that you understand that before we talk."

"You've made that perfectly clear."

239

"I'll be in Corpus next weekend. Maybe we can have dinner together like two old friends."

"Like two old friends." I thought to myself, she didn't say no; that's a beginning.

"I plan to call Sarah while I'm in Corpus too."

"I'll be glad to tell her you're coming to Corpus. She'll be delighted. She misses you almost as much as I do."

She glanced at her watch and said, "Let's say goodbye here, Jeremy. I have to run. I'll see you next week." With that she turned and disappeared through the electric door.

I spent the rest of the weekend with Joan. Grace and several other friends dropped in for short visits, but for the most part, we were alone. The house seemed empty without Angela. Tim and Carolyn stayed on with their father, so Joan and I had plenty of time to talk. Joan told me that she was seriously thinking of accepting a teaching job out of the country next semester, and I realized that she would always be a peregrine, and I'd better get used to the idea.

On the flight home, I sat next to a young woman who wanted to talk, so I pretended to be asleep. Soon she was engrossed in her book, and my thoughts flew back to my conversation with Meggie. I felt that she had been swayed by the events of the moment, and I wasn't sure she ever wanted us to be together again. Maybe she already had someone else and just was afraid to tell me. Perhaps it was Frank. He was meeting her at the airport. I wasn't ready to give up yet, but I knew that I had to be prepared for her answer, whatever it was. For the first time I was ready to accept most of the blame for what had gone wrong between us. But what if she says yes to a reconciliation? Now I had to decide if I could make the commitment she always wanted. Was I ready to marry her? She was right. Both of us had much thinking to do before next weekend.

When I arrived home, I pulled into my parking space in the back of the building and grabbed my bag from the seat next to me. Just as I was about to enter the building, I saw him leaning casually against a stone pillar holding up the overhang near the door.

"What are you doing here?"

"Waiting for you, Greystone."

"How did you know I'd be here? I just got back in town."

"Shall I simply use the old cliche, I've got my sources?"

"So what do you want?"

"I know all about you and Linda. She told me everything."

"I don't know what she told you, but there's nothing going on between your wife and me."

"She told me you were sleeping together. Is that nothing? She won't like hearing you described it that way."

I gasped but tried to remain cool. "I don't know why she told you what she did, but we are not sleeping together. In fact, we have no relationship at all." I hated to parse words, but I knew the violence Harvey Stone was capable of. He was probably carrying a gun, and I wasn't.

"She said that if I want proof, all I have to do is look in your apartment, and I'd see some of my things there, some of my Audubon prints, for example. Do you want to take me up there right now, Greystone?"

"Look, there's nothing going on between us. And I have no plans to ever see her again."

"If you value your life, you'll keep your word. I'm only going to warn you this once. If I catch you hanging around her again, you're a dead man."

I knew this would probably be the only chance I'd ever have to question Harvey about Sharon, so without any preparation I plunged in. "Is that what happened to Sharon? She made you angry, and you decided to collect that insurance money that you had taken out on her?"

Harvey measured me for what seemed like a minute, and I could tell he thought I came up wanting. For some reason of his own, he decided to play the game. "So you think I killed Sharon for the insurance money. Can't you do any better than that?"

"Perhaps you were angry over her involvement with her married boyfriend."

"Not good enough, Greystone; she was leaving him and returning to the apartment. I thought a college professor might have some real insights, but I guess I was just as wrong about you as Linda was."

"I don't expect you to admit the truth to me, but I hear that Sharon was telling a number of people that you and she had an inappropriate relationship. I guess I don't have to go any further than that. You know what I mean."

He laughed and said, "Are you afraid of the word, 'incest,' Greystone?" He paused, trying to stare me down. Then he added, "You've been reading too many dirty novels. You're way off base; you really didn't know her very well, did you? Don't let her good looks fool you. Sharon made accusations like that about a lot of people to manipulate situations for her own use. She wasn't a saint. In fact, in many ways she was a lot like me. I've always understood her better than anyone else. That's what I liked most about her."

"Then why did you kill her, and how did you do it?"

"Why did I do it? Maybe because she talked too much." He looked at me as if he were trying to make a point that I should consider. "And how did I do it? If I had anything to do with Sharon's death, it wouldn't have been too difficult. She told me she was going back to Ben's house to pick up the rest of her things. All I had to do was follow her over there and wait for the opportunity to get her alone. I knew the gun was on the table by the door. She told me that herself."

"So you waited until you were sure she was alone in the house and went in and shot her. How did you make it look like a suicide?"

"That would have been the easy part. Remember I'm an expert with guns. I didn't even have to worry about getting rid of her body because both the Hayneses had been fighting with her that evening. It would have been impossible for them to prove to the police that one of them hadn't shot her. They both had a motive, and besides, nobody would believe them if her body was found in their house."

"So are you confessing to me that you killed Sharon?"

"Why would I confess anything to you. I just find it amusing that you believe you've figured the whole thing out."

"Then why tell me this story?"

He laughed and said, "Because I know that nobody else who really counts will believe a word you say about me, my being the wronged husband of your lover. And perhaps I want to let you know that I don't make empty threats."

"What if I go to the police anyway and tell them what you just told me?"

"I wouldn't do that if I were you. Nor would I say anything to Sarah either. She's a lovely young woman, but she has the same problem you do — she's overly inquisitive. I'd hate to see something terrible happen to her because of you."

"When you threaten Sarah, I take it personally. Nothing had better happen to her."

"Greystone, I'm a peaceful man. I'd never do anything to hurt either one of you, but I know people who don't have the same scruples. Just a few dollars to one of them and you never know when you or she might meet with an accident. Nobody knows when he's getting ready to buy it."

"Stone, one of these days you're going to get caught and end up where you belong."

"And where is that, Greystone? Do you believe you can beat me at this game? You're messing around with the wrong person." He looked at me with contempt. "You're so gullible. You simply think in terms of black and white, that only villains commit violent acts. Read the newspapers. Even good people snap when they're provoked enough. It happens all the time."

He turned to leave and then looked back and said, "For the last time, Greystone, if you value your life, stay away from me and my wife. I've got my informants, and they'll be watching you from now on." Then he turned again, climbed into his Jaguar, and sped out of the parking lot.

❧ 28 ❧

That night I was awakened around two o'clock by a caller who did not speak. I tried to go back to sleep, but my mind was full of images: The caller was either Linda full of the malevolence of the woman scorned, determined to destroy me. Or it was Harvey or one of his spies checking up on me, determined to keep me off balance. I wondered what they had planned for me next. I spent the rest of the night thinking about how I was going to handle these two. I was not going to put up with either their harassment or their making nuisances of themselves. By morning I was exhausted, and I wasn't sure I had enough energy to teach my classes.

When I got to my office, Royall was already working on his notes and handouts for his students. He told me that Sarah was anxious to talk to me. When I asked him what she wanted, he said he'd better let her tell me herself. Then his phone rang, and I went to the English office to pick up my mail.

After my classes were over for the day, I thought I'd call the station to see if Sarah could talk for a few minutes. I wanted to invite her out to lunch and tell her about Meggie's coming to Corpus this weekend, but she was out on a shoot. I was just gathering my books and papers into my briefcase when someone knocked on my door. When I opened the door, I was surprised to see Ben Haynes.

"What are you doing here, taking classes?"

"I've been trying to get in touch with you for days."

"I've been out of town for a few days. What can I do for you, Ben?"

"I thought we agreed that you were not going to go to my house and disturb my family. Doesn't your word mean anything, Mr. Greystone?"

"Of course, it does, and I've kept my word. I haven't been anywhere near your house."

"Just like an English teacher — playing with words."

"What's eating you, Ben?"

"Clair told me that you sent that woman reporter friend of yours nosing around and asking questions about Sharon's death. I told you Clair was still upset about my relationship with Sharon, but that doesn't matter to you. What are you trying to do, ruin my marriage?"

I told Ben to close the door and sit down, and he slammed it and sat down in my reading chair.

"Of course, I'm not trying to hurt your marriage. Sarah, the reporter, just thought that Clair could answer a few questions about Sharon since she was in the neighborhood anyway taking a survey."

"I might not have a fancy education like yours, Mr. Greystone, but do you think that I'm stupid enough to fall for that bull?"

"She was sent there by the station. She probably explained that to Clair."

"I called the station. There's no survey. And don't think I didn't report her to the station manager. She was pretty mad when she heard that she was questioning some of my neighbors too. I hope she gets into big trouble. She ought to lose her job for doing something like that."

"To be frank with you, Ben, the reason Sarah went by the house that day was that she thought that it may be the place where Sharon died."

"Why would you think that?"

"A number of reasons. First, Sharon told three people that

night that she was heading back to your house to pick up the rest of her things because you had threatened to throw them away if she didn't get them out of the house that night."

"Maybe she never made it back to the house."

"She had to get back there because she had left her gun on your living room table. That was one of her reasons for going back."

Ben took a deep breath and looked like he was searching for some explanation. My knowing about the gun surprised him.

"She must have come back while I was still at Clair's mother. I never saw her," he said at last.

"Let me ask you some other questions as long as we're discussing that night. When did you redecorate your house and buy new furniture?"

"What's that got to do with anything? I thought you wanted to talk about that Thursday night."

"You've just painted the inside of the house. There's new carpet and furniture. I thought you were broke. Didn't you have to use Sharon's money to pay the bills?"

"We did all that redecorating while Sharon lived there."

"That's not what you told me last time we spoke. You said that Sharon complained about the old rug and the smelly brown couch. Don't you remember?"

"I think you're remembering wrong. We did all that redecorating when Sharon was living there because she complained so much."

"Where did you get the money to redecorate? From what both Sharon and Clair said, you were having money problems?"

"The landlord put in the new carpet and paid for the paint and supplies. I did all the other work myself."

"Clair told Sarah that the two of you bought the new furniture on credit and were making monthly payments."

Ben looked down at the floor as if he were searching for answers in the tiles. "I did that as a coming home present for my wife and daughter. You can't make anything sinister out of that."

246

"That sounds more like the truth to me. But didn't you do all the recarpeting and painting and buying new furniture to cover up any traces of the murder scene? Haven't you made it almost impossible for the police to investigate the crime because everything has been changed and cleaned up?"

"Listen to me, Mr. Greystone, I told you this before, and I'll tell you again: I never killed anybody."

"Things don't look too good for you right now." Just then the phone rang. "Excuse me; I'll get rid of whoever it is."

"I have to be going anyway."

"Just a minute." Then I picked up the phone. "Hello, I can't talk right now. I'll call you back." It was Sarah, returning my call. "You have four-wheel drive on your truck, don't you, Ben?"

"Sure. I need it for driving on the beach to get to my surfing locations."

"Did you move Sharon's body and her gun to the beach after she was shot?"

The blood drained out of Ben's face, and he started to speak but stuttered something unintelligible.

"Did you move her dead body to the beach, Ben? Did you take her car to Padre Island and park it in front of the apartment complex? Who helped you? Where are the keys to that car?"

Ben stood up and said, "I never shot anyone. I'll take a lie detector test to prove it."

"You'll take a lie detector test?"

"No. I've changed my mind. I don't trust you. You're trying to hang this on me."

"Did your wife help you get rid of the car?"

"I told you to keep my wife out of this."

"Was she there when Sharon was shot? Is that why you're afraid to let anyone talk to her?"

"Nobody from my family was with Sharon when she got shot. She killed herself. The autopsy proved it. Clair is not guilty of anything. I've always done my best to keep her away from Sharon. Sharon was very upset that night. She said she was going to use the gun on herself. She had threatened to kill herself before many times. I didn't believe her, but this time I was wrong. She was probably alone when she shot herself, or someone would have stopped her."

"Why didn't you tell all this to the police?"

"I don't know anything to tell the police. Why are you talking about the police? You're trying to make me take the rap for something I didn't do. I'm through talking to you. I'm warning you. Just leave me and my family alone if you know what's good for you." With that he stumbled out of the chair, caught himself, and bolted out the door.

I sat stunned for a few minutes, thinking over what Ben had just told me. I was sure now that Sharon had died in that house, but I couldn't prove it. He certainly was not going to confess. The police would just say I was conjecturing. There was no way they'd take me seriously without any evidence. But I knew I was getting close to the truth. Ben was mistaken if he thought I was going to quit now. I dialed Sarah's number, but the operator told me she had already left the station. I picked up my briefcase and went home.

When I opened the door of the apartment, I saw the chaos immediately. A chair was turned over, the drawers from end tables had been emptied on the floor, and the bird sculptures and Audubons were gone, leaving empty picture hangers on the wall. The bedroom was in no better shape with clothes from the closet and drawers strewn all over the floor. Water was running in the bathroom, and I got there just in time to turn it off before water from the bathtub had flooded the apartment. Whoever was in here must have just left a few minutes ago. Where were the cats? They were nowhere in sight. I started calling them frantically, but they didn't come. I looked under the bed, behind the furniture, and in the kitchen cabinets, which had been opened, dishes and pots dumped all over the floor. Tony and Cleo were nowhere to be found. Then I heard a muffled noise coming from the closet. At first I saw nothing, even with the light on. When I looked on the shelf over the clothes, I saw Cleo perched in the farthest corner behind some shoe boxes. I gently lifted her down. Still holding her, I kept calling Tony. Finally I found him hiding behind my suits, where he was sure nobody could see him. Now holding them both, I called the manager, who came at once to see the damage.

"How did whoever do this get in?" she asked.

"I don't know." I wasn't sure which of my enemies was the perpetrator, but I was determined to find out and stop him or her before this went any farther.

"Did you leave the door unlocked?"

"Of course not," I answered, acting a little insulted.

"Then you gave someone the key," she said in the same tone.

"It's too late for recriminations now. All I want is to change the lock to prevent whoever it was from getting in again."

"Whoever it was," she scoffed. She then assured me that she'd change it immediately. Still unfriendly, she asked, "Is anything missing?"

"I don't think so, but I haven't had time to look."

"It looks to me like there are pictures missing from your walls, or haven't you noticed the empty hangers?"

"You're right. I did notice that."

"Well, I hope you have insurance."

After she left I started to clean up the mess, when the phone rang. I thought it was Sarah, and I was going to ask her to come over and see the apartment, but it was another woman's voice. Clair Haynes asked me if I remembered speaking to her on the phone. I said that I did. She said that she needed to see me immediately. She wanted to tell me something important before I went to the police. She asked if we could meet somewhere today before she lost her courage. I asked her where she had in mind. She told me that it wouldn't be safe for me to come to their house. Ben would find out from somebody that I'd been there. I asked her if she wanted to meet at my office. She said that she'd rather come by my apartment, if I didn't mind. She wouldn't stay long as she would be leaving Nancy with her mother. I looked around the apartment. It was such a mess, but I thought that with a couple of hours, I could clean it up, at least the living room and kitchen.

She said it was important that no one see us together. I looked around at the mess again, and with some reluctance, told her to come around four P.M. Then I started in the living room and worked as fast as I could picking things up. I was surprised at how quickly I was able to make things right again. As the clock struck four o'clock, I was ready to receive my guest.

❀ 29 ❀

A nervous looking Clair soon arrived, and I led her to a chair in the living room by the window. I offered her coffee or a cold drink, but she said she didn't want anything. Her blond hair was pulled into a pony tail, and she wore jeans and a baggy shirt. I tried to put her at ease by letting her play with the cats for a few minutes. Then I asked her why she wanted to see me.

"Mr. Greystone, I know that you think that Ben shot and killed Sharon, but you're wrong. That's not how it happened. Ben was not even there when Sharon shot herself."

"Is that what he told you, Mrs. Haynes?"

"Please call me Clair. I know where he was at the time that she did it. He had come by the house to see Nancy and me. We were trying to get back together again. Ben told me about their last fight and how he had told her to take all her things and leave the house. I was so happy that it finally would be over, and Nancy and I could go home."

"Perhaps when he got home after your visit, he found she was still there, and they began fighting again."

"That's not what happened. Ben told me that he had tried to make Sharon leave many times before, but she always found a way to change his mind. She usually apologized and took most of the blame for their fighting, and if that didn't work, she'd try to get him into bed with her. Once he told me that she even threatened to kill herself, and that stopped him."

"So what do you think happened that night, Clair?"

"When Ben was describing their fight, he mentioned the last thing she said to him. He had told her to get out and take all her things, and she answered, 'Don't count on it.' Mr. Greystone, I knew then that she wasn't going to leave. It was going to be just like every other time they had a fight."

"So what happened next?"

"I decided to go over there and talk to her myself. I wasn't going to do anything violent. I was just going to explain to her that Ben didn't want her there any more and that Nancy and I had agreed to come home. We wanted our family to be together, and she was standing in the way."

"Did Ben know that you were going to the house to talk to Sharon?"

"No, of course not. He never would have let me go. I had wanted to talk to her before many times, but he forbade me to have anything to do with her. He said he'd take care of it himself. But he never did. I have to admit I was desperate to get out of my mother's house. I told Ben that I was driving to a convenience store to buy some milk, so Nancy could have cereal for breakfast. I said I'd be right back."

"So what happened when you got to the house? Was Sharon there?"

"When I saw her in my house, I just snapped. We said terrible things to each other. It was probably mostly my fault. All my anger came out. I didn't even recognize the sound of my own voice. Then I told her to get out. She told me that my husband had told her that he didn't love me and that the only reason he was taking me back was because of our child. I screamed at her again to get out of my house, and she laughed at me. Then I saw the gun. It was lying on a table by the door. I don't know why I picked it up. I'm afraid of guns. I don't know anything about them, but I thought I could scare her, and she would leave. We stood there for a minute, looking at each other. She wasn't laughing any more. I could see the gun was shaking in my hand. I didn't even know if it was loaded.

"I aimed it at her and told her to get out before I shot her. I could see Sharon was scared. She didn't know if I would shoot her or not, but then she noticed that my hand was shaking, and she said, 'You don't want to do this. Put the gun down. Put it back on the table.' At first I just held it. I didn't know what to do. I thought that if I put it down, she might grab it and shoot me. I've seen plenty of police shows on TV. My fingerprints were all over the gun. Then she could shoot me and say that it was my fault. She started to reason with me and said again, 'Somebody is going to get hurt with that. Put the gun down where you found it. Think about your little girl.' I thought about Nancy, and I knew I couldn't do it. I didn't want to shoot anybody, not even her, so I put the gun back on the table. Then slowly, without my realizing it at first because she was still talking calmly, Sharon edged toward the table and started to pick the gun up. I tried to grab it again, but she knew how to handle it better than I did. We both had our hands on it, and before I could think what to do, we were fighting over the gun. I tried to get my hand away, but I couldn't get loose. When the gun went off, I thought that I had been shot. I never heard such a loud noise in my whole life."

"Guns like that don't go off by themselves, Clair. Did you pull the trigger?"

"No, I'm sure I didn't. I swear, it was an accident. Then Sharon slumped down on the floor, and I realized that she was the one who got shot. I didn't know if I should call an ambulance or the police. I didn't know what to do. There was blood everywhere, all over her and me. She was lying there, and I didn't know if she were alive or dead. So I called Ben, and he came right over. He had been putting Nancy to bed, but he left her with my mother. He took her pulse, and he told me that she was dead. By that time I was hysterical. At first I thought all the noise from the yelling and the gunshot would bring the neighbors out, but nobody came. We stood in the living room with blood everywhere, and we didn't know what to do next."

"Wouldn't it have been better at that time to call the police?"

"I think Ben really believed that I had shot her. He thought about what would happen to Nancy without a mother. He had had a rough childhood, and he wanted to protect her. There were lots of reasons not to call the police."

"But if it was an accident?"

"We couldn't afford a good lawyer, and we were afraid that the Stones wouldn't stop until the courts gave me the death sentence. They're rich and powerful people. Ben always told me that. We panicked, Mr. Greystone. All we could think of was how lucky we were that nobody had heard the shot. It gave us time to get her and the gun out of the house and put her someplace where nobody would find her until we cleaned up the blood and the rest of the mess."

"Did you go with Ben to Padre when he took Sharon's body there?"

"Yes, I did."

"And did you help him dispose of the car?"

"I drove her car to Padre Island. I parked it in front of that big apartment complex and locked it. I forgot to leave the key in it. I threw it out the window on the way home. After I left the car parked in front of the building, I walked down the street a ways, and Ben picked me up in the truck. We had wrapped Sharon in an old tarp Ben used for deer hunting and put her in the back of the truck. If someone had stopped us, it would have been all over if they had looked back there. But our luck held out. We buried Sharon so the coyotes couldn't get her. Ben said a few words over her. I was so nervous that I can't even remember what he said. Then he cleaned the gun and left it buried beside her grave."

"Why did you decide to tell me this today?"

"Because Ben told me that you think he shot Sharon and are probably going to the police with the story. All Ben did was try to help me get out of the mess I got myself into. Please, Mr. Greystone, don't go to the police. I swear to you, nobody killed Sharon. It was an accident. She was struggling with me for the gun and shot herself."

After Clair left I thought about what she had told me. I was going to call Sarah again to tell her about Clair's visit. Just as I was reaching for the phone, the locksmith knocked on the door. He quickly changed the deadlock and gave me a couple of spare keys. I hoped this would put an end to Linda's breaking into my apartment. By now I was convinced that Linda had made a duplicate key while she was staying at the apartment, and it was she who trashed the place. I felt certain that this was not Harvey's style. He could have insisted that night when he met me downstairs on seeing the apartment and looking for proof that I had been given some of their pictures and other items by his wife, but he chose not to.

Later I called Joan to check on her. She had a few friends keeping her company, so we didn't stay on the phone long. Then I tried Sarah again, but she was still out, probably with Royall. I had a quick dinner, fed the cats, and went to bed early. I hadn't got much sleep the night before.

When the phone rang, I thought it was the middle of the night, but it was only nine o'clock. For a minute I expected it was another nuisance call, but there was a man on the other end, who answered my greeting in a loud whisper. I didn't recognize his voice at first.

"I have to talk to you right away."

"Who is this and what do you want?"

"You have to see me, Mr. Greystone. There's something you have been trying to find out. I'm ready to tell you the whole story now."

"Is that you, Ben? Why are you whispering?"

"I don't want to wake Clair and Nancy. Can I come to your apartment?"

"I'll see you tomorrow after I finish my classes. You can come by my office."

"Too many people hang around that building. Besides, I need to talk to you tonight. Clair told me that she came to see you. You won't be sorry that you talked to me."

"I'll meet you at the Pub in twenty minutes."

When I arrived, he was already sitting in a booth in the back. I slid in across from him. "What's so urgent that it couldn't wait until tomorrow?"

"I know what Clair told you this afternoon. She's not very good at keeping secrets from me."

"Are you here to try to keep me from going to the police too?"

"I'm here to tell you the truth about what happened that night."

"Another truth. Why should I believe you now?"

"Because you're a smart man, and you'll know the truth when you hear it. I promise not to leave out any of the details this time."

"Okay, you tell me your version of the truth, and we'll see what I believe."

"Clair said that she told you that she went back to the house that night to talk to Sharon and that she was there when the accident happened. She said that to protect me. It's true that Clair went to the house to see Sharon and ask her to leave, but the visit did not go well. That's why I always told her not to have anything to do with Sharon. They'd only end up fighting, and nothing would change. Clair said they got into an argument almost immediately. They said some pretty bad stuff to each other. When Clair told Sharon to leave, Sharon just laughed at her and told her she had been planning to leave, but their conversation had changed her mind. She had started taking her things to her apartment, but now she was going to bring them all back."

"Was she just trying to get under Clair's skin?"

"That's what I thought. Clair came back home crying and told me what happened. I was pretty upset with her for going to the house, but then I couldn't blame her either. I told her I would go back to the house and take care of it. When I got back home, Sharon was still there. She said that she had been thinking and realized that she didn't want to leave after all. She asked me to give her one more chance. She said that she still loved me more than anyone in the world. She admitted that our problems were mainly her fault, but she said it was because she was so insecure. Because I kept running back to Clair all the time, she never knew if I really loved her. Then she said that she loved me enough for both of us and begged me to give her another chance."

"What did you tell her?"

"I had seen her change her mind like this a dozen times before. This time I said no. Mr. Greystone, I tried to reason with her. I told her that it was nobody's fault that it didn't work for us. There were too many obstacles. We'd had too many fights. She wasn't any more happy with me than I was with her. There were her parents, and there was my daughter. Nancy needed me, and I wanted to be with her. All we had in common was sex, and as good as it was, it wasn't enough to keep us together with all the other stuff."

"Did she agree with what you were telling her?"

"No, she wasn't listening to a word I said, but I never raised my voice to her. We weren't fighting. She finally said that we should have sex again, one more time, and then she would go. I felt uncomfortable saying no to her, especially about the sex, but I did. I had never been able to do that before. When she could see that I meant it, she grabbed the gun off the table and threatened to shoot herself. She had done that before too. I tried to talk her into putting the gun down, but she said she was going to kill us both."

"Are you saying that you believed that she was going to shoot you too?"

"To be honest, I wasn't sure what she was going to do. After several minutes of my reasoning with her, she said that she would give me a chance to leave the house before she used the gun on herself. I reminded her that she had told me she never would die like her father did. She said she guessed she was her father's daughter after all."

"You mean you had the chance to walk away and you didn't take it?"

"I wanted to, Mr. Greystone, and maybe I should have, but I didn't hate her. I didn't want her dead. I still thought maybe there was a chance that I could talk her out of it, so I said, I'd stay."

"It's hard to believe you'd put yourself in jeopardy like that."

"I've thought about it a hundred times, and now I think I must have been crazy. But I'd talked her out of killing herself before. I thought I could do it this time too. Now I may go to jail for a crime I didn't commit."

"What happened next?"

"I put my arms out for her to come to me like I always did, and when she came closer, I reached for her, but she stepped away from me. I thought I was close enough to grab the gun, but she struggled to hold onto it. Just as I let go of her, the gun went off. I don't believe she meant it to happen. I know I didn't. I bent down to check her breathing and her pulse, but she was gone. I was scared that I would be blamed for it. I expected the whole neighborhood to come running over because the noise had been so loud, but nobody came.

"Just then the phone rang. I didn't know whether to answer it or not. I thought it was one of the neighbors who heard the shot, so I answered it, but it was Clair. She wanted to know if I had got Sharon to leave yet. I told her what happened, and she rushed over. We stood there in the room with Sharon's body, and we didn't know what to do."

"It never occurred to you to call 911?"

"I would have been accused of murder. My fingerprints were all over that gun. Sharon used to tell me what a powerful man Harvey Stone was. He wouldn't stop until he saw me dead. We didn't have the money or friends to fight him. I know it was a mistake now, but all we could think of was getting rid of her body and the gun."

"So you got your wife to help you do that and also to get rid of the car?"

He hesitated, probably not wanting to implicate her any further. Then he nodded his head.

"The rest of what she told you was the truth about how we drove in my truck to a secluded area and buried her there. But Clair had nothing to do with Sharon's death. She shouldn't have to pay because I got mixed up with Sharon and couldn't find my way out before this terrible thing happened."

"And this story is the truth?"

"I swear, Mr. Greystone, on the life of my child, that neither I nor Clair shot Sharon Ames. I never wanted her dead. I would do anything if I could go back and change what happened."

❀30❀

The next morning I finally reached Sarah and told her Meggie would be in Corpus during the weekend and was anxious to see her. Sarah asked me to have lunch with her. She had something to tell me, but she also had questions she wanted to ask about Joan and the funeral. I hadn't talked to her since I had spoken to Harvey, Ben, and Clair. I was curious about what her reaction would be to their stories. We met at a small Chinese restaurant close to the college. We both ordered the special for the day, and she leaned back in her seat and looked at me, waiting for me to ask the question.

"All right, out with it. What's the news you're so anxious to tell me?"

"Royall and I've set the date. We're getting married on June seventh, in Dallas. I'm taking him home with me this weekend to meet the family. I'm sorry, Jeremy; I won't be in town when Meggie comes."

"She'll be disappointed."

"The reason that I'm giving you the news before the rest of the family is that both Royall and I want you to be in the wedding. After all, we'd never have met if it weren't for you."

"I'm delighted."

"Delighted to be in the wedding or delighted we met?"

I paused for a minute. "Both, of course. My aunt always said that when a woman asks you if you like the hat she's wearing, that if she hasn't purchased it yet, answer honestly. But if she has already bought and paid for it, you like it."

"I asked for that one. But you're going to have to learn to like Royall. He'll soon be a member of the family."

"And you like every member of your family?"

She thought for a minute and then said, "I thought I did before this conversation started. So can we count on you to be in the wedding?"

"Why not? If I remember your mother and aunt accurately, they will make it the social event of the Dallas season."

"Enough. Let's sign a truce, at least for lunch. Now tell me about your trip to Dallas and how Joan is holding up."

I described the funeral and told her that I had seen Grace there and later at the house. Joan was doing as well as she could but was lonely. She was spending time with friends whom she hadn't had time to see during the last months of Angela's illness. I told her that Meggie had come for the funeral and that we had a short visit when I drove her to the airport.

"How does she like living in Austin?"

"She says she does. She likes her job and the people she works with. She's glad not to be teaching right now."

"Does she like living in a townhouse, and has Harold adjusted to his new environment?" Sarah said with a smile.

"She likes it for now, and you know Harold. He's the quintessential alpha-male. As long as Meggie does whatever he wants, he's a happy poodle."

"You've always been a little jealous of Harold."

"Jealous of a dog. Ridiculous."

"I don't know why; maybe it's because Meggie loves him so much."

"I have my cats, but at least I don't spoil them."

"I'm not even going to go there. I plan to call Meggie and ask her to be in the wedding too. Do you mind?"

"Why should I mind?"

"You always answer questions with a question. Has anybody ever told you that?"

"I'm always happy to be with Meggie. I'm just afraid that it's over between us. I haven't been ready to face it yet, but I will if I have to."

Just then the waiter came with our lunches — egg rolls, fried rice, sesame chicken, and a large pot of jasmine tea. While we ate, we talked about Sarah's job; she was finally getting some good assignments of her own. She told me some things about Royall's childhood in California and his family. In all the time we had shared an office, I didn't know anything about his past life. After we had finished eating and were drinking the second pot of tea, I told Sarah about my meeting with her good friend Harvey Stone and how he had threatened me. I left out the part about her because I didn't want to scare her. I was convinced that his including her had been a bogus threat to get me to do what he wanted.

"You're not afraid of him, are you? Are you still involved with his wife?"

"Of course not. But she told him that we were sleeping together."

"I'm disappointed that you weren't more careful in your choice of lovers."

"She was never a lover. As far as I'm concerned, it's over. I hope I never see her again."

"I'm sure Harvey was just making empty threats. He'll get over it."

"I just thought I'd mention what your buddy is really like."

"Do you want me to talk to him for you?"

"Absolutely not. I can take care of myself."

"You said that you have finally figured out the Sharon Ames case. Tell me what you found out. Is it something I can use on the news hour?"

"I've tried to call you. I wanted to congratulate you. Your visit with Clair started it all." I told her about my two meetings with Ben and my one with Clair. She was surprised that they had given me so much information.

"Their stories are close, but who really was with Sharon when that shot was fired?"

"I don't know for sure." Then I told her what Harvey had said about following Sharon back to the house. He seemed to know too much about what went on there that night to be guessing. He said he waited until Ben and Clair were out of the house and shot Sharon, making it look like she did it herself — that it was either a suicide or an accident.

"So now you've heard three stories; any one of them could be true. Which one do you believe?" she said.

I wanted to hear her opinion first, so I said, "You want to be an investigative reporter. Tell me what you think first. I've been mulling it over so much I could use a fresh perspective."

She rested her arms on the table and looked down for a minute. "I'll have to think about it. I know you don't see him the way I do, but I still can't believe that Harvey would kill Sharon. Even if what you think about their relationship is true — and I'm not sure it is — he wouldn't have hurt her. She was the one person whom he really loved."

"And men don't kill what they love, Sarah? You're being pretty naive if you think that."

"I know they do — sometimes. I'm not convinced that he did, even though he threatened you. But you be careful. You could be in danger if he still thinks you're involved with his wife."

"No chance of that, I promise you. But I've been told that anybody who's a threat to Stone is in mortal danger, including his own children. Sharon was beginning to hint to people about some things in their relationship that would have ruined him in this city."

"That's still a big question mark to me. I'm not sure I believe her."

Remembering my conversations with Harvey and Linda, I said, "Maybe you're right. Both her mother and stepfather have told me that Sharon was a great manipulator, that she had made accusations about others before that were only partially true or exaggerated, that she was no saint. Harvey said that's what he liked most about her. But no matter what her character flaws might have been, not everyone saw her that way. Randy and Jim certainly never said anything like that about her. When she was in my office, she looked honest and sincere. Either that or else she was a great actress. None of that matters anymore; she didn't deserve to die like that."

"You're right, but can we go back to the Haynses for just a minute? Clair gave you such specific details that it is hard to believe that she wasn't telling the truth. Ben might have come to you afterwards to protect her. He doesn't want her to go to prison, or worse, because of their child needing her mother. Remember there is the death penalty in this state, and the system's not afraid to use it on women. Of course, Clair may be trying to protect Ben too. Perhaps she thought she could appeal to your chivalrous nature, and you would not report it because she was the one who was with Sharon when she was shot."

"Then you believe it was an accident?"

"It'll be hard to prove it was anything else. The entire house has been redone, and the autopsy shows that Sharon had shot the gun."

"I don't agree with you about Harvey. I think he's quite capable of committing murder. I believe he's done it before. Ben and Clair played right into his hands. Each of them thinks the other did it, and they're trying to protect each other and their daughter. They also know that if they admit the truth, one or both of them could go to prison as accessories after the fact or for tampering with the evidence. And since Sharon's body was found on a national seashore, both the state and federal courts could consider the case under their jusrisdiction."

Sarah wasn't ready to give up yet. "What about Ben? He knew Sharon was depressed and had talked her out of suicide before. Maybe he made a bad judgment call and thought he could handle the situation again. What he failed to realize was that it was different this time. He hadn't given her any hope that he would remain with her."

"So you're saying that Sharon really loved Ben."

"When she was about to lose him to Clair, she probably thought she did."

"I believe that all Ben really wanted was to be rid of Sharon and get back with his family."

"Maybe you're just projecting how you felt after you lost Meggie."

"Could be, but I don't think so. I don't know why, but when I looked into his eyes, I was sure Ben was telling me the truth about that much."

"And when you looked into Harvey's eyes?"

"He's a lot harder to read. I know you've talked to him more than I have, but I've a gut feeling about him. I believe he's the one, but I can't prove it."

"So now what are we going to do?"

"I talked to a couple of police officers in my class. They asked me about the evidence. I don't have anything I can give them. Everyone is telling a different story. The police said it was all hearsay. They can't do anything with a case like that. I went to a lawyer, and he told me that unless we get a confession, there's no way to prove there was even a murder. Remember, the coroner's investigation called it a suicide. And you may be right; it could have been an accident with either Ben or Clair."

"That means there's no news story either, but Jeremy, there is something."

"You've thought of something else?"

"I've just realized that you kept your commitment about finding out what happened to Sharon. You pursued the truth when everyone else stopped looking."

"Someone needed to pay attention to the victim. After someone dies like she did, people are anxious to get back to their own lives; they want to forget what happened. They think, she's gone. No more we can do here."

"You never thought that. But, Jeremy, she is gone."

"The one thing that will always haunt me is that I could have done something differently and perhaps saved her life the day she came into my office."

"Life is full of regrets. Sometimes we give ourselves too

much credit — too much power or too much blame — when we become involved in events like this."

"I guess I'm looking for some closure for her and for me. There are still too many unanswered questions: Was Randy just a friend of Sharon's like he said, or was he guilty of harassing her? He kept calling her after she asked him to leave her alone. Were her parents in any way responsible for her tragic end? She was trying to be independent, yet they still controlled her with their money. Did her problems begin with her father's suicide? Teresa says that he didn't die by his own hand. Maybe Harvey murdered him too."

"In the search for the truth, Jeremy, some of our questions are going to remain unanswered."

"You're right. Harvey Stone suggested something to me that I've been wondering about myself. He said that I couldn't see the truth because I think too much in terms of black and white."

"To me, you think more in terms of the tension and attraction of opposites, such as those between black and white, truth and lies, good and evil. It's what makes you a good teacher, and when I develop that ability someday, it will make me a better reporter."

"He also said that sometimes even good people snap and commit terrible acts. Since human beings tend to rationalize their own deviant behaviors or try to blame them on someone else, maybe in his own way, Harvey was trying to make me understand him."

"You're never going to let him off the hook, are you?" she said, shaking her head.

"In the end I don't have to. What Socrates said 2,400 years ago is still true today: If people do not live well, they cannot be happy. Injustice by definition cannot bring happiness."

"What all your unanswered questions show me is that we can never know the whole truth about anyone else's life, only what a person is willing to reveal or unable to hide."

"And that truth is subjective. You're right. Maybe it's time to let it be."

I heard from Meggie Friday afternoon. She had driven to Corpus with Harold, and they were staying at the Regis even though Phillip and Jenny Jones had invited her to stay with them. I asked her to have dinner with me at the apartment that night. The rest of the afternoon I spent on preparations. I ran to the store to pick up two sirloin steaks and baking potatoes. I found a package of washed lettuce and filled two plastic bags full of cherry tomatoes and mushrooms. I found a jar of Meggie's favorite salad dressing. As I was getting ready to check out, I passed a large display of candles and threw several into the basket.

When she arrived, the apartment was ready. The shutters were open, so she could see the lights of the city. Chopin was on the CD player, the lights were low, but not too low, and the table was set with my new dishes and glasses. Candles were lit in the living room letting off a light floral aroma.

When the doorbell rang, I felt like a sixteen-year-old on his first date. I opened the door, and she stood there, beautiful in a forest green velvet jumpsuit, her red hair shining in the hall light. She immediately noticed the changes in the apartment and approved of everything. Like Sarah, she asked who did the decorating, and I changed the subject as a way of getting by without answering. She immediately noticed the empty picture hangers on the wall and asked what happened. I told her that I had hung some pictures that weren't appropriate. That was true. Before dinner we sat on the sofa, and the cats jumped up next to us. They acted as though they were happy to see her.

She wanted all the news from the college. She asked about some of our colleagues, and I filled her in with the information I had, which wasn't much. Then she wanted to know about Sarah, and I told her about the upcoming marriage. Meggie smiled and asked me how I felt about it. I said it wasn't up to me to have an opinion.

I had prepared most of the dinner in advance and just had to put the steaks in the broiler. Since we both preferred them medium-rare, they were finished in ten minutes. When we sat down at the table, I poured the merlot and brought in the salads. Meggie commented on how long it had been since I had prepared dinner for her. We had always enjoyed cooking for each other. While we ate she told me about her job and some funny stories about her new clients. She described her townhouse and complained about the traffic on the Austin freeways.

I asked about Harold, and she said that he had discovered a new friend, a female black miniature poodle living next door. She was afraid that Harold was in love; most of the time he sat in front of the living room window waiting for her to come out. "Whenever he sees her, he tries to get out the door. If I don't let him out, he cries pitifully. I don't believe in giving him medication to calm him down as the vet suggested, but I'm afraid both our sanities are in jeopardy."

After strawberry shortcake and coffee, we sat together on the sofa, and she asked whether I was still investigating Sharon Ames' death. I brought her up-to-date on what Sarah and I knew about it.

"So Sarah believes it was an accident?"

"We'll probably never be sure, but if it's true, Ben's version is the most convincing of the two to me. Sarah disagrees. She's sure that Clair told me the truth."

"You don't sound too persuaded by either story. Now tell me what you really think."

"I suspect that Harvey not only shot Sharon, but he made it look like an accident. Sarah says I feel that way because I don't like him. I don't; I know too much about him. He lives by a personal code that is both immoral and narcissistic, but one of these days, he's going to commit another crime. I hope the next time he does that he makes a mistake, and they get him. When that happens, I want to be around to see it."

"You just may be," she said. "I've seen others who thought they were above the law finally get theirs."

"I went by the cemetery a few days ago to say good-bye to Sharon and to tell her that I was sorry I failed to get justice for her. It was cold and windy, with dark clouds hovering above; a Texas norther had just unexpectedly blown in. Someone had been at the graveside shortly before me, for in the vase attached to the gravemarker were a dozen freshly cut yellow roses. I read the name sandblasted on the pink marble stone: Sharon Ames Castillo. That must have been her legal name, and underneath, only the years of her birth and death."

"And nothing more?"

"Nothing. Then I noticed something else lying near the pink marble marker. One of the roses looked like it had been deliberately pulled out of the vase; someone had crushed the petals and laid or dropped it beside the stone."

"How do you know the wind hadn't simply blown it there?"

"At first I thought it had, but when I looked closer at how carefully the others were arranged, I knew it was neither nature nor an accident that had placed it there. The rose looked as if someone had crumpled the petals in anger. I guess it's just one more thing I'll never understand. I picked it up to remove it from the graveside, and one of the thorns cut deep into my hand. You can still see where it went in."

She took my hand in hers and examined the wound and then gently massaged it. "I think it's going to leave a scar."

"I think so too. Standing by the grave in the cold wind, holding the rose in my bloody hand, I thought about why Sharon's death had been such an important event in my life. All of us, including me, bore some responsibility for what happened to her. I finally had to admit my own culpability. The others involved collaborated through their actions; but I participated, though an unwilling part of it all, through my inability or reluctance to act. I feel so deeply the regret of a lost opportunity."

"Are you saying that we're all responsible for what happens to everyone we know?"

"Just as we're the recipients of all that has come before us, we're connected to all those around us whose lives we touch. We're touched by each other in ways we never know and are often unaware of how we've affected someone else's life. We happily receive the good from others, but we must not turn our backs on the pain, as we're a part of that too."

"You're right. We do share a sense of responsibility for each other. We hear what happens to another person, even a stranger, and we're moved by it. So what's next?"

"Sarah and I agreed that our involvement should be over now. The legal experts say that this is one of those cases that will never be brought to trial without new evidence. Let me rephrase something that Tolstoy once wrote that fits this case: 'Pure and complete truth is as impossible to know as pure and complete joy.'"

Meggie nodded and said, "I like that, and what else did you learn — that you would like to give up teaching and become a private eye?"

"Let me think, what have I learned?" I leaned back on the sofa, my head resting against the back and closed my eyes for a minute. "I learned that while you go through traumatic experiences, you don't have time to evaluate them. You're too busy acting and making the best choices you can, influenced by so many things — the past, your family, your friends, and your ambitions or lack of them. It is only after you are no longer in the midst of the action that you have time to think about what you've done. And if you're smart, you learn from your mistakes even more than from your successes."

"Are you talking about yourself now?"

"About myself and all the people involved in Sharon's life and death."

Meggie curled up in the corner of the sofa, so she could look at me more directly. "And what else did you learn?"

"I learned how two of the great themes in literature pertain to my life. To paraphrase them, What appears true is not necessarily so, certainly not entirely so; and reality is perception. All the people I spoke to, including Sharon, believed they were telling the truth, for the most part, but their stories were full of contradictions."

"I'm not sure that you haven't been manipulated by some of these people, including Sharon."

"Neither am I. I learned how important every relationship can be; I looked closely at marriages, lovers, parents, children, and siblings. I was reminded how flawed we are, but the good news is that there's hope. We can do better if we really want to."

"I thought you always said that nobody can change. That all we can do is put on a facade, which comes right off when we're under pressure."

"I believe that idea comes from fear, the fear of being disappointed and the loss of trust. The most important things I learned are to face life without fear, to learn to trust, and to forgive — all this has come to me in the last few months since that day when Sharon came to my office."

Meggie smiled and said, "I think that this is what you wanted to talk to me about."

"I also wanted you to know that if you choose not to be with me, I won't like it, but I'll understand that you've moved on without me."

Meggie nodded. "I see. How about another cup of coffee?" She stood up and went into the kitchen to get us both some more. When she returned with the cups, she sat down on the chair by the sofa. "I don't think we're really here tonight to talk about Sharon or Sarah or themes in literature, are we?"

"No. I've wanted to tell you for a long time how wrong I was on Thanksgiving night when we had that talk that changed both our lives. I've regretted what I said every day since. Can you ever forgive me for hurting you like I did?"

"I've thought about that night too, and these weeks have given me a chance to look at my own part in what happened between us. It wasn't all your fault, Jeremy. I'm not a victim in this relationship. I expected something from you that you weren't ready to give, and I gave you no way out. I was wrong to do that."

"But after all the time we'd been together, you had every right to expect we would get married."

"I think I've grown quite a bit since that night. I know that all love stories don't end in marriage, and I can accept that."

"I do love you, you know; I've never stopped."

"I've always known that. That was never the problem."

"Then why did you leave like that? Why wouldn't you give me another chance. You had never made an ultimatum before. It was like you were changing the rules without letting me know."

"We're not here to blame each other for the past, are we?"

"No, but the past is never the past. We can't pretend that it didn't happen."

"No, we can't, but something happened to me too. When I got to Austin, I decided to go to church again."

"Really."

"I can understand your surprise. It had been a long time since I walked into a church. At first I thought it would be a good way to get involved in the community. I'd join a single's group and meet new people to go with my new life. Soon I realized that I wasn't interested in dating someone else. I felt like I would have been betraying you." She smiled at me.

I thought about Linda and felt a twinge of guilt. I wondered if I should ever tell her about that.

As she had always been able to do, she guessed what I was thinking. "I know all about Linda Stone. But that'll have to wait for another conversation. The church had a young minister whom I really liked. I found myself listening to what he said. It was as if he were speaking directly to me. He was telling me to look deeply within myself and hear the voice of God, speaking to me. I had been afraid to look within myself for a long time, and I'd almost forgotten how."

"And what did you find there?"

"I found myself again. I'm not telling you this to frighten you," she smiled, "or even to impress you. I just want you to know what has happened to me since we were together here."

"I'm beginning to see that we both needed this time by ourselves." I said.

"When I heard you give the memorial speech at the funeral, I realized how much I still cared for you. What we've always shared was our friendship. Jeremy, I don't want to lose my best friend. Perhaps we can build on that."

"Best friends are hard to come by. They take years to grow. Can we be that for each other with so many miles between us?"

"Frank told me he was opening a branch of his accounting firm here in six months. I asked him if I could run it. I'll be back here after tax season to set it up."

"Did you decide to come back because of me?"

"I'm coming back for many reasons, including you. But, Jeremy, maybe it won't work out for us. We'll have to see what happens."

"I'm more optimistic about us than you are. Are you going to buy another house?"

"I still have the house. When the first deal fell through because the buyer didn't qualify, I raised the price $20,000. Nobody wanted it at that price. I guess I never did want to sell it. That's why the sign was removed. Then I took it off the market when Frank told me about the Corpus branch. I can't wait to get started in our new offices. Frank told me to pick out the location while I'm in town and locate an interior designer to help me configure it to suit my needs. He has a list of Corpus clients that he also wants me to contact. He says they've been asking for a long time to have someone in this city do their work for them."

As she continued talking about the future, I reached over and took her hand and gently pulled her back onto the sofa. We sat there with my arm around her shoulders looking out at the city lights. In some ways this moment reminded me of those many times in the past when we used to sit together talking about our dreams for the future and our plans to achieve them. We had always thought we'd be together then. Now that seemed like a long time ago. Neither one of us was the same. Meggie stopped talking and looked up at me.

"Do you believe in fresh starts?" I asked her.

"Yes," she said softly. "I think I do."